THE PART ABOUT THE DRAGON WAS (MOSTLY) TRUE

SEAN GIBSON

Edited by Rebecca Milhoan, Alyssa Barber, Mary Westveer

ISBN: 978-1-956136-47-0

Parliament House Press

www.parliamenthousepress.com

CHAPTER 1

A CLASSIC BEGINNING...

Few indeed know the paralyzing terror of a mighty dragon's roar or the skin-blistering heat of its fiery breath. Few, I say, for most who do experience such things know them for but the briefest instant before they are consumed by flame, burned beyond all hope of recognition, their hopes and dreams turned to smoke and ash.

Such was the horrible fate of many who called the village of Skendrick home on the fateful day when the great red dragon Dragonia first painted the evening sky red and orange with searing gouts of fire, raining death upon men, women, and children without distinction or hesitation, the tallest and smallest alike unable to withstand the dragon's terrible fury.

One small girl huddled in the corner of her family's home, a wooden structure made from loose planks held together by crooked nails and covered with tarpaulin, shivering and shaking with fear. She clapped her hands over her ears as she tried in vain to silence the screams and wails of agony that knifed through the air and pierced her heart. Her mother must surely be among them, for the woman had gone to the market that morning, and the girl knew *that the dragon would strike there first, at the heart of the village. On market day, half of the villagers gathered in the town square to trade goods and gossip—a teeming mass of conveniently clustered humanity that would make an irresistible target for an insatiable wyrm.*

The girl cried and prayed, beseeching aid from gods she had never believed in but turned to now in desperation, hoping against hope that divine intervention might spare her life and, somehow, someway, bring back those who had died so horribly.

Her prayers went unheard, or at least unanswered, for it was only moments later that her own ramshackle dwelling was engulfed in flames, and the girl, clutching her most beloved doll, wailed in agony as slithering tongues of fire kissed her feet and proceeded to consume her, leaving nothing behind but a bleached pile of bones and the ashy corpse of a blond doll.

The dragon left some alive that day—it would never kill them all, not when it wanted survivors to spread the word far and wide of what had happened, how the town had burned, how the people had suffered, and how no one could resist its awesome fury. For then, perhaps, the encroachment into its territory would cease, the disturbances to its slumber would end, and it could sleep, finally, in peace.

The great wyrm wheeled and turned overhead, leaving the smoking crater of the village behind as it flew north to its lair. The raging beast had no doubt that some foolhardy adventurers would soon come calling in the hope of righting this terrible wrong, but it would be ready.

Those brave souls would die in agony just as the villagers of Skendrick had died that day for daring to defy it, and for the simple crime of living too close to the home of an angry dragon.

CHAPTER 2

...IS NOT HOW IT ACTUALLY WENT DOWN

Being in the business of barding, one must not be bothered by blurting bull...excrement. (Though one should occasionally curb one's love of cursing.)

I mean, it's our job. Every once in a while, though, the truth turns out to be far more interesting than the tales bards tell in taverns; it's just rare that bards actually know the truth behind the songs they sing, and so the ale-swilling public misses out on some truly epic—or, at least, epically weird —stories.

Hi, my name's Heloise. I am, if not the most well-known bard in Erithea (yet), arguably the most talented, and unarguably the cleverest. I also wouldn't quibble if you suggested that I'm the most beautiful, but that's just because I'm very agreeable (and beautiful). I'm no stranger to telling a tall tale or two. However it just so happens that I know the truth about what happened that fateful day in Skendrick when the dragon attacked and the shocking events that followed, and let me tell you: the tavern version, even though it's superbly written and exquisitely melodious, isn't half as entertaining as the truth.

Because I'm an ethereally gorgeous (not my words, mind you—that's how noted seer Llendarlin Wayfender once described me, and even though he's blind, he's a venerated font of knowledge, so who am I to argue?), half-elf, I may not look it, but I'm approaching one hundred and forty years of age. Over the years, I've had more than a few adventures. Decades ago, I was sworn to secrecy regarding the true story of the great and terrible "Dragonia," but recent developments have released me from that promise, and so I can finally tell the tale.

I'll warn you up front, though—those of you who think you know the story will scarcely believe the truth. You'll be shocked, stunned, surprised, and staggered. The faint of heart should stop reading right now, close the book, and proceed to the nearest public garden or quiet pub to watch butterflies or enjoy a hoppy pint. Or maybe both.

For those who have the stomach—and I realize I'm mixing my metaphors here, because it's entirely possible to have a weak heart and a strong stomach, in which case I leave you to make the decision whether to proceed at your own peril, or, at least, after consultation with the nearest physician, witch doctor, or oracle—however, you'll enjoy a tale the likes of which has never been told before, and is unlikely to be told again. Well, not until I get paid to write another book, anyway, or at least booked into the pub nearest you.

So read on, brave souls...adventure awaits. And shenanigans. There will definitely be shenanigans.

CHAPTER 3

HOW IT ACTUALLY WENT DOWN

There *was* a lot of dragon fire that day, and there really was a terrified little girl clutching her dolly, and it actually was market day, so all of the residents of Skendrick were standing around like cattle in the middle of the town square, just waiting to be turned into crispy sticks of human bacon. But, no one actually died, and the only casualties were Farmer Benton's livestock, a development that, understandably, upset him.

"Away wi' ye, ye durn ha'-wit gi'nt beastie! Ye guin druve me durn unta th' pur hus!" screamed Farmer Benton at the departing dragon after it had torched his fields and barns. I should note that Farmer Benton's accent was so thick that not even his mother could understand him, and I'm really only speculating that he was unhappy with the dragon based on his gestures and facial expression.

This wasn't the first time the dragon, which the very practical residents of Skendrick referred to as "the dragon" (and not "Dragonia," which was an invention by a very literal-minded bard somewhere along the way), had wheeled through the skies over Skendrick and rained down fire, and it consistently attacked the farms that circled the village like a very delicious donut.

Livestock were frequent casualties, as were the fruits and vegetables that the townsfolk relied upon for both sustenance and trade with other villages. No one could say why the dragon seemed to have such an obsessive need to destroy Skendrick's food supply, but the residents had mixed feelings on the subject: on one hand, it would have been nice to have a bacon cheeseburger every once in a while without having to pay an entire gold piece for it because the scarcity of the components needed to make a bacon cheeseburger—namely beef, cheese, and bacon—had driven up the price to insane levels; on the other, the townspeople generally preferred to want a bacon cheeseburger and not have one than to not be able to want one at all, on account of having been immolated by dragon fire.

This particular attack caused the good people of Skendrick to reach something of a tipping point, however. Exhorted to action by the furious Farmer Benton, the village council held an emergency meeting at the town hall to figure out what to do.

You may have noticed, and possibly been driven crazy by, the fact that I'm referring to Skendrick as both a "town" and a "village." First and foremost, if you *did* notice and are bothered by that fact, you are an insufferable pedant and the type of person I like to affectionately refer to as a "kremlaut's face:" kremlauts being a unique kind of horse found in the southern regions of Erithea whose faces look like the hindquarters of other varieties of horses, only without the tail. But, I don't want you to get the idea that I'm imprecise with language, so, for those of you who are not tremendously obnoxious kremlaut's faces, please indulge me as I explain why I keep going back and forth.

It all began with an event that took place in Skendrick

about 200 years ago known colloquially as "The Word Fightin'" (in order to distinguish it, of course, from "The Pointy Things Fightin,'" which occurred some two hundred and fifty years ago, and which cost more than one Skendrickian an arm, leg, eye, or other doubled-up body part). The real reason for the rift is now lost to time, but the primary point (no pun intended) of the argument (The Word Fightin,' that is) was whether to incorporate the living area now known as Skendrick as a town or village. There were, to be fair, logical reasons for doing both—towns generally have larger populations than villages (requiring at least twenty thousand or so residents to officially obtain that designation), but villages possess more farmland within a twenty-five-mile diameter. Each status confers certain benefits—towns, for example, are all highlighted in guidebooks to the region, thereby enhancing tourism, while villages receive special subsidies from the crown in order to grow more food for the kingdom. Some settlements meet the criteria for both designations, but they have to be one or the other on the royal tax rolls, and their location may make one a more logical choice.

Skendrick, however, was well-positioned for tourism—being less than a day's ride from Bethel, which draws thousands of pilgrims each year to its shrine to Helvetica, the goddess and patron deity of printers (an odd bunch, those typesetters), and having a proud printing history of its own—and farming, with its vast tracts of highly productive land, which accounted for a third of the region's barley crop and supplied some of the area's finest whisky distillers. That said, far be it for me to judge anyone who...

No. Screw that. I'm judging. The people of Skendrick are *morons*. Or, at least, the people who were on the town council during "The Word Fightin'" were morons. This type of decision is worth about ten minutes of discussion at a town hall meeting, and that includes pauses for participants to shove donuts into their mouths, with the end result for those on the losing side being a win-some, lose-some shrug and the consumption of another donut. Instead, three straight days of heated arguments ensued, broken up only by brief periods of rest for the verbal combatants to sleep and feed their pet chickens (which tells you something, perhaps, about which designation Skendrick should have chosen). For a brief moment, cooler heads prevailed and someone pragmatically suggested the portmanteau "townage" as a solution. He was promptly shouted down, however, and the battle raged on. Pitchforks were raised in anger (again, pointing toward "village" as the obvious solution; no angry town-dweller has ever threatened someone with a farm implement), though I should note that I always have a hard time telling the difference between a pitchfork being raised in anger and one being raised in joy.

After far too many arguments, threats, and breaks to feed the ingredients of a future bowl of chicken noodle soup, the stalemate was finally broken when one enterprising young council member proposed an external designation of village (to settle the benefits question in a way that was more advantageous to the settlement as a whole), but, in a concession to the highly cosmopolitan "Townies" (as they came to be called, as opposed to the "Villains," which was not a term those who supported the village designation particularly appreciated), suggested that, internally, they use whichever term they preferred. To sweeten the pot, he got the village/town's leading farmers and bakers to agree to provide a steady stream of *kellgaso*, the village/town's most well-known delicacy (a delicious mixture of pears, pastry, pecans, and persimmons...as for why the name of the food itself doesn't start with '*p*,' well, consider the collective brainpower of the governing body), to the owners and operators of the town's most touristy attractions as a means of further attracting visitors. ("Come for the boring lesson on the history of printing, stay for the sticky bun!")

Finally, some semblance of logic had prevailed, but only after the Townies insisted on formally memorializing in writing that, despite Skendrick's official designation as a village, they, and their descendants in perpetuity, would be able to refer to it as a "town" as long as they were within the village limits, and that the gathering place of the village council be called the "town hall." The Villains agreed to this provision, a deal was struck, and perhaps the most ridiculously stupid three-day town hall meeting in the history of stupid town hall meetings came to a close.

Now you, like me, have the burden of knowing far more about Skendrickian politics than you ever cared to, and, if you're like me, feel considerably less bad about the prospect of a dragon digesting and subsequently defecating each and every resident. At the very least, you now have some understanding of the level of competence of the august body that gathered to discuss what to do about the dragon.

"I don't see as how we have much choice," said Alderman Wooddunny, the leader of the council, after he called the meeting to order following much harrumphing from the villagers. "That dragon keeps destroying our crops, we'll have nothing left for trade or to eat. We need to, ah, take action."

"Ye kin hoowel and scram ull ye're wantin'; we'll gae no peece like we ha' way bick win we was gooin' a lick 'em but good," added Farmer Benton.

Alderman Wooddunny looked at his fellow council members and, seeing blank looks on their faces, around the room at the gathered villagers, who showed not even the faintest flicker of recognition that what they'd just heard had in any way constituted human speech. He licked his lips. "Ah, yes, Farmer Benton. Of course. Well said."

Farmer Benton nodded vigorously.

"So," said the Alderman, "in light of Farmer Benton's stirring, ah, words, I propose that we put to a vote our options."

"You haven't given us any, you nitwit!" shouted the Widow

Gershon, maybe a little more disrespectfully than was proper.

"The Widow Gershon have the right of it, she does!" shouted an indignant and nameless Skendrickian whose only contribution to the historical record was that grammatically regrettable outburst.

"Right," replied the Alderman, "I was getting to that. Patience, good people, patience." The crowd quieted as the Alderman held up two fingers. "Now then, as I was about to say, we need to put to a vote our options, and I see those as being two in number.

"The first is to assemble a band of hearty villagers to confront the dragon when next it descends upon us."

This option was greeted with boos, hisses, and a cry of *'sign me up!'* from one man who sheepishly declared that he thought the Alderman had said to assemble "randy, horny pillagers" instead of a "band of hearty villagers." Given the slim chance that a group of men in need of erotic fulfillment would deter the dragon, most of the villagers agreed that it would be good to hear the second option.

"The second is to hire a crew of brave adventurers to seek out the dragon and slay it in its lair. What say you? Option one or option two?"

A chorus of responses rang out, with most seeming to shout *"Two!"* except for a few lusty, and apparently still confused, fellows shouting *"One!"* The resulting cacophony made it impossible to definitively declare a winner.

"Call for a show of hands, you brainless goatherd!" shouted the Widow Gershon helpfully.

Alderman Wooddunny, who was, in fact, a goat herder (one amongst many of his talents and occupations), cleared his throat and held up his hands for silence. "The Widow Gershon is, once again, correct." He bowed to the frowning woman. "Thank you, Widow, for your, ah, helpful suggestion."

"Get bent!" replied the Widow Gershon, spitting a wad of tobacco near the Alderman's right foot.

"Of course, madam," said the Alderman, somehow remaining polite. "Raise your hands if you support option one."

About a quarter of the people in the room raised their hands. The Alderman nodded. "Hmmm. You do understand that there is no sexual congress involved, correct?" Most of the men lowered their hands. "Now then—raise your hands if you support option two."

The remainder of the people in the room raised their hands, including one man who had already raised his hand for option one.

"I'm sorry, Gerard," said the Alderman, "but you can't vote for both options. It won't affect the outcome, but, ah, given that this is on the record, I'd like to make sure the tally is accurate."

Gerard gave him a blank look, scratched his head, scratched his crotch, and then sniffled. "What was the question?"

It really wouldn't have been a tragedy if the dragon had chosen to eat everyone.

"We'll call that a vote for option two," said the Alderman. "Very well—it is decided: the Village of—"

"Town!" shouted a bearded man near the back of the room.

For the first time, the Alderman showed a hint of annoyance. "Fine. The Village, the Town...whatever...of Skendrick hereby declares that it will seek aid from a group of adventurers to slay the dragon that has plagued our fair vil...er, tow...ah, place that we live, to be rewarded from the city's treasury." He turned to an elderly woman seated in the front row. "Loalia," he said, "how much do we, ah, have in the coffers for this purpose?"

The Village Treasurer rose shakily to her feet with the aid

of a cane. She couldn't have been a day over four hundred years old. "Once we pay for the damage caused by this most recent attack...well, let's just say we'll have to hope there are some hard-up adventuring groups running end-of-year sales. Then see if we can get a discount."

The Alderman, as enterprising a person as there was in Skendrick, which is a little bit like saying he was the kindest orc in the grope ("grope," of course, being the technical term for a group of orcs, for reasons it doesn't take much imagination to figure out), ran his hand over his chin in a pondering pose that would have been hackneyed if it wasn't being described by a bard of such incomparable skill. "Well, how about we think of it as an opportunity for an, ah, up-and-coming group of adventurers to make a name for themselves, and the real reward will be the reputational benefits that will redound to them if they defeat the dragon. Oh, and all of the treasure they can plunder from the dragon's lair, of course."

CHAPTER 4

IT IS A RARE BREED THAT CAN COMPLETE AN EPIC DEED

Truly legendary warriors are not born; they are forged in the crucible of combat, tempered in battles that call for fire in the heart and ice in the veins. Sure, they build their skills in the same way a fletcher or wheelwright might, starting with the basic building blocks and gradually learning more and more sophisticated techniques. The stakes, however, are much higher for adventurers—failure means not merely the loss of occupation or income, but rather the loss of limb, or even life. Thus, it is only the bravest and heartiest (and, some might suggest, foolish) individuals who seek this path, for what sane person wishes to face down a dragon's fire, dodge a bolt of lightning flung from an evil wizard's staff, or take on a horde of orcs who threaten to overrun the land of civilized folk?

Fortunately, there are those among us who are willing to take on such challenges, and who have the courage, instincts, and talent to survive their earliest adventures so that they might mature into the types of warriors who can complete even the most impossible quests. It is just such a noble group that this tale is about, a group that came together at just the right place and just the right time, driven together by a combination of coincidence and necessity.

Before those heroes were ready to aid the good people of Skendrick, however, they needed to complete another quest, one that would test their mettle and their commitment and instill them with the confidence they needed to take on an even more daunting mission.

If, that is, they could survive...

CHAPTER 5

NOW, I'M NOT SAYING THEY WEREN'T HEROIC, MIND YOU…

Bards smooth the rough edges of reality and make even the most bumbling idiots look like heroes. We like to think of ourselves as beacons of knowledge, illuminating every corner of the world by sharing insightful tales of the human condition, but, really, we're just glorified ale sellers. Ultimately, our job is to entertain patrons whom the owners of the taverns in which we ply our trade would prefer to drink heavily. Each story has a comforting rhythm to it, a familiar cadence that soothes and lulls unsuspecting patrons into having a third (or fourth, or fifth) ale. To do that, we obscure and ignore certain facts, particularly the mundane and boring parts of adventuring (with rare and generally perverted exceptions, no one wants to know how and where heroes pee), while taking a little creative license to jazz things up. In this instance, though, I think the boring and mundane parts are pretty entertaining, and you're still welcome to drink heavily while I tell it.

The adventuring group that would eventually answer

Skendrick's call for help was undeniably brave, but they were far from legendary, or even particularly experienced. In fact, the group had only recently come together through circumstances that, in and of themselves, would make for an interesting tale, though I'll save it for another occasion. (That's right, printers—there's already a prequel ready and waiting for you; I'm the kind of woman who thinks ahead...or, behind, I guess...and maybe occasionally about behinds, but only if they're really spectacular, and generally only if they're dwarven.) I will, however, tell you about an incident that happened just before they took up the quest to slay the dragon, which will give you some idea about both the group itself and the adventuring life in general.

Rumscrabble Tooltinker, all four feet and nine inches of him, stood in the center of a public square in the city (not to be confused with a town, village, or townage) of Velenia, surrounded by a group of people not much smaller than himself. Unlike Rumscrabble, a very rare half-dwarf, half-halfling (quarterling?), those around him were human children, notwithstanding the presence of a few mothers—of the children present, as opposed to people who just happened to be mothers standing near children who were not their own, which would be weird. Rummy, as he was known for numerous reasons (in addition to being shorter and easier to say than "Rumscrabble," it also described his disposition and the generally spicy scent—not necessarily unpleasant—of his breath), held the rapt attention of his audience, who oohed and aahed at each new feat of prestidigitation he performed.

Side note: I don't generally use a two-gold-piece word when a copper piece word will do, but in certain parts of Erithea, "prestidigitation" is the technical and professional term for sleight-of-hand tricks performed solely through non-magical means. Some street magicians are literally magicians, and their tricks and conjurations involve everything from simple, environment-affecting cantrips to elaborate illusions; others, however—generally less successful, but no less abundant—rely solely on quick hands, nimble fingers, and misdirection to wow their audiences, and Rummy falls into that group. The only thing magical about him was his ability to consume liquor in quantities that would fell a Cormanthian yak beast and still be able to pull off a successful shell game, complete with snappy patter. I'm not even sure *I* would dare to get into a drinking contest with him. I think it was his rare genetic heritage; the dwarven side gave him a higher level of tolerance than most and the halfling side gave him ample room to store it—I swear, it's like they've got a hollow leg.

It was easy to see why the children couldn't take their eyes off of Rummy—with his muttonchops, wiry goatee, sunny smile, dark brown skin, and a pair of golden, wire-framed spectacles perched on the bridge of his bulbous nose, he looked like your favorite uncle (just shorter), and his charisma was matched only by his deft sleight-of-hand skills. The children's mothers were no less enraptured, and Rummy worked both children and adults into his act, asking them to hold onto birds that disappeared beneath silk handkerchiefs, instructing them to draw cards that then showed up elsewhere later in the performance, and making them hold still while he pulled increasingly (and comically) larger coins from a range of ears. An observant bystander might have noticed him performing a higher proportion of ear-pulling tricks with the mothers and lingering a bit longer with them than the children, and that bystander might assume that it was simply the behavior of a lascivious quarterling who had a thing for human women of a certain age.

Rummy, however, was anything but a ladies' man, having rarely, if ever, shown any interest in the fair sex; his interest in the mother members of the audience was less lewd, lascivious, lustful, lecherous, or libidinous than it was financially motivated (or maybe "larcenous").

Incidentally, why are women the "fair sex"? What does that even mean? I resent the implication that because I lack a dangly part, I'm expected to be fair in any sense of the word —I mean, I *am* undoubtedly fair in the sense of my complexion, and if one takes "fair" to mean "attractive," well, that's certainly true, too (objectively speaking). I'm certainly not gentle, demure, or deferential, however, and goodness knows I'll just as readily punch someone—man or woman, incidentally—in the crotch as I will the face in the middle of a bar brawl. I'd suggest that we refer to women as the "superior sex," but that would be sexist of me (albeit factually accurate).

After concluding his performance with an astonishing feat that involved the apparent transformation of a pair of pigeons into a jar of cookies that was then passed around to a cheering audience of sugar-addicted kids, Rummy took a bow and sauntered on down the street. As he walked, an elven woman sidled up next to him and matched his pace, though neither looked at each other and, for a moment, they walked in silence.

The woman was tall and striking by human standards with long blond hair and pale blue eyes, though on the plain side by eleven standards. She walked with the ease of someone who is confident in her ability to handle both the longbow slung over her shoulder and the very sharp sword that hung from her belt. She wore plain leathers, well cared for but worn with use, and her skin was freckled from long hours spent in the sun.

After the pair turned a corner, the woman glanced over at Rummy and said, "How many?"

"Ho ho! Whatever are you implying?"

"I'm not implying anything. I'm straight asking how many mothers of young children you just robbed."

Rummy shook his head and frowned. "Such an ugly word, *'robbed.'* That's something hoodlums do." He sniffed.

"And what are you?"

"An entertainer who simply collects payment for his performances in a discreet way that saves audience members the hassle of having to stand in line to purchase a ticket or the unseemly embarrassment of handing money over directly."

"How many?"

"There were eleven paying customers for today's performance, which I humbly submit was a very fine one."

"Unwilling paying customers."

"I would suggest we call them 'unwitting' paying customers instead—who's to say how they feel about it? It's entirely possible, given the thrills they experienced during the show, that they might have wished to pay even more than they unwittingly did. And, they got cookies, so there's that."

Nadinta Ghettinwood shook her head, both exasperated and amused. "You didn't take too much, I hope?"

Rummy shook his head vigorously. "Never, dear Nadi! I love those wee lads and lasses, and I'd never take the food out of their mouths. A pittance! *Far less in coin than received in pleasure.*' Which, apparently, is the motto of the local house of ill repute."

Nadinta frowned. "And how do you know that? We haven't even been here for a full day."

"Only because I can read—don't fret." Rummy pointed across the street to a sign with that very motto hanging from the balcony of a classy building that looked out of place in the rundown neighborhood through which they walked. "I assume that a place called 'The Soiled Peacock' is a house of ill repute, anyway." He scratched his beard. "I suppose it could it could be a bathhouse for birds, in which case the motto might still be readily, if a bit less aptly, applied."

"Speaking of birds...you're an odd one."

"So I've been told." The pair walked in silence for a few more minutes before Rummy spoke again. "Do we have a plan?"

Nadi took a deep breath, then blew it out slowly. "I'm working on it. I have an idea, but it's not fully baked yet."

"Where are Whiska and Borg?"

Nadinta rolled her eyes. "I'll give you two guesses."

"Ah, I've always been good at guessing games! Now, let me think." Rummy tapped his fingers on his chin as he walked. "Let's start with Borg: he must be at the Feed Bag. Still."

Nadinta nodded. "Got it in one." The Feed Bag was a well-known experimental restaurant in Velenia, one in which, for a fixed price (two silver pieces and five copper), a patron could eat as much as he wanted, refilling his plate over and over until he was satisfied. Everyone thought this was a risky venture until it proved profitable mere weeks after opening, but the arrival of rock giant Borgunder Gunderbor seemed sure to change that situation. Rock giants, of which Borg was a particularly impressive example, stand about nine feet tall, weigh upwards of a full five hundred pounds, and essentially look like a miniature mountain come to life. They have considerable appetites, particularly when it comes to sweets. The Feed Bag's pastry chef would be working overtime.

"As for Whiska...hmmm. Cockfight?"

Nadinta shook her head. "Not this time."

"Bear fight?"

"Not legal in Velenia."

"Yes, laws and regulations are always such effective deterrents when it comes to preventing sick people from making animals fight to the death," said Rummy with his most sarcastic edge, which, truth be told, was not particularly edgy, given his habitual cheerfulness.

"Fair point, but no—she's not at a bear fight."

"Cage fight? Wrestling match? Boxing bout?"

"She doesn't only go to violent events, you know."

"So, then, she's drinking."

"Yes." Nadi sighed. "And possibly trying to start a praying mantis fight."

"Those aren't illegal here?"

Nadi shook her head again. "Frowned upon, but no, not technically illegal."

"Well, what's our next move?"

"You get Whiska and Borg and meet me at the inn—I've got one more clue to chase down."

"Why do I have to get them?"

"Because you're much more persuasive than I am."

"You just don't want to do it."

"That's true."

"Fine." Rummy sighed. "But you owe me one."

"How many times retrieving Borg from a restaurant and Whiska from a bar is saving your life worth? Because I think it's probably more than one," responded Nadinta as she walked away.

Rummy pursed his lips and nodded. "Fair point. I suppose I owe *you* one, or a few, then." He shrugged and headed off in the opposite direction, whistling a jaunty tune.

THERE'S a tricky balance storytellers need to strike between offering sufficient details to build the scene, establish the characters, and give you the information you need to enjoy the twists and turns a good story takes while not boring you by describing every single thing characters do. Borg's bathroom habits, for example, probably shouldn't factor into our tale, and we won't spend time detailing exactly what Rummy has for breakfast every day—unless, of course, either of those things is relevant to the story. (Which, unfortunately, they are in the former case.)

The songs we sing in taverns are the best bits of a story, but they're not the whole story. In writing down this tale, I can tell more than you'd get in a song, and I think those extra parts are worth the price of admission (hopefully a fairly high price), but I also promise not to abuse the power of my unabridged platform by telling you anything that doesn't relate to the story. Okay, well, that's a lie—I'm going to tell you all sorts of things not related to the story. But, none of them will be boring or mundane.

Sometimes, I'll exercise my right to skip over those boring parts, provide a brief summary, and move onto the next good part.

I don't just break hearts, people—I break fourth walls.

CHAPTER 6

WHAT HAPPENS IN VELENIA STAYS IN VELENIA (HOPEFULLY)

After some difficulty, Rummy managed to round up his charges and deliver them to the inn where the group was staying. Nadinta was there waiting for them, pacing back and forth in the common room. "What took you so long?" she asked, ushering them to a table and signaling the innkeeper for food.

"Do you know how long it takes to get a rock giant away from a buffet?" asked Rummy as he settled into his seat. "Only slightly less time than it takes to get a Ratarian away from a glass of champagne."

"It was prosecco, you mouth-breathing midget!" replied Whiska Tailiesen sharply. "You'd think that being the unwanted offspring of two alcoholic races, you would know that, but I guess that's what you get when an ugly dwarf lets a halfwit halfling into her very loose knickers."

Rummy smiled at Whiska before turning his head toward Nadinta and raising an eyebrow. "Can you remind me why we keep her around?"

At that moment, a cockroach skittered across the floor. Whiska pointed at it, uttered an arcane syllable, and a bolt of blue energy shot from her finger, incinerating the bug and leaving nothing but a tiny pile of smoking ash. She cackled with glee. "*That's* why. Because that spell works just the same on orcs."

I should note that Whiska was a Ratarian, a rather interesting race of beings primarily found in southern Verdusk. As a people, Ratarians tend toward belligerence, rudeness, and coarseness. Whiska made most of her people look like choir boys (as opposed to chorus boys, which are a very different thing, and more in line—at least in some respects—with Ratarians). She was, however, a wizard of not inconsiderable power, though her raw ability outstripped her training. When you're an adventuring group just starting out, though, you take what you can get, and it never hurts to have someone along for the ride who both enjoys killing things and is good at it.

"I can't imagine you're still hungry, Borg," said Nadinta as the innkeeper set bowls of stew before them, "so if you don't want yours..."

"I still want...stew. I like...eating. Mmmm," replied the rock giant. Borgunder Gunderbor was a particularly immense representative of his people. His skin was rock hard (obviously) and nearly impenetrable to most mundane weapons (and even some spells). Rock giants aren't stupid, but they *are* slow, both in terms of thought process and speech pattern, which makes them frustrating conversational partners. Despite their size and strength, they aren't usually skilled fighters; they're much better at taking punches than throwing them, and Borg was less adept than most at dealing out pain. Still, they can absorb such absurd amounts of punishment that they're indispensable adventuring companions, and most of them (Borg included) are very sweet. As a result, he was, generally speaking, singularly exempt from being the target of Whiska's ire.

"Well, then, eat up," said Nadi. "You too, Whiska—we need your head clear before we head out."

"This tastes like deer feces," replied Whiska, loudly slurping her stew.

"Sorry it's not to your liking—it's all they've got tonight," said Nadi.

"I didn't say I didn't like it," replied Whiska, sopping up some stew with a piece of crusty bread. "I just said it tastes like deer feces."

The companions finished their meal in silence, notwithstanding the unappetizing sounds Whiska made as she worked her way greedily through her bowl. After a few moments of quiet digestion punctuated by the unique gurglings of a Ratarian stomach, which sound a little bit like an elephant choking on a ham, Nadi cleared her throat and unrolled a parchment on the table, revealing a crisscrossing maze of tunnels. "I think I found a way in—a discreet way."

The companions leaned forward, both to get a better look at the map and to hear Nadi, who lowered her voice as she continued. "On the south side of the city, there's an entrance to the sewers that isn't used by the sanitation crews anymore—partly because they don't want to go into that neighborhood, and partly because there's not much need. Apparently, the residents there tend to use pots, streets, and people they don't like as toilets, which means there's not much use for the sewer other than for storm runoff. Since it rarely storms in Velenia, well, that's not a huge concern." Nadinta tapped the map. "That's our way in."

"You're sure no one will see us?" asked Rummy.

"I'm sure someone will," replied Nadi, "but they're unlikely to be the civic-minded type who would notify the authorities. They're more likely to be the stabbing type who steals purses."

"I'd like them try to steal something off of *me*," cackled Whiska. She pointed to the still-smoking cockroach corpse and crooked her finger.

"I'd prefer we didn't leave a trail of death behind us," replied Nadi, shaking her head. "We need to do this stealthily. We're not being paid by the body."

"We're not *not* being paid by the body though, right?" asked Whiska.

"I guess that's technically accurate, but...just don't kill anyone unless it's absolutely necessary, all right?" said Nadi.

"Humans!" seethed Whiska.

"I'm an elf."

"Whatever! All you pink hairless ones look the same to me."

"Assuming we get into the sewers without incident," interjected Rummy, "then what? Where do we start looking for the statue?"

"Dr. Phelonious believes it will be located somewhere in the sub-sewer of the eastern quadrant of the city," said Nadi.

"Well, that narrows it down. Shouldn't take us more than a year to thoroughly inspect all of those tunnels." Rummy frowned. "I know the good doctor is paying us well, but not *that* well." He raised a finger and smiled. "Maybe we can talk him into a retirement plan!"

"Relax—he gave me a magical amulet that will guide us to the statue."

"How?"

"It's supposed to glow brighter as we get closer. He said it'll work like a charm." Nadi shrugged. "I guess it is a charm, technically."

"The food...doesn't taste...like feces," said Borg. He looked thoughtful. "Not deer feces...anyway."

"Thanks for catching up, big guy," said Rummy, patting him on the arm. "Well, then, I guess we have a plan. When do we head out?"

"Midnight," replied Nadi. "So, no more drinking." She looked at Whiska, who harrumphed loudly. "Go get some rest and we'll meet back here in a couple of hours."

✢

IT WAS JUST past midnight when the quartet of adventurers left the inn and made their way through the darkened streets of Velenia. Despite her size, big for an elf, Nadi moved gracefully and silently, and Rummy did a passable imitation of her stealth, though his rumbling stomach would have earned more than one disapproving glare from Nadi if not for the fact that Borg, on account of having feet the size of a mastiff but the coordination of a newborn deer, and Whiska, on account of not really caring all that much about remaining silent and being much more interested in muttering imprecations about everyone she would obliterate if they got in her way, drew all of her attention.

After a while, Rummy shrugged and stopped trying so hard to mask his footfalls, even going so far as to start to whistle. Nadi gritted her teeth and walked faster. Rummy increased his own pace to catch up to her. "Hey, don't worry so much—no street thug in his right mind is going to jump a rock giant and a Ratarian."

"Borg's about as dangerous with a weapon in his hand as a fish is with a sword strapped to it."

"Yeah, but no one knows that...all they see is nine feet of gray muscle. The only one who might possibly be interested in accosting us is a drunken lady with a weird rock fetish. Or a drunken gent with one—I don't judge or discriminate. Though, I must say, you'd have to be a little, well, off to want to make love to *that*." He nodded toward their granite-jawed (and bodied) companion.

"That may be true," replied Nadi, "for now, at least. Things will be different when we get underground."

"You think there are things underground that are going to want to want to make love to Borg? Gross."

"I give up," said Nadi, throwing her hands in the air. The group walked the rest of the way in relative silence, coming to a stop when they reached the alleyway in which they would, according to the map, find the seldom-used entrance to the sewers.

Borg, whose strength matched his physique, removed the iron cap that covered the entrance, and the four adventurers fell back as they were pummeled by the stench of the after-meal remnants of a thousand unhealthy pub-goers. After a few moments of gasping and wiping watery eyes, Borg spoke. "I think...this is...the sewer."

"Or Nadi's mom's boudoir," said Whiska.

"My mother is nine hundred years old," replied Nadinta, nonplussed.

"Exactly!"

Nadi shook her head. "I don't understand Ratarian humor."

"Ratarians understand humor?" asked Rummy innocently.

"Bah! Hairless dragon food!" Whiska shook her head. "Come on." She started to climb down into the hole, scrabbling down the ladder that led into the sewer.

"Age before beauty," said Rummy, motioning to Nadi to go first.

She stuck her tongue out at her diminutive companion, but moved quickly down the ladder.

"You're up, Borg. Or down, I guess," said Rummy.

"I'm not...dragon food. Just...hairless."

"She was trying to be funny, big guy."

"Just correcting...factual errors."

"Always good practice." Rummy watched Borg descend and then followed suit, stepping gingerly off the ladder into an inch-deep slurry of human waste. (Sometimes it's fun to be the adventurer; more often than not, though, it's much, much more fun to be the storyteller, especially if you prefer to keep your shoes free of feces. Which I do.)

Nadi nodded at her companions and took the lead, walking straight for fifty yards before taking a right turn, continuing on for twenty-five more yards, and then hooking a left, following the instructions on the map. Given that everyone in the group had some form of night vision, no one suggested they light a torch, which was just as well; the accumulation of excremental gases in the sludge they trudged through would have exploded the moment a spark touched the ground. Contrary to their approach aboveground, they walked in silence through the sewers, focused on inhaling as little of the filth as possible (except for Whiska, who not only found the stench bearable, but wistfully noted that it reminded her of both a former lover and her mother's cooking).

A few moments later, Nadi raised her hand, signaling her companions to halt. Rummy gave her a questioning look, but she just shook her head and pointed to her ear. She leaned forward, listening intently, while Rummy, whose hearing wasn't nearly as acute, nervously gripped the handle of his mace, a weapon that looked too large for him and about as comfortable in his hand as a quill snake. Whiska's ears perked up and she raised her staff. Borg scratched an itch that appeared to originate in his crotch, but ran all the way up to his lower abdomen before making its way back to his crotch.

Nadi's brow furrowed for a brief second before her eyes shot wide open. "Come on!" she shouted, racing down the corridor and looking frantically left and right. The rest of the group followed, confused by her sudden urgency and struggling to keep up. Eventually, however, they found Nadi standing in the center of a large chamber. She had her sword out and a grim look on her face. "Circle up—Rummy on my left, Whiska on my right, Borg at my back."

"What's going on?" asked Rummy, dutifully trotting to his designated spot.

Borg followed suit, though Whiska took her time, pausing to extract something from her whiskers, sniff it, and then pop it into her mouth. "What?" she said in response to Nadi's disgusted look. "Part of a grasshopper."

"Never mind—just get in position. We're about to have company."

Whiska shrugged and took her place, and the four waited silently. Nothing happened. They waited another minute, tense and ready. Still, nothing happened.

"Um, Nadi?" asked Rummy.

"Quiet!"

"Sure, but, uh, any idea what we're waiting for?"

Nadi relaxed slightly. "I thought I heard something."

"Was it rats?" asked Whiska. "You think it was rats."

"Well, Whiska," said Rummy, "we are in a sewer, and they do tend to..."

"It wasn't rats," interjected Nadi. "At least, not just rats—though I think I heard some of those too."

"You humans...always so afraid of the rats!" Whiska grunted. "As well you should be—a single rat could gnaw your leg off, given enough time."

"I'm not a *human*!" yelled Nadi, instantly regretting it.

"Hairless pinkie. Hmmph."

"Just be quiet! All of you!"

The four of them looked around, seeking the source of Nadi's concern, but they still heard nothing.

"I...wasn't making...noise," said Borg a moment later.

Nadi ground her teeth and relaxed her stance. She was about to tell her companions that they should start moving again when all four of them heard a long, low growl. Nadi whirled around. "Tell me you all heard *that*, at least."

Rummy nodded. "What *was* that?"

"It was...that giant...cat bush," said Borg, pointing toward where they'd entered the chamber.

The creature they faced looked like a cross between a panther and a shrubbery, all sleek black muscles and twiggy, leaf-covered spikes. Or, something that looked like leaves, anyway—they were actually razor-sharp projectiles that could be hurled by the beast and regrown over the course of a few days. Not exactly the kind of thing you want to run into in a dark sewer tunnel, or anywhere else for that matter.

"Okay," amended Rummy, "what *is* that?"

The creature shot a pair of leaves toward the group, which Borg stepped in front to deflect, the missiles bouncing off him and doing no apparent harm. Nadi, sword at the ready, circled around Borg and yelled, "I don't know, but maybe let's figure it out after it stops trying to kill us!" as she rushed the beast.

"Relax," said Whiska, sifting through pouches at her belt for spell components, "it's just a bushlinks."

"Really looks more like a panther than a lynx to me," said Rummy, looking doubtfully at his tiny mace and then at their foe.

"Links—with a 'k,' you mostly hairless twit!" Whiska yelled in concession to Rummy's beard. "Subterranean scavengers, mostly. They've got sensitive eyes, so they really hate it when you do this." Whiska muttered two syllables and then hurled a handful of powder toward the creature's feet. The instant the powder landed, a bright light flashed through the cavern, searing the retinas of everyone unfortunate enough to be looking at it, which was everyone except for Whiska, who had closed her eyes. "Close your eyes!" she shouted.

Rummy, clawing at his eyes, screamed, "Why not just punch me in the face and then tell me to duck?! Instructions come first, Whiska—instructions come first!"

"Oops," said the Ratarian sheepishly, offering a shrug no one could see.

Nadi, who had closed swiftly on the creature, lashed out blindly with her sword in the beast's general direction, which was fairly easy to locate due to its furious yowls. She felt the tip of her sword strike home, so she readjusted the angle of her blade and thrust forward hard, feeling it sink deeply into something soft and yielding. The creature's yowls turned to yelps and Nadi opened her stinging eyes, blinking back tears as she twisted her sword and pushed in deeper.

A moment later, the beast's yelps became whimpers; shortly after that, it ceased making noise entirely.

"Well," said Rummy, rubbing his eyes and blinking rapidly, "I guess that's one way to take care of a bushlinks. Bushlink? What's the singular form?"

"I'm more concerned with whether there are any others nearby," replied Nadi, squinting as she looked around the chamber.

Whiska shook her head. "Bushlinks travel alone—they're very territorial."

"How do you know all this stuff about bushlinks?" asked Rummy, curious.

"Oh, I don't know, because I'm not a moron? Because I've read a book? Because if you don't know how to kill what wants to kill you, you end up getting killed?"

"All good reasons," replied Rummy cheerily. "Shall we?" He motioned for Nadi to continue on.

Nadi blinked her eyes one more time and nodded, resuming her position at the point and leading her companions on as directed by the map.

Over the course of the next two hours, they killed two snakes (neither of which was poisonous); got peed on by a snizzard (a breed of lizard that likes to hang out in urban subterranean areas and is known for both its disproportionately large and prominent genitalia and exceedingly voluminous bladders—yes, bladders, plural); heard some goblins snickering but didn't see them; trudged through excrement and waste that was, at times, hip-deep for a less-than-thrilled half-dwarf, half-halfling; and found treasure that amounted to three buttons, a broken wine glass, half a spool of string, a few rotten apple cores, and two copper pieces, both of which Whiska gleefully laid claim to despite the party's preexisting agreement to split all treasure equally. (Two coppers, incidentally, would be just about sufficient to purchase the apples they found the remains of, so it wasn't exactly a windfall for the wizard; it probably had more to do with Ratarians' love of shiny things, which they defensively insisted had nothing to do with their rodent heritage.)

There's a saying amongst adventurers: it's not a quest until you're covered in snizzard pee and have shit on your knees.

Finally, tired and smelling like a furyak's breath in the morning, the brave heroes reached the chamber that the map indicated held the statue they sought. They burst in, weapons and spells at the ready, expecting some fierce guardian, only to find dust, cobwebs, and about one hundred and fifty statues of similar size and appearance.

"Dragon balls," muttered Nadi as she looked around in a vain effort to identify the statue. "I was sort of hoping it would be the only thing in here, or have a note on it or something. Is that too much to ask after wading through feces for the past few hours?"

"Stop worrying, you shaven sow," said Whiska, picking up the nearest statue and dropping it on the brick floor, where it exploded into pieces. "Magical items are tougher than most." She picked up another statue and shattered it alongside its unfortunate predecessor. A third soon followed. "Whichever one doesn't break is the one we're looking for."

"I can...help." With one mighty sweep of his massive arm, Borg sent a dozen statues tumbling to the floor; every one shattered. He smiled. "Nope." He moved to another shelf and cleared it with the same result.

"Are we really sure this is the best way to find it?" asked Rummy, wincing as Borg sent another ten statues to their doom.

"You got a better idea?" replied Whiska, smashing a statue.

"Well, no, but maybe you've got a detect magic spell, or something that might—"

"Found it!" Whiska sang out, scooping up a statue Borg had dropped that didn't show the slightest crack or dent.

"Are you sure that's it?" asked Nadi.

Whiska shrugged. "What's it supposed to do?"

"Cure illness and disease."

Whiska scratched her ear with her tail. "Can't really test that easily."

"No." Nadi furrowed her brow. "You can't think of any magical ways to figure out whether this is really the right statue?"

"What do I look like, an oracle?"

"Not really," replied Rummy. "I always picture them having wings. And maybe the face of a cat or lion."

"You're thinking of a sphinx, you ninny."

"Really? Huh." Rummy scratched his head. "I need to bone up on my sooth-saying beings."

"Can we focus?" asked Nadi, exasperated. "I'd rather not have to come back down and do this again."

"If we ever *do* do this again, Nadi, maybe we can get our employer to draw us a picture," said Rummy.

"Let's just take the statue and get out of here," said Whiska. "The smells down here are making me hungry—I need to get something to eat."

"That statue," said Borg, gesturing to the one Whiska held, "didn't break. When it fell."

"Right you are, Borg," Nadi sighed. "Come on—let's go."

After another long slog through feces and other, even less savory things, our heroes returned to the surface and stopped by their inn to cleanse themselves (though short of burning off their skin, there was no way to get rid of the stench that clung to them entirely), change their clothes, and, in Whiska's case, inhale a plate of leftovers that the innkeeper managed to find in the kitchen. They then headed to a quiet home in one of the tonier neighborhoods of the city to deliver the statue to their employer.

He opened the door himself when Nadi knocked, which surprised her; given the size of his house, she had expected a servant to greet them. "Come in, come in," said the man, hale and hearty despite his gray hair and wrinkles, motioning them inside. He wrinkled his nose as they passed, a testament to the lingering stench of adventuring success, but didn't comment. He closed the door quickly once they were inside and clasped his hands together, his eyes shining eagerly. He eyed the bundle of rags Nadi cradled to her chest. "Is that it?" The man reached for it, but she turned deftly, and subtly, away.

"We believe it is, Doctor, but there was an...unexpected complication in retrieving it."

"What? What was it?" The man's tone shifted from warm and friendly to sharp and shrill, and his sudden twitchiness contrasted sharply with the geniality he had displayed when he had hired Nadi the previous day to retrieve the statue.

"Your directions to the statue's location were very helpful, and, we believe, proved correct, in that we found a statue," said Nadi.

"And we got to wade through shit to get to it, too, which was great," added Whiska.

The doctor blinked. "Perhaps I'm just not very familiar with Ratarians, but do you not know how to include a particular inflection in your voice when you say something sarcastic?"

"Who said anything sarcastic?" replied Whiska. "I love shit. Smelling it, rolling in it, taking a little taste...all of it. It's all good."

Whiska looked around, but no one could quite bring themselves to make eye contact with her. "Well, this is awkward," muttered Rummy. "Rolling in it? Really?"

"You said you found *a* statue," said the doctor, clearly eager to get the conversation back on track. "Did you find *my* statue? Show me!"

Nadi looked taken aback by the doctor's intensity, but nodded and unwrapped the statue. "We found dozens of identical statues, maybe even hundreds. We relied on the counsel of our, ah, wizard,"—she inclined her head toward Whiska—"to determine which was the one we were looking for, and we believe this is the right one."

The doctor practically ripped the statue out of Nadi's hands, pulling it close and holding it up before his face. He muttered a couple of unintelligible words and the statue began to glow red. The doctor threw his head back and laughed, a joyous roar that echoed off the walls.

"You've got admirable enthusiasm for helping people, Doctor," said Rummy. "A real passion for curing the sick. That's what this thing does, right? Because I've got this bunion..."

"*FOOLS!*" roared the doctor before throwing his head back and laughing again. "You have no idea what you've done!"

"Not quite what I pictured when you called him a 'nice old man,' Nadi," said Rummy.

Nadi drew her sword. "What's going on?"

"This statue can no more heal your bunion, dwarf, than it can the common cold," said the doctor.

"Half-dwarf," said Rummy. "Half-halfling. It's the beard that throws people off."

"Then what does it do?" asked Nadi, dropping into a battle stance.

"This!" bellowed the doctor, pointing the statue at Nadi, who dove to the side just as a bolt of energy whistled out of the statue's mouth and immolated a credenza that had, a second before, stood behind her.

"The doctor...is not a...nice old man," said Borg.

"Whiska—now!" Nadi yelled as she rolled back to her feet.

Whiska muttered an incantation and held out her fingers, unleashing a torrent of magical projectiles at the doctor. She cackled with glee as they struck him, but stopped when the doctor, too, started laughing before pointing the statue at her, seemingly unfazed by the barrage of magical energy that had just exploded against his chest.

"Mother fu—" The rest of Whiska's eloquent response was drowned out by a rush of energy from the statue, which blasted her in the stomach, and her own screams of pain.

Nadi surged forward, sword leading, and hacked at the doctor, who grinned as the sword bounced off his thigh without doing any damage. "That's not good," she muttered.

The doctor turned the statue in her direction and unleashed its power; fortunately for Nadi, Rummy was a step faster, diving into her and bringing her to the ground just before the blast reached her. Nadi grunted as she hit the floor, the wind knocked out of her, and Rummy moaned and grabbed a very bruised right elbow.

"Borg," Nadi managed to gasp, "help!"

Borg nodded and moved slowly to stand before the doctor, who smirked. "You'll fall just as hard and as quickly, you overgrown pebble!" The statue glowed and released its energy once more, striking Borg squarely in the chest.

"Heh. Tickles...a little," he said, looking down curiously

at where eldritch energy crackled down toward his abdomen. "Stings, too."

The doctor looked confused. "What are you?"

"What are *you*, you maniac?" growled Whiska, climbing slowly, and painfully, to her feet. "You owe us money!"

"Maybe," said Rummy, cradling his injured arm against his body, "we worry less about the debt the good Doctor owes us and more about our ability to remain alive, without which, I'm told, it's difficult to spend money anyway."

"No way! This sack of excrement owes us gold. We're not leaving here until—" The rest of Whiska's comment was cut off once again as a tendril of energy snaked around Borg's blocking body and hit her tail, making it spasm and twitch as she yowled. "Fine! We'll do it your way!" She bolted for the front door.

"I think our rodent friend has the right idea, Nadi." Rummy backed slowly toward the door, his mace clutched in his hand, though, for the second time that day, he looked down at it and shook his head, thinking that he would be just as well equipped for this fight if he were holding the rotting carcass of a particularly ugly muskrat. "Come on!"

"I'm not leaving Borg!" Nadi circled around the rock giant and stabbed with her sword; in return, she took a hit from the statue that sent her tumbling. She came to rest at Rummy's feet.

"You mean the guy who said that the thing that just knocked you on your backside tickles? I think he'll be fine. Come on." Rummy grimaced as he reached down to help Nadi to her feet, the energy from the statue coursing up his arm and giving him a painful jolt.

"That's it...run, little dwarfling, and take your haughty companion with you!"

"Haughty? Really?" Rummy shook his head in a rare display of disgust. "Do you want to call me industrious and avaricious while you're at it? Because all elves and dwarves have the same character traits, right, you power-mad racist? Well, the joke's on you, because I'm not even a little industrious." He looked at Nadi. "I'm not such a big fan of this guy. Why did we agree to work for him?"

Nadi gritted her teeth as she got back up. "It's not my fault! He came highly recommended—he was supposed to be one of the city's most prominent leaders, a doctor known for his kindness and efforts to help the poor!"

"Oh, I plan to help them, all right—help them to die in agony! Ahahahahaha!" The doctor threw his head back and cackled, honestly cackled, in the way that only a delighted and insane wizard, or maybe a hen laying a double egg, can.

"Borg!" yelled Nadi. "We need to go—you've got to get out of there!"

"I don't think...the wizard...is going...to pay us," replied Borg.

"Borg's keen powers of observation appear to remain intact even when he's under duress," noted Rummy as he ducked out the front door.

Nadi reached into a pouch on her belt and pulled out a tiny pellet. "Borg, when I say now, run!"

The wizard cackled again as he hit Borg with another jolt of energy; this time, the giant grunted, apparently beginning to feel the cumulative effect of so much magical energy. "Running is...hard."

"Just do it!" She threw the pellet at the doctor's feet; smoke exploded from it, obscuring everything in the room and turning the doctor's shrieks of laughter into coughs. "Now!"

Nadi hurried toward the door, holding her breath and waving her hand in front of her face to try to clear her stinging eyes. A moment later, she emerged into the night air, coughing and hacking and looking anxiously behind her.

Whiska and Rummy were nearby, weapons at the ready. "Where's Borg?" asked Rummy.

"He should be right behind me—I told him to run."

"You know that a rock giant's top speed is about as fast as a snail's saunter, right?" replied Rummy.

"Come on, Borg," muttered Nadi. "Come on!"

Finally, after what seemed like an hour, the rock giant's massive silhouette appeared in the doorway and he strode toward them. "Smoky," he said.

"Let's not dilly-dally, shall we?" said Rummy.

Nadi stared hard at the house; smoke billowed from the front door and obscured the view through the windows. "Where is he?"

"Taking a smoke break?" Rummy looked at his companions. "Come on, that's funny!" He shook his head when no one laughed. "Let's go."

"Hold on," said Whiska. She held her staff up and pointed it toward the door, launching a massive fireball that exploded when it hit the doorframe. "Heh heh. Fire."

"Coming, Nadi?" said Rummy.

Nadinta tore her gaze from the house. "We need to stop him."

"Look, generally speaking, you know I'm on board with righting the wrongs and stopping the bad guys. It's why I decided to give this adventuring thing a go. Well, that and the treasure...though we haven't found much of that. And some of us are hoarding what little bit we've found." Rummy looked pointedly at Whiska, who sniffed and harrumphed. "But...this guy's out of our league. If it hadn't been for the fact that we're traveling with a giant rock"—he inclined his head toward Borg—"we'd all be smoking corpses right now. I know we haven't been doing this very long, but if there's one thing I know, it's that sometimes you just need to walk away and live to fight...or run away again, I guess...another day."

"I hate to say it, but pube-beard is right," said Whiska.

"Pube-beard?" muttered Rummy. "I admit that it's not as thick as a full-blooded dwarf, but I think that's a little bit—"

"I don't think any of my magic is going to be much good against the old bag of skin," said Whiska, ignoring Rummy, "and I'm the most powerful weapon we've got. We need to run, Nadi."

Nadi ground her teeth. "What do you think, Borg?"

"Smoke break. Heh. That's...funny."

"See? I told you," said Rummy.

Nadi rolled her eyes. "Fine, but we're coming back at some point. We just gave a lunatic a weapon of immense power, and every single person he hurts with it is on us."

"Maybe we need a better vetting process when it comes to our potential employers..."

"Not now, Rummy. Come on—before he comes after us." Nadi sheathed her sword and strode off at a brisk pace, matched by Whiska, with Rummy and his little legs, and Borg and his inability to move with anything resembling haste, struggling to keep up.

CHAPTER 7

A CLARION CALL FOR NOBLE AND HEROIC WARRIORS

The steadfast and resilient residents of the village of Skendrick sent forth a call for aid and succor from a band of heroic adventurers whose might and courage would enable them to sally forth and seek out the mighty wyrm in its lair and, by virtue of their strength at arms and magical might, slay the awesome beast and lay claim to its treasure hoard.

Far and wide went the call, and many famed adventuring bands, from the Company of the Dancing Scimitar to ThreeD (the Death-Dealing Dwarves) to the Barbarian Horde of North Babador, heard the summons and considered whether they could help the good people of Skendrick in their hour of need.

But, while the task was worthy of the most renowned adventurers, many of those noble bands of heroes were already engaged in epic quests of their own, and so it was that a lesser-known band of hearty warriors would ultimately come to answer the call, their desire to build a name for themselves as a distinguished adventuring company surpassed only by their desire to ensure the safety of the people of Skendrick.

It would, however, take the heroic efforts of one of Erithea's most celebrated bards to bring the adventurers to the good people who so desperately needed their assistance.

CHAPTER 8

A CLARION CALL IS MET WITH INDIFFERENCE, BUT FINALLY ANSWERED IN AN UNEXPECTED WAY

It's true that a who's-who of adventuring companies heard about Skendrick's call for help, albeit weeks later and after the dragon had ravaged the surrounding countryside a few more times. But reactions to the desperate plea were indifferent at best. The Company of the Dancing Scimitar, for example, snorted at the lack of reward and then went back to snorting various narcotic powders. The Death-Dealing Dwarves were too drunk to do anything more than giggle over the word "Skendrick," which, in the dialect of the dwarven stronghold from which they hailed, referred to the very special (and odiferous) type of sweat that builds up beneath a dwarf's nethers after a hard day at the forge, as in, "Ach! It's been a long day workin' the bellows, and me giggle-berries be covered in skendrick; might be that it's time for a washin' before the alehouse." And, while the Barbarian Horde of North Babador discussed the matter seriously, they concluded by raising a toast to the dragon in recognition of its might and contemplating the prospect of looting the corpses of the villagers if the dragon made a particularly deadly assault.

In short, powerful adventurers weren't exactly stepping on each other's mother's throats for the chance to help the good people of Skendrick. So, the Skendrickians waited, and it was in their hour of greatest need that they showed their true spirit. Alderman Wooddunny called a townage hall meeting to address everyone's concerns.

"Gi' th' blurnin' widdah the wee burn a' th' stake afore th' beast strikes agin! It's all hur doin', what wi' sayin' nay t' doin' a wee bit o' th' double-backed beast wi' a man's as honest as a day's long, and him bein' twice as much so!" exclaimed Farmer Benton heatedly to start the proceedings.

"While we appreciate your opinion, as always, Farmer Benton," replied the Alderman smoothly, "I'm quite sure that it's not the Widow Gershon's unwillingness to, ah, lie with you that's causing the dragon to attack. As such, burning her at the stake is unlikely to resolve our situation."

"Ach! How do ye ken fer suren? Might culd be her munthly bleed!"

"I haven't had a monthly bleed in fifteen years, you tiny-todgered pig lover!"

"Thank you, Widow Gershon." Alderman Wooddunny massaged his temples. "Now then, does anyone have any, ah, more constructive suggestions as to how we might find some capable, or at least willing, adventurers to come to our assistance?"

The citizens of Skendrick looked at each other blankly. Finally, after several moments of awkward silence in which the snuffling and snorting of a piglet in Farmer Benton's lap lent credence to the Widow Gershon's accusation of porcine affection and prompted a "Likes 'em young, you see?" comment from the Widow, a young man stood, cleared his throat nervously, and said, quietly, "Maybe we could...I dunno...offer a bit more of a reward?"

"Now, that's not an unreasonable solution to propose, Goodman Youngman," replied the Alderman, "but, I'm afraid our coffers are, ah, rather less well apportioned than would be ideal—due in large part to the lost sales of the crops the dragon has destroyed."

"Th' harrible crecher took a shine ta th' Brussels in me field, it did! Wiped 'em but clean," said a bewildered Farmer Benton, apparently, and perhaps justifiably, mystified by the dragon's particular focus on his fields of Brussels sprouts.

"Yes, well, be that as it may," replied the Alderman, "I fear that offering more money is, ah, not an option we can pursue." He paused and looked slowly around the room. "Does anyone else have an idea? Anyone?"

More awkward silence followed, broken only by a pig's squeal, an urgent shushing sound, and a low rumbling from the seat of Goodman Breakwind.

Alderman Wooddunny sighed. "Very well, then. I suppose we shall, ah, just continue to wait and hope that the missives we sent out will—"

The Alderman was interrupted when a young girl stood up and said, "Excuse me, Mr. Alderman, sir?"

The Alderman raised an eyebrow in surprise. "The floor recognizes Betty Sue Etterkin. You may address the floor, Miss Etterkin."

Seven-year-old Betty Sue Etterkin looked around with unsettling poise and more maturity than most in the room could have mustered. "Well, Mr. Alderman, sir...maybe we need a little marketing help."

"Marketing?" replied Alderman Wooddunny, confused.

"Yes, marketing."

"What do you mean '*marketing*'?"

"Something hip. Something catchy. Something sexy. We live in a boring village that—"

"Town! We live in a boring town!" someone shouted,

which resulted in five minutes of yelling and grumbling before order was restored.

"Please continue, Miss Etterkin."

"Thank you, Alderman. It's just, who would want to come rescue a boring village that's losing a bunch of boring vegetables, especially when the call for help we sent out is so dull?"

The Alderman, who had authored the call for help, frowned. "And just what would you propose?"

Betty Sue shrugged. "I don't know. I'm seven years old, remember? Shouldn't you all be coming up with ideas?" Everyone in the room looked at each other sheepishly, but no one said anything. "I'm just saying that we could probably sex things up a little."

"Harlot!" shouted the Widow Gershon.

"Thank you, Widow," said the Alderman.

"What if we, I don't know, hired a bard to spread the word?" said Betty Sue.

"A bard?" said Goodman Youngman. "Won't that cost money?"

Betty Sue shrugged again. "Like I said, I'm seven. Figure it out, grown-ups."

Alderman Wooddunny rubbed his chin. "It's not a bad idea. And if the bard is good enough..." His voice trailed off as he considered the girl's suggestion.

When he still hadn't spoken a moment later, the Widow Gershon kindly reminded him that they were still waiting by shouting, "Finish your thought, virgin!"

"I was just thinking," replied the Alderman, refusing to rise to the Widow's bait, "that if the bard is, ah, persuasive enough, perhaps he, or she, can emphasize the dragon's considerable hoard of treasure, and while I wouldn't go so far as to suggest that our messenger lie, per se, a judicious embellishment of the truth might suggest that the dragon's gold and jewels might be sufficient enough reward."

"Well, then, get a song whore in here and be done with it!" shouted the Widow Gershon.

"It does sound good in theory, certainly," replied the Alderman, "but that leaves us needing to find a bard...I don't suppose anyone here knows one?" he asked, his tone somehow both hopeful and doubtful.

"I was in Borden just last night," offered a slouching, middle-aged man who smelled faintly of stale ale and had a stocky frame now gone to seed, his paunch jutting just over the lip of his belt. (In other words, a representation of my core audience straight out of central casting.) "At the tavern there, Big Bob's, was an elf girl...had a real pretty voice. Funny, too, but bawdier maybe than the Widow Gershon might like." He nodded in the Widow's direction.

"Elven song whore!" yelled the Widow Gershon.

"Had a real nice can, too, if it's not improper to say," continued the man.

"It actually is," replied the Alderman. "Exceedingly improper, in fact."

The slouchy man nodded. "Well, all the same, her can was just the sweetest."

"Mebbe we brang the wee lass wi' the swee' can aboot so might she sing the fowel beastie inta slumbrin' times, what say?" said Farmer Benton.

"I'm not sure we're focusing entirely on her best and most relevant credentials," said Alderman Wooddunny, "but it seems as though she may be about as good of an option as we can hope for. And, at least she's nearby." He raised his hands and then dropped them, a gesture that could have been an expression of either exasperation or an involuntary twitch. "You say she was in Borden last night, Goodman Drunk-man...do you know where she was headed afterward?"

The man shrugged. "Not sure, Alderman, but can't imagine she's gone far. Maybe I could go back round to Big

Bob's and feel her up to see if she's interested, if she's still there."

"Feel her out, you mean. Not up," replied the Alderman.

"Right. Feel her out."

"Well, ah, I would suggest that you go as quickly as possible. Goodman Youngman—please go with him. I empower you both to offer her the sum of up to ten gold pieces from the town's coffers."

"We'll leave right now, Alderman," replied Goodman Drunkman, sipping from a flask he had produced from somewhere beneath his gut.

"One last thing," Alderman Wooddunny said as the men moved toward the door, "what did you say this bard's name was?"

"Heloise."

And that's when the *real* hero entered the story.

CHAPTER 9

THE MODEST BARD ENTERS AND HUMBLY OFFERS HER SERVICES

And so did Goodman Youngman and Goodman Drunkman, Skendrick's capable and clever emissaries, depart for the town of Borden to seek out the bard known variously as Heloise the Beautiful, Heloise the Tuneful, and Heloise of the Sweet Can. They found her there, in the common room of the inn where Goodman Drunkman had seen her the evening before, strumming her lute and bringing it into perfect tune.

They made their impassioned entreaty, describing the horror-filled shrieks and rivers of blood that ran through the streets of Skendrick as the mighty and fearsome Dragonia ravaged their land, and the brave resolve of the townspeople in the face of such pain and suffering. They told her of the town's desperate plea for help and the heroic attempts made by some of Erithea's most legendary adventuring groups to render their aid, only to be detained or delayed by other, even more epic quests. And they begged her to lend the vastness of her storytelling powers in the *service of the town, to save its people from certain extinction should the dragon be permitted to continue its ravages unchecked.*

The humble and self-effacing bard nodded as the townsmen spoke, expressing her sincere sympathy for their plight, and she rose boldly to her feet as they finished their tale, exclaiming passionately and for all in the crowded inn to hear that she would not only aid the good people of Skendrick in finding their champions, but would hear no talk of reward or payment for her services —the people needed her, and so she would risk life and limb to find the heroes the town so desperately sought in its hour of need simply because it was the right thing to do.

Goodman Drunkman fell to his knees and wrapped his arms around the great bard's legs, sobbing his thanks, as Goodman Youngman, overcome with gratitude and emotion, sank into the closest chair just before he fainted.

Heloise the Bard calmed and soothed the men and raised their spirits high, making them feel as they had not felt since before the terrible dragon's wrath had been unleashed upon Skendrick. She brought them both back to their feet and bid them follow her, leading them out of the inn on a mission to find their saviors.

She knew she would not fail, for she could not—lives hung in the balance, an entire town depended on her, and so the noble bard with perhaps the world's silkiest hair would rise to the occasion.

CHAPTER 10

**IN REALITY, THE PEERLESS BARD RESPONDS
INDIFFERENTLY TO AN ABSURD LOWBALL
PROPOSAL**

If this were a performance and I were describing Borden, I'd probably call it tranquil and idyllic, but those are really just polite ways of saying boring and filled with lazy people, and since I don't need to be polite here, I'll say this: Borden is a boring place full of lazy, and frequently chauvinistic, people. On the plus side, lazy chauvinists do love to drink, and so the few taverns there tend to do a rousing business, though where the patrons get the money they spend every night on drink and what is, in all honesty, a pretty homely bunch of hookers is beyond me. I assume that something illicit is involved, but have never been inclined to do any sort of actual investigating.

Suffice it to say, Borden's not exactly a star-making destination for bards on the rise, but it does consistently offer gigs with solid pay, so if I'm in the region, I make it a point to stop over for a night or two. Around the time the people of Skendrick were so desperately seeking assistance with their little dragon problem, I was in the middle of a two-night stint at Big Bob's, the nicest tavern in Borden, which is a little bit like saying it's the least drunk sailor in a dockside bar. Still, the disappointingly regular-sized Robert, the proprietor and namesake of the establishment, didn't ogle me, paid performers well, and at least had a decent selection of ales, so it was my preferred stop when I was in Borden.

After an epic performance the night before that had featured a packed house pitching in on a rousing singalong of "Back to Borden" as well as four black eyes (all of which were gifts from me to a cheeky Arachnidian who decided that all eight of his legs would be best served attempting to touch various parts of my person...I should note that the spider-like Arachnidians also have eight eyes, so I was kind enough to leave half of them uninjured), I was enjoying some downtime in the taproom with a cold ale as I thought through which songs I would perform for my second show later that evening. There were maybe three or four other patrons scattered across the room lazily sipping drinks, half-asleep in that late afternoon hour at which the body is naturally inclined to want to doze—though, to be fair, I think that description applies to every hour of the day in Borden.

My quiet reverie was interrupted when two men burst through the door, both panting and wheezing. One, young and scrawny, had a scraggly brown tangle on his chin reminiscent of the type of hair you hope never to find in your bed at an inn. The other, red-faced, bulb-nosed, and stocky, shook slightly, though his tremors stopped the moment he spied the ale taps. Nerves restored, he turned his eyes to the room's most beautiful occupant and stumbled over, his pubescent, pube-faced friend in tow.

"There she is! She's the one I told you about—Hermione, Hermione the bard!"

"Sort of close," I said by way of response. "Lot less nerdy, little classier, just as smart—it's Heloise, actually." I directed this comment at the younger man.

It could have been a combination of awestruck wonder at my beauty or simply a lack of intellectual horsepower, or maybe both, but the only response the lad could muster was to say, "What is 'nerdy'?"

"I'd show you, but I don't have a mirror handy just now," I said, finishing the last swallow of ale in my mug. I signaled to the barmaid for a refill.

"Me too!" the older man shouted as she turned toward the bar. "I'll have one, I mean."

"And you're buying, right?" I said.

The two men looked at each other.

"Are we?" asked the younger one.

"Alderman give you any money?"

"Just what we said we'd give her."

"Then yes, we're buying."

"That's very kind of you," I replied. They stood awkwardly next to my table, the older one fiddling with his fingers and the younger one shifting his weight from left to right and back. "Would you care to sit?" I looked at the younger one. "Or maybe pee? Because there's a privy in the back..."

Scraggly chin mumbled something incoherent and bolted to the back of the tavern, slamming the privy door behind him. The older man sat down as the barmaid brought our drinks. I nodded my thanks and took a sip; the man did the same.

We sat in silence for a moment. "We need your help," the man said finally, after he'd drained more than half of his drink. He seemed considerably less fidgety.

The younger man, looking both relieved and embarrassed, returned and sat down. The barmaid motioned toward the ale I was drinking and looked at him. He turned bright pink, looked at the table, and mumbled, "Not old enough." The barmaid sniggered and left us alone.

"So, you need help," I said. The older man nodded. "With what, and why me?"

"It's our town!" blurted out the younger man. They proceeded to tell me about the dragon, the attacks, and their inability to find a group of willing adventurers to take up the quest to slay the beast.

It wasn't quite a tale as old as time, but it wasn't exactly the *Foriginia* in its originality either. (The *Foriginia*, for those who don't know, is a recent stage phenomenon that features a company of elves pretending to be dwarves pretending to be dragons pretending to be flowers. It's unlike anything else. It's also pretentious, terrible, and unwatchable.) Consequently, I wasn't particularly moved by their plea for help. "Well, gee, gentlemen, I'm very sorry to hear that," I said with what I hoped was convincing sincerity.

"You have to help us!" pleaded the younger man.

"The only thing I *have* to do is find out who brewed this ale, because it's delicious," I replied. "Maybe we should back up a step—you haven't even told me where you're from, what your names are, or why, beyond being a humanitarian of the first order—which I'm actually not, incidentally—I should help you."

The two men looked at each other. The younger one, clearly deferential, nodded to his older companion. "Well," said the older man, draining the rest of his ale, "I'm Goodman Drunkman, and this is Goodman Youngman. We're from Skendrick."

"Seriously?"

"Skendrick is a fine town, a fine town!" bristled the younger man.

"Skendrick is mildly less boring than Borden, which is one of the five most boring places I've ever been to, and I've been to a lot of places," I replied. "Though it's a perfectly valid place to be from. I wasn't seriously-ing your place of origin; I was seriously-ing your ridiculous names."

"Well, now, Ms. Heloise," replied Goodman Drunkman, "it may not be so in other areas you frequent, but 'Goodman' is a pretty common form of address in many towns around—"

"Oh, come on! You can't possibly be this thick."

The two men looked at each other. Youngman's eyes were wide, and Drunkman just shrugged.

"Or, maybe you are." I sighed, but Drunkman's attention was on the barmaid, attempting to get her to bring more ale, and Youngman was looking down as he fiddled with a button on his tunic. "Fine. Goodman Youngman and Goodman Drunkman of Skendrick, tell me why I should help you, and exactly how you think I can do that. Because, amazing though I am, dragon-slaying is not, at least as of yet, among my accomplishments, and, frankly, it's not likely to be anytime soon, mainly because I'm a pretty big fan of not being killed."

"Don't...don't all adventurers help people out of the goodness of their hearts? And because they want to right wrongs and fight injustice wherever it may be found?" asked Goodman Youngman tentatively.

"Bwahahahahahaha!" Maybe not the most ladylike response I could have offered, but, under the circumstances, I thought it was at least more polite than some other things I might have said. "You're sweet, Youngman. Completely misguided and an idiot, but sweet."

The barmaid brought another ale for Drunkman; after he sucked the head off and downed a generous portion of the mug, he sat back and sighed, seeming fully relaxed at last. "Hey, he's young, right?"

"It's right there in the name, yes."

"Listen, Ms. Heloise," said Drunkman, leaning in. I immediately leaned out, overwhelmed by the rank stink of ale on his breath. He took no offense at my attempt to distance myself, but neither did he pull back. "We've got gold."

Well, a girl does need to eat. And boots. A girl needs boots. "I'm listening..."

"Here's what we want you to do," continued Drunkman. "Spread the word about our town. How we need help. Write a song and make it sound like this is the greatest opportunity ever for a group of adventurers. Convince them that if they don't come to Skendrick, they're missing out on the adventure of a lifetime. And the treasure of a lifetime in the dragon's lair."

I nodded. "I could do that. I could do it for...how much gold did you say you were offering?"

"I have been authorized by the town council of Skendrick to pay five gold pieces to hire you."

Before I could respond that five gold wouldn't even buy a night with Drunkman's mother—just a negotiation tactic, because it certainly wasn't true (I'd bet you could have had Drunkman's mother for no more than three silver)—Youngman interrupted. "Excuse me, Goodman Drunkman, but Alderman Wooddunny gave us ten gold pieces to hire Ms. Heloise."

"You're mistaken, lad," said Drunkman, an edge in his voice. "It was five."

"No, I'm pretty sure it was ten," replied Goodman Youngman, pulling a small purse from his belt. "See here?" He dumped the contents onto the table, drawing the attention of the few other patrons in the room. "One, two, three, four, five," he counted, methodically picking up each coin and putting it back into the pouch, "six, seven, eight, nine, ten!" He plopped the bag in front of me, a look of triumph on his face. "I knew it was ten—I wouldn't forget a thing like that! My mother says I have a head for sums." He smiled sheepishly.

To his credit, Drunkman, though clearly dismayed at the opportunity to potentially pocket five gold, rolled with it. "I guess I misremembered. Yes, it looks like we've been authorized to offer you ten gold pieces to help us."

I looked at the purse, but didn't reach for it—yet. "And how much of a reward are you offering adventurers to slay the dragon?"

Goodmen Drunkman and Youngman looked at each other awkwardly. "Well, about that," began Drunkman slowly, "we were sort of hoping you could play up the size of the dragon's hoard and convince people that it's so huge that it would seem like a big draw just by itself…"

"Not offering anything, are you?"

"We don't have much to spare, given that the dragon keeps destroying our crops," said Youngman.

I mulled the offer. On the one hand, I didn't think I'd have much luck getting any adventurers worth their weight in mithral to bite on this "opportunity"; on the other, all I had planned for the next couple of weeks was bopping around to various towns and villages in the area to perform, and this wouldn't prevent me from doing that, and would put some extra gold in my pocket besides—and all I had to do was whip up a new little ditty, which I could do in the bath. So, that made the decision pretty easy. "All right," I said, "after careful thought and deliberation—"

"You've only been thinking for like two seconds," said Goodman Youngman.

I gave him the same look I once gave a rabid were-owlbear that tried to get handsy with me. Youngman blanched in the most satisfying way. "As I was saying, after careful thought and deliberation, I will take up your cause." I picked up the purse and tucked it securely inside my shirt. "In part because I feel for the good people of Skendrick and wish to help free your town—"

"Village," said Goodman Drunkman.

"Village," I amended, "from the oppressive yoke of the dragon, but mainly because you're paying me, and I'm not really in a position to turn down ten gold pieces right now, the economy being what it is."

Goodman Drunkman drained the rest of his drink. "We'll give you half now and half when you've managed to get us some adventures. Adventurerersh. Adventurers. That's a hard word to say," he said, his speech slurred.

I tapped my impressive bosom, not to point out its impressiveness (well, not solely for that purpose), but to indicate where I had sequestered the purse. "You do realize that you've already given me all the gold, right?"

The two men looked at each other. "You were just supposed to give her half," said Drunkman. He hiccupped.

"I've never done this before," replied Youngman.

"I have a feeling that's true in more ways than one when it comes to interactions with members of the opposite sex," I opined.

A moment of awkward silence ensued. "Well, what happens now?" asked Goodman Youngman.

"Now I finish my drink, take a nap, and then get ready for my performance tonight."

"And what about helping us?" he pressed.

"I'll get to it. I need to write a song first. And then I'll sing it everywhere from here to Kazaloon."

"Where's Kazaloon?" asked Goodman Drunkman.

"Next to Pluradia."

"Where's Pluradia?"

"You guys don't get out much, do you?"

"This is the first time I've ever left Skendrick," said Goodman Youngman.

"Me too," said Drunkman. "Except for when I was here last night. And all the other times I've come here. Which is pretty often." He hiccupped again.

"I'd tell you to enjoy your time in Borden," I said, "but that would require getting your hands on substances that aren't usually available for sale in Borden. Though I do know a guy." I finished my drink and stood up. "Gentlemen—or, rather, Goodmen—it's been...well, if not a pleasure, certainly financially rewarding. Whatever. In either case, it's time for my nap. You're more than welcome to stick around for the show tonight."

"We need to get back to Skendrick," said Goodman Youngman. He looked at Drunkman. "And we don't have any more money to stay the night anyway."

Sometimes I hate my tendency to want to help every stray dog that wanders into my path. I ground my teeth. "I will cover a room for you if you want to stay."

"Can we?" asked Goodman Youngman, the excitement evident in his voice.

"We really should get back to Skendrick..."

I sighed. "I'll cover your bar tab, too—within reason."

"Then again, it's always good for a young man to expand his horizons," said Drunkman enthusiastically. "All right—we'll stay."

I secured a room for them, tossed them the key, and then retired to my own room. I really did need a nap, and I needed some quiet time if I was going to write a song to help the good people of Skendrick dupe some idiotic adventurers into taking on (and most likely getting immolated by) a red dragon.

Fortunately, if there's one thing I'm good at, it's writing songs that appeal to idiots.

CHAPTER 11

THE HEROIC ADVENTURERS MEET THEIR DESTINY

*B*ruised and battered, but not deterred, from their mission to seek justice for all those in need, Nadinta and her companions arrived in the sleepy town of Napperville. *Rather than seek solace in the bottom of a bottle or a house of ill repute, however, the stolid adventurers, eager to set right the misfortune that had befallen them in Velenia, made their way to the town square, where those in need of assistance of all kinds gathered to find aid. Farmers came to seek help in harvesting crops, builders to find laborers to help them build and repair homes, and merchants to find those who could make deliveries. Adventurers, too, gathered in the town square on occasion, ready to lend their strength and skill at arms to those unable to defend themselves from the evil creatures that lurked in all corners of Erithea.*

In truth, however, there was seldom a need for the services of such noble heroes in Napperville, and so, after determining that no one would call upon them for help, Nadinta, Rummy, Borg, and Whiska walked to a quaint inn to recover their strength and prepare for their next quest.

That evening, over a simple meal of stew and bread, the

companions learned of a village in dire straits indeed, one in need
of heroes to rescue it from the ravages of the savage red dragon
Dragonia. The entertainer that the inn had retained that evening,
the legendary bard Heloise, painted such a vivid and heart-
wrenching picture with her beautiful words and honeyed voice
that the heroes were overcome with a desire to provide succor to the
good and valiant people of Skendrick, and so they approached the
bard after she had finished her tale and, near tears borne of their
compassion for the Skendrickians' plight, expressed to her their
desire to aid the village, and begged her to take them there straight
away so that Skendrick would not need to suffer one day more at
the hands of the foul beast.

The noble and humble bard recognized that the group before
her was formidable indeed, and so she raised them up from their
prostrate positions, comforted the suffering Nadinta with a gentle
touch on her shoulder, and told them that she would lead them to
Skendrick, and that she felt deep in her bones that the worthy
adventurers would prove mighty enough to slay the dragon.

CHAPTER 12

ALCOHOL + DESPERATION = BAD DECISIONS

Their flight had been neither swift nor heroic, but at last Nadinta, Rummy, Whiska, and Borg reached a sleepy hamlet that they considered far enough from Velenia to be safe from pursuit from their prior employer.

"As farm implements go, maybe a scythe would be better, eh?" said Rummy as they waited to enter the village, checked by a bored guard armed with a garden hoe.

The guard shrugged, jerked a thumb over his shoulder, and said, through a yawn, "There's an inn down the road a few blocks that way—The Dancing Dozer. Can't miss it. Unless you do. Which you won't."

"Dancing Dozer?" replied Rummy. "That seems danger-ous. I've heard of sleepwalking, but dancing while you're asleep seems like it would—"

"Come on, Rummy," said Nadi. She nodded to the guard. "Thank you."

"So, what do we do now?" asked Whiska as they walked.

"We go to the inn," replied Nadi.

"I meant after that, you pointy-eared tree hugger."

"I...don't know. One thing at a time." Nadinta shook her head, seeming unsure of herself.

They arrived at the inn a few moments later and reserved two rooms, deciding to double up to conserve their meager supply of coins. After taking some time to clean up and refresh themselves, they reconvened in the very sparsely populated common room of the inn, just in time to catch a glimpse of the most spectacular backside any of them had ever seen, which was attached, incidentally, to a bard of no small skill, as they would soon come to learn.

"So, what do we do now?" asked Whiska as they sipped drinks, an indulgent purchase given their financial circumstances.

"We go to the inn," said Rummy after taking a long pull of his ale.

"We're already at the inn, you hairy molerat."

"Oh, sorry. I thought we were just having the exact same conversation we had half an hour ago."

"We have to go back," said Nadi as she stared into her wine glass.

"To Velenia?" asked Rummy.

"Yes."

"Where there's a homicidal wizard with an incredibly powerful weapon who has every intention of turning us into shish roundabobs?"

(Shish roundabobs were an ingenious invention that was revolutionizing food service across Erithea; unlike shish kabobs, which are pointy and pose constant danger throughout a meal, to the point (pun fully intended) where you can't really relax and enjoy the lovely combination of meat and vegetables they offer, shish roundabobs are fashioned from a stick that has a pointed end in order to slide easily through food, but the pointy part snaps off once the food is on to reveal a soft, round tip that is much less dangerous if you happen to poke yourself in the eye with it.

Even better, the stick is hollow, and can be filled with whatever substance best compliments the meal you're eating—yogurt sauce, hot sauce, garlic sauce, lizard blood...whatever you fancy. It's been whispered that the woman who invented them once lost an eye while eating a shish kabob, but I met her, and the worst injury she ever suffered eating a shish kabob was a tiny scratch on the roof of her mouth that took about a minute and a half to heal; she's an exceptional marketer, however, so she generally wears an eyepatch wherever she goes—often switching it from one eye to the other so that she doesn't strain her vision—and lets people make assumptions about the dangers of shish kabob consumption, leading, in most cases, to an uptick in sales for her invention. She's pretty amazing.)

But, I digress.

"He's our responsibility, Rummy."

"Like hell he is!" shouted Whiska, drawing stares from the few other patrons who occupied the taproom. "I didn't hand him some sort of crazy magical weapon!"

"No, you just found it," said Rummy. "And gave it to the person who gave it to him."

"We're all culpable," said Nadi.

"I like...shish roundabobs. Do you think...they have any?" said Borg.

"I'm not entirely sure they have running water in this...this...well, I was going to say backwater, but that would sort of undermine my point. Anyway, I'm not sure they have running water here, Borgy, let alone fancy inventions like shish roundabobs," said Rummy, shaking his head sadly.

"This is ridiculous. I'm not doing this!" Whiska stood up. "If you decide to come to your senses, I'll stay. Otherwise, you're on your own, you ridiculous tailless top feeders!" She stormed off in a huff, slamming the door of the inn behind her.

"I'm not sure that calling us the opposite of bottom

feeders is as insulting as Whiska thinks it is," mused Rummy. "And all of her stuff is still up in her room."

"She'll be back," said Nadi. "I hope."

"Whiska seems...upset," said Borg.

"Sure does, big guy," said Rummy.

They ate and drank in silence for a few moments before Rummy spoke again. "Look, Nadi...it's not that I agree with Whiska, mind you—I mean, I don't think you look even a little ridiculous without a tail, for example. But, I'm not sure we're quite ready to go back to Velenia." Nadi started to say something, but Rummy held his hand up. "Please—let me finish."

"That's what...she said," said Borg.

"Not now, Borg," said Rummy. He paused. "Though that was pretty good."

"I don't get it," said Nadi.

"Never mind." Rummy finished his ale. "I agree that it's our responsibility to try to stop that madman." He spoke softly. "But we're not ready. I barely even know how to hold a weapon. Borg is basically a giant, sweet punching bag." He looked at Borg. "No offense, big guy."

"I have...to poop."

Rummy pointed toward the commode. "Please do it back there."

Borg squinted. "That is...a small room. I will...wait." He looked pained.

Rummy looked uneasily at his giant companion and shook his head. "Anyway. Whiska's got power, no doubt, and she's clever, but she's got no idea how to work with other people."

"And me?"

"You're perfect, Nadi."

"Rummy."

Rummy shrugged. "You're smart, calm, fair, honest, and

skilled with weapons. You've got all the qualities of a good leader."

"But? And be honest."

"But, you doubt yourself too much, you have an overactive conscience, and you're not assertive enough."

"I see," replied Nadi. "Anything to add, Borg?"

"Getting punched...doesn't really hurt."

Nadi smiled. "Glad that's true for one of us, at least." She looked at Rummy. "Though there are different kinds of punches, and sometimes the ones that aren't physical hurt more."

Rummy grimaced. "You said be honest! Look, we're never going to become successful adventurers unless we trust each other and are truthful about our shortcomings. We're new to this! Of course we're not perfect. Some of us are less perfect than others." He nodded toward the door through which Whiska had departed. "Some of us have a tendency to poop too much, but are too big to use normal bathrooms, which makes it awkward to be in public with others." He nodded to Borg, who nodded solemnly in return. "And some of us have to speak truth to those in positions of power so they don't end up like Emperor Halsted."

(Emperor Halsted was the key figure in an old legend about power's ability to corrupt and blind those who possess it to the truth. In most versions of the story, the Emperor is convinced by a shady con artist to buy some expensive new clothes from him, only it turns out that there are, in fact, no clothes at all, and the Emperor ends up parading naked throughout his kingdom, but no one is willing to tell him the truth. In some versions of the story, most likely written down after years of oral recitation had garbled the original tale, the Emperor ends up wearing "newt clothes," which, as might be expected, make him look like a giant, bipedal newt. I've always been partial to the newt version, even if the moral of that story is less clear.)

Nadi smiled wryly. "It *is* difficult not to let the power go to my head, leading such a fearsome and dangerous group." She blew out a long, slow breath. "What do you suggest we do, truth speaker?"

"Right now? Have a drink. Enjoy the fact that we're still alive. Get a good night's sleep. We can figure out our next move in the morning. Whatever that move is, we need to get a lot better at not almost getting killed before we go back to Velenia."

✦

NADI, Rummy, and Borg spent the next couple of hours nursing drinks, but even the slow rate of consumption left them more than a little impaired by the time my show started. They, along with several other already inebriated patrons—well, not *that* many; this was Napperville, after all, and there couldn't have been more than a few dozen people in the tavern that night—rocked drunkenly in their seats, singing along to my first few songs, all well-known favorites, in the characteristically loud, confident, and off-key voice of the overserved.

With the crowd sufficiently warmed up, I decided it was time to debut my newest work, though given the typical Nappervillian crowd (not to be confused with The Nappervillain, a well-known local crime lord who trafficked heavily in black market wool), I didn't hold out much hope that there would be any eager adventurers among them.

I strummed my lute and motioned for the crowd (such as it was) to be quiet. "Those of you who have called this region home for any length of time know well the danger and hardship that a ruined crop can bring; imagine, if you will, what it would be like if decimated vegetables were the least of your worries, and that you had to spend your days and nights looking to the skies for fear of death being rained down on you from above.

"That is the plight of your friends and neighbors in Skendrick, not so very far to the north, and they are in need of aid. I have taken up the cause of the good villagers and would like to dedicate my latest composition to them, and urge you, if you know any brave and worthy adventurers who might aid Skendrick in its darkest hour, to come forth after my performance and tell me so that I might lead those hearty souls to the place where they are needed most."

With the exception of a few soft, drunken belches, the room had gone quiet, the mood shifting from loud and raucous to quiet and somber. You might think that trying something like this would kill the mood entirely and would be an idiotic move for a performer who relies on tips generated by goodwill to make the evening worthwhile, and you'd be right—if you were talking about a lesser bard. Fortunately, I'm not a lesser bard.

I began to sing soft and low, without accompaniment.

Gather round friends, and hear tell my tale

Of love, of loss, of pain

When I am done you will know full well

A sorrow that will drive you insane

It was a little darker and heavier-handed than I normally like to go, but I'd written a jaunty melody to counterbalance the bleakness. There are few things in life so bad that a catchy whoa-oh! chorus can't make at least a little better.

The Dirge of Skendrick

Written in the key of persuasion

Take heed, my friends, for all in this life

Can be taken in the blink of an eye

When the bulk of a massive red dragon

Rains fire and death from the sky

· · ·

FOR SO IT HAS HAPPENED, and is happening still
  In a town just like your own
  Where people are screaming and crying for aid
  As flesh is charred to the bone

NEAR SKENDRICK DOES a red dragon dwell
  A beast who blots out the sun
  He wheels in the sky and lets out mighty roars
  As he gobbles up babies for fun

THE DRAGON SOARS and the dragon flies
  When the dragon roars, everyone dies

TAKE UP YOUR SWORDS, your axes, your bows
  And use them in service to good
  Though the day seems dark indeed
  We must do what noble folk should

THE DRAGON SOARS and the dragon flies
  When the dragon roars, everyone dies
  Who will save the day?

THE CALL GOES OUT, who will answer it now?
  Send us your warriors, your heroes, your fighters
  The night is so dark
  But the dawn will be brighter

HERE IS the chance for a brave band of heroes
  To enter the realm of legend and myth

By slaying the dragon who's killed so many
Men and women, kin and kith

THE DRAGON SOARS *and the dragon flies*
When the dragon roars, everyone dies
Who will come to save the day?
Will it be you who enters the fray?

THERE IS MORE *than just gratitude*
And stories to be told,
For the heroes who answer
Will be showered in gold

THE DRAGON'S *treasure is legion*
Ten feet high and wider than tall
And the brave heroes who slay him
Will lay claim to it all

THE PEOPLE *of Skendrick are in dire need*
Of champions to save their town
Who will become heroes and legends
Before all is burned to the ground?

THE DRAGON SOARS *and the dragon flies*
When the dragon roars, everyone dies
Who will come to save the day?
Who will boldly enter the fray?

IT MAY JUST BE...YOU.

.   .   .

I DREW out the last note and let it hang in the air, turning my (bewitching) eyes toward anyone and everyone who looked like a possibly competent warrior. In such a small audience, there were really only a few likely suspects, and two of them sat next to each other—a capable-looking elven woman with a bow slung over her chair and an enormous rock giant. I didn't have particularly high hopes, though—an elf carrying a bow is a bit like a chef wearing an apron; it's a standard accoutrement and not necessarily an indication of aptitude. Let's face it—there are some apron-wearing chefs who are pretty hopeless when it comes to making a decent meal. Plus, while rock giants may look tough and powerful and intimidating, most of them are pretty passive, and they're about as skilled at fighting as the average Skendrickian is at speaking coherently.

Still, they represented the most promising possibilities in the room, so after I finished my performance (to rousing cheers, numerous whistles, calls for an encore, a marriage proposal, and an exceedingly loud belch (the timing of the latter might have just been coincidence; I don't think it was a commentary on my show, though I still took it as a compliment)), I went to the bar for the usual post-performance complimentary ale and then made my way over to the table where the elf and the rock giant sat, stopping along the way to acknowledge compliments and star-struck expressions of adulation.

A small, scraggly looking dwarf sat with the elf and the giant, but the fourth seat at their table was open. "May I?" I asked, inclining my head toward the unoccupied seat.

The elf looked surprised, maybe even a little bit flustered, but nodded and I took a seat.

"Fine performance," said the skinny dwarf.

"Eh," I replied. "Not my finest, but I have a pretty high floor."

"Golden voiced *and* modest," murmured the dwarf.

"Hush, Rummy," said the elf.

"The bard wants...to sit...with us," said the rock giant.

"She already is, big guy," replied the dwarf.

"So," I said, taking a sip of my ale, "I'm Heloise."

"I am called Nadinta Ghettinwood," said the elf, her tone and bearing formal, almost stiff. "My companions are Borgunder Gunderbor and Rumscrabble Tooltinker." She gestured toward the rock giant and then the dwarf.

"Not yet charmed," I replied, "though I'm sure I will be." I gave Rumscrabble the once over. "Normally, I have a thing for dwarves, but you've got nothing going on back there, do you?" I pointed toward Rummy's seated backside.

He nodded pleasantly. "I'm only half-dwarven. I'm also half-halfling."

"Ah, that makes more sense," I said. "I can see which parts are halfling. Most of them, anyway."

To his credit, he didn't blush or show even the slightest hint of embarrassment. "Those that you can't see are decidedly halfling as well, unfortunately. And you can call me Rummy."

"I'll think about that," I replied.

"The genetic heritage of my covered parts, or addressing me by a diminutive?" he asked.

"Both."

"Fair enough."

I gave them a very obvious once over. "You're either adventurers or have terrible fashion sense."

"Are those things mutually exclusive?" replied Rummy. I was starting to like that one.

"We are indeed adventurers," cut in Nadinta. "And we really did enjoy the performance." She frowned. "I...*we...*

would offer to buy you a drink, but we're a little short of funds right now."

"How'd you get those, then?" I asked, nodding toward their drinks.

"Borg helped unload a shipment of ale earlier," Nadinta replied. "Took him less than half the time it would have taken the owner, so he offered to stand drinks for us this evening."

"Or, if not real drinks, the cheapest—and most watered-down—ale he has," added Rummy cheerfully. "But, as they say—any port with a deep enough harbor not to bump into anything when you're taking on water."

"No one says that," I responded.

"They should," said Rummy. "Though I guess it could be pithier."

"This ale...tastes like water," added Borg.

I signaled the barmaid, pointed to my glass, and held up three fingers. I figured the least I could do was buy them a real drink if I was going to try to talk them into getting themselves killed by a red dragon. "Let's get you something stronger, Rocky."

"You don't need to do that," said Nadinta.

"But we won't say no," said Rummy.

"My name...is Borg," said Borg.

The barmaid brought the drinks, and my companions looked noticeably happier. After a few moments of sipping and small talk, I leaned forward. "Let's talk seriously for a moment."

The three of them put their drinks down and leaned in as well. I kept my voice low, more for effect than because I cared if any of the few remaining patrons, all of whom had just heard me publicly invite adventurers to take up the quest I was now about to talk my new friends into, listened in on our conversation.

"The people of Skendrick need help," I said. "And you, clearly, need coin."

Nadinta nodded, but didn't say anything.

"I know it seems daunting…"

"Taking on a dragon? Pshaw," said Rummy. "I've had blisters that were more daunting. Mainly because it's very hard to prestidigitate when you've got a blister."

"Not now, Rummy," said Nadinta. "Heloise…there's no question we could use the money. Our adventures so far haven't exactly been lucrative, but—"

"So far?"

"We haven't been together very long," she admitted.

Advantage: Heloise.

"Getting started is tough. Killing a dragon is probably tougher. But what better way to both fill your purses and ensure that you never lack for commissions in the future? Not that you'd need to go questing anymore after you've got all of that dragon gold."

"I'm pretty sure Nadi was coming to a '*but*,' and I think, or maybe just hope, that the but was that we can think of better, or at least safer, ways to fill our purses," said Rummy.

"This is…good ale," said Borg.

"Why did you decide to start adventuring?" I asked Rummy.

He shrugged. "Prestidigitating is a young man's game. And I'm getting older."

I nodded. "So you weren't very good at fake magic —got it."

Rummy smiled, but not the smile of someone who is offended. He reached into a pouch at his belt and withdrew a pack of cards. He took his time removing them from the box, bringing them close to his nose and inhaling deeply before casually shuffling them with blinding speed in ways I can't even begin to describe (and I'm a good describer). After a moment, he fanned them out on the table, looked at me, and said, in the time-honored tradition of street swindlers, "Pick a card. Any card."

I raised an eyebrow, but did as he asked, reaching for a card toward the middle of the deck.

"Not that one," he said.

"You said any card."

"Any card other than that one."

"Okay...this one." I reached toward another card.

"Not that one, either."

"This is the worst card trick I've ever seen." I threw my hands up, exasperated.

"That's because it's not a card trick."

"Huh?"

Rummy raised his right hand, which had been resting on the table, to reveal five gold coins. "I think these might be yours. I know they're not mine. Though I'd like them to be. May I keep them?"

I'm sure my eyes went wide as I reached down into my purse and found it considerably lighter. About five gold coins lighter. Okay, exactly five gold coins lighter. "How in the name of the Seven Devils of the Serenthem did you do that?"

"I'm pretty good at fake magic." Somehow he was neither smug nor proud. It was a simple statement of fact.

"Noted. And, agreed." I was genuinely impressed; I hadn't even suspected he was going for my purse. He might not have an ass, but he sure had balls. "But no, you can't keep them."

Rummy shrugged and slid the coins across the table. "Worth a shot."

"The reason I asked why you decided to start adventuring," I said, "is because, other than the risk of possible death, hunting this dragon in Skendrick is pretty much everything you could hope for—adventure, excitement, a chance to make a name, heaps of treasure, helping people...whatever your motivation—and I don't buy for a second that you chose to become an adventurer because you're getting old, because that's just ridiculous and absurdly counterintuitive. This has to appeal to you on some level."

"Except for the risk of possible death," said Rummy.

"Right. But, isn't that a risk regardless of what you do as an adventurer?" I looked at Nadi. "You don't have anything else lined up, right?"

"Well," said Nadi, "there is actually something else that we need to take care of, something that happened because we—"

"Nadi!" said Rummy, cutting her off. "I don't think Heloise is all that interested in our heretofore mundane adventures."

I shrugged. "Probably not. I am a storyteller however, so I'm always on the lookout for new material."

"Dragons have...lots of treasure. But they are...big," said Borg.

"There is something we need to do." Nadi looked at Rummy and shook her head before he could interrupt again. "It's our responsibility." She blew out a deep breath. "But, maybe we're not ready to tackle that just yet."

"So?" I prompted.

"What do you guys think? Should we go slay a dragon?" asked Nadinta.

"I'm not particularly inclined to get eaten or burned beyond recognition, but I'm also not sure what our next step would be otherwise, because I agree that we're not ready to... go back and deal with that, ah, thing we need to do. So...why not?" offered Rummy.

Nadi nodded. "Borg?"

We sat in silence for two minutes while Borg took a sip of his drink, looked around the room, scratched his nose, stretched, let out a soft belch, and cracked his knuckles. "Sure."

"What about Whiska?" asked Rummy.

"Who?" I replied.

"Our erstwhile wizard," said Nadi.

"Are we writing her off?" said Rummy.

"Yes. No. I don't know." Nadi sighed and looked at me.

"Whiska is...challenging. She stormed out of here just before your performance, and I'm not sure if she's coming back."

"Having a wizard at your side when fighting a dragon would be helpful," I suggested (helpfully).

"I'm not sure we can do this without her. She's got more juice than any of us," said Rummy. "If she's not coming back..."

Just at that moment, the door of the tavern burst open and in walked a giant rat holding a staff with a crystal on the end. (In truth, she didn't actually come in until about ten minutes later when we were in the middle of a conversation about the bathroom habits of rock giants, but I've chosen to slightly edit the timeline of the story for dramatic purposes. And, believe me, if you'd heard Borg rambling on about which foods have adverse effects on rock giants' digestive systems, you'd thank me.)

"Elf. My seat. Move. Now," said the rat.

"Half-elf, actually," I replied. "Whiska, I presume?"

She gave me a once over, which was one of the more uncomfortable moments of my life. Between her beady eyes, the disdainful sniff she gave, and the stink of stale ale hanging on her like a wet fur cloak, she knew how to make a girl feel unpleasant. And that's not even counting the fact that her staff was crackling with energy, and I had the distinct impression that she could have turned me into a cackleroach, a disgusting (and disgustingly giant) bug that, when stepped on, emits a shrill burst of laughter before exploding into a puddle of green goo. I hate cackleroaches.

"Who's the new wench? Are you trying to replace me already? With *this*?" She shook her head. "Give me one good reason I shouldn't turn her into a cackleroach."

"Cackleroaches are disgusting, she's not a wizard, she's not a replacement, she might have a job for us, and she bought us ale." Rummy ticked off each point on his fingers. "That's at least four good reasons."

"Five," I corrected.

"Well, I'm not sure 'cackleroaches are disgusting' is all that good of a reason. I mean, they're gross, but that doesn't really give Whiska any incentive not to turn you into one."

"Neither does the fact that she bought all of you drinks," replied Whiska.

"Okay, so, three good reasons," said Rummy.

I signaled the server to bring Whiska a drink. "Four."

Whiska nodded and sat down. She took Borg's drink, which was still a quarter of the way full, and drained it in one swallow. She wiped a sleeve across her foamy whiskers and looked at me. "What's this about a job?"

"Well," I responded as the server delivered a drink to Whiska. "How do you feel about the idea of killing a dragon?"

"How much does it pay?"

"As much treasure as you can carry."

"Nothing upfront?"

"If you knew how much treasure this dragon was sitting on, you wouldn't be worried about upfront payment. Besides, even if you do get paid something upfront, what good does it do you if the dragon kills you anyway?"

"Hmmm...fair point, I guess. Though we could use some capital for supplies and equipment."

"I wasn't...finished," said Borg. "With my...drink."

I signaled the server for another drink for Borg. This was really starting to eat into my profits. "Well, I can think of one way you could pick up a little cash on the road to Skendrick."

"How's that?" asked Nadi, who stared at me a little too intently. I couldn't figure out if she was just intense, had a vision problem, was sort of drunk and trying to pretend to be sober, or some combination of all three.

"There's an orc encampment just off the road to Skendrick, maybe a half day's ride out of the way. Granted, orcs aren't exactly known for their legendary wealth—nor for being clean, literate, or pleasant, for that matter—but if you clean that place out, you should at least be able to cover expenses, and you were just saying that you could use a little more seasoning before you take on a dragon..."

I was going to need to ask the Skendrickians for a bonus; they hadn't mentioned the encampment, but I knew it was a problem for several of the surrounding towns, and I couldn't imagine that they'd be too upset to see a reduction in the number of bands of marauding (and very handsy) orcs roaming the countryside.

"Orcs?" Nadi set her jaw. Definitely intense. Probably drunk. Unclear about the eye problem.

"Orcs?!" Whiska's face lit up. "They explode great. It's the green blood—looks great on dirt. Very lush."

"Orcs." Rummy looked like he had just smelled something unpleasant.

"Oh, come on," I said, "even you could manage to hit an orc with that oversized child's toy of yours." I motioned to his mace. "Besides, don't dwarves hate orcs just as much as elves hate them?"

"Sure, but halflings really hate getting dirty. I think my dislike of getting dirty outweighs my hatred of orcs, who, truth be told, have never really done anything to me."

"Orc raiders killed my father," said Nadi quietly.

Everyone turned to stare at her. "Nadi...Nadi, I'm sorry. Oh, dear," said Rummy.

"We'll get revenge!" shouted Whiska gleefully.

"Nadinta—I'm sorry. I didn't know." I reached over to pat her shoulder. She started to draw back, but then leaned forward and allowed me to comfort her.

"It's okay," she said. "None of you knew." She narrowed her eyes. "I certainly wouldn't object to paying a visit to this encampment before we go to Skendrick."

"Good." I nodded. "It's settled. Be sure to tell the good people of Skendrick that Heloise sent you. And that maybe they should pay her more."

"You're not coming with us?" Nadi looked crestfallen.

"Orcs make funny...noises when...you squish them," said Borg.

"It's a beautiful sound, isn't it?" I replied. I looked at Nadi and shook my head. "Places to go, stories to tell, I'm afraid. You guys will do great, though." I stood up and stretched. "Turns out it *was* a pleasure after all. Good luck." I stood up to go to my room, but was stopped before I could get more than two steps.

"Heloise." Nadi stood and grabbed my arm. "Wait. I have...I have an idea."

I arched an eyebrow, an expression that has quailed emperors, frightened children, and aroused dwarves (though not simultaneously, because that would just be weird). "I'm listening."

She blew out a deep breath. "I haven't discussed this with the others, obviously, but...what if you came with us—to, uh, tell our story?"

Rummy looked curious. "What are you thinking?"

"Well," replied Nadi, rubbing her forehead, "one of our problems is that we don't have a reputation as an adventuring band yet, right? If we slay a dragon...that's the big leagues. That's legitimate legend territory, but it's not enough just for the people of Skendrick to know what we did—not if we want to become as well known as we want to be and get the kinds of quests we want to get. Everyone needs to know, and what better way for that to happen than for our legend to be spread by a beaut...er, talented bard?"

"Beautiful would be accurate, too," I said magnanimously.

"We don't need the dead weight," said Whiska. She looked me up and down and then focused on my hips. "Emphasis on weight."

"Whiska!" Nadi looked furious.

"It's okay," I said, motioning for Nadi to stay calm. "Body

image issues don't plague me. Unlike, say, the plague, which plagues a lot of people, and thanks for that, Whiska."

More than anything, Ratarians hate being associated with the pestilence rats spread, mostly due to the (allegedly) mistaken belief that it was a Ratarian, not a rat, who brought the fleas that caused the Great Plague of the Year of the Crooked Spear into the port city of Dagobar. You can always count on it to be a sore point with them, and I wasn't disappointed as Whiska flew out of her chair and reached out her hands to throttle me.

"Stand down!" yelled Nadi, stepping between us and grabbing Whiska's hands. Whiska fought her for a second before sitting down with a huff, grumbling something about elf kabobs under her breath.

"I like this plan generally," said Rummy, "though I see one major issue, apart from the possibility of Whiska trying to kill Heloise."

"What's that?" asked Nadi.

"Well, if I was a bard that a relatively inexperienced adventuring band had just asked to accompany them to fight a savage red dragon that will probably kill them (and me) so that I could tell their story afterward on the off chance that they survive, I'd probably want to be paid something. And we aren't really in the position to make that kind of, what do they call it in the merchant world? Capital investment, I think."

"The assless dwarf makes a point," I said.

"What if," said Nadi slowly, "we offer you an equal share of the treasure? One-fifth for all of us. You don't have to fight —just bear witness."

"Deadweight sits around and diddles her strings while we get burned to a crisp and gets the same amount of treasure? Not a chance!" Whiska crossed her arms, which, as short as they were, made her look both ridiculous and uncomfortable.

"Body shaming...isn't nice," said Borg. "Don't do it...again."

"Thanks, big guy." I patted him on the shoulder. "What happens if you guys get melted like candles before you get to the treasure? Or offed by orcs? That doesn't work out so well for me."

"I know it's a gamble," said Nadi, nodding. "I won't pretend that it's a sure thing you'll get paid out. But, if your claims about the treasure are true, you'd come out of this with considerable wealth for doing nothing more than writing a song."

Well, this certainly put me in an awkward spot. I had no idea whether the treasure was as big as I claimed; I was taking the word of two barely functional semi-adult men, neither of whom had seen it themselves. On the other hand, it was an attractive—and exciting—opportunity, and I didn't really have anything else going on. If nothing else, I figured I could start out on the road with them and, if they seemed incompetent, bail before we got to the dragon. They weren't paying me, so it wasn't like I had any obligation. And, besides, I thought—it might make for one heck of a story (spoiler alert: it did).

Still, I didn't want to seem too eager.

"It's possible," I said, casually, "that you'll earn other treasure along the way—if you take out the orc encampment, for example, you'll probably stumble into a few gold coins. Or, at least copper. Maybe just some old bits of fuzz. And human ears. But, something." I looked at Nadi. "How about if I get a one-fifth share of anything you find along the way, not just in the dragon's lair?"

"No. Absolutely not!" growled Whiska. "This is ridiculous." She stood up. "Good luck slaying a dragon without me —I'm gone!" She started to walk away, then realized she'd already done this once before today. "Again! And for good!"

"You don't...have any...gold," said Borg.

Whiska stopped. She glared at the rock giant, but didn't say anything.

"The dragon...does. You are...powerful. We...need you."

If Whiska were an actual rat instead of a race of creatures that just happen to look like rats, I might have thought she was preening, the way she suddenly began to groom her whiskers. Given her apparent love of smiting things, however, I decided not to point this out.

The rock giant's words mollified Whiska in a way nothing else had. She sat back down, looked at Borg, nodded, and then downed the rest of her drink.

"So...Skendrick?" I asked.

Nadi looked at Rummy, who nodded, then at Borg, who did the same. When she looked at Whiska, the Ratarian just licked her lips to get the last of her ale off of them, but we all took that as a sign of assent.

"To Skendrick," replied Nadi. "With a detour through the orc encampment." She looked grim. "We leave at first light."

CHAPTER 13

SO WERE SLAIN THE FOUL ORCS OF THE GLOOM FOREST

The heroes set off on their journey to Skendrick to lay claim to the quest of slaying the foul beast Dragonia, but not before first stopping to destroy the encampment of orcs deep in the heart of the Gloom Forest, whose vile presence was a threat to all of the goodly folk of the area.

After three days' ride, our heroes, saddle sore but spirit strong, reached the edge of the wood and did fierce battle with the orc outriders, defeating them handily and preventing them from giving their foul kin warning of the heroes' coming. With stealth and poise did Nadinta lead her charges into the heart of the encampment, shying not from the combined might of the orc forces, knowing that the righteousness of her cause and the combined might of her company would be proof against all resistance the wretched orcish forces might muster.

The heroes crept in under cover of darkness, and the mighty Whiska woke the foul creatures with a display of raw power, sending bolts of lightning and great balls of fire springing forth from her staff, such that many perished before they could even rise from their filthy bedrolls.

Whiska's companions were not idle in the midst of this maelstrom of destruction, for Nadinta's sword rose and fell a hundred times, and a hundred orcs lay dead at her feet afterward. The mighty Borgunder stood as a bulwark against those orcs who tried to fight, deflecting blow after blow and sheltering his companions as they rained death upon the orcs. Even Rumscrabble struck repeatedly at the terrible creatures with his mace, his fury driving him on and giving him power that he had never known he possessed.

Through it all, an unassuming bard witnessed their display of courage and sang out at the top of her lungs (showcasing impressive octave range), exhorting and encouraging the adventurers to new heights of glory, her music giving them strength and stamina to ease the strain of a battle fought so long and so hard.

When the sun arose many hours later, when the first of its pink rays dared surmount the horizon to bathe the world in the soft glow of predawn, our heroes finished their virtuous work, a blow from Nadinta felling the last of the despicable monsters.

The companions paused, each laboring to draw breath after their exertion, but knowing that their efforts would save the lives of countless individuals, for never again would these base marauders raise their rusty and wicked blades against an innocent.

For a few moments they rested, reflecting upon their mighty deed, and then, with a deep breath, they continued on the road to Skendrick, knowing that each moment they delayed was another moment that the dragon might strike.

CHAPTER 14

OKAY, FINE, SO IT TURNS OUT THAT THE ORCS WEREN'T REALLY ALL THAT FOUL

Full disclosure: I was pretty much raised to hate orcs.

Elves and orcs are like fire and ice, salt and wounds, or Janiperian turnip plants and codswattle bugs. The whimsical, nature-loving tendencies of the elves contrast sharply with the literal-mindedness and casual disregard for the world around them orcs tend to display. But, there's a chance that orcs' bad reputation is as much a result of the fact that there are very few orcish storytellers (most orcs can't read or write and wouldn't have the faintest desire to learn how to do so even if they had the opportunity) and very many biased elvish (or, in the case of your lovely narrator, half-elven) bards and poets as it is because of the orcs' own actions.

So, while I don't like the fact that the orcs may not come off as evil and disgusting and gross as I would like them to in this story, I promised you the truth, and so the truth you shall have, even if it ends up making you feel kind of bad about how much you used to hate orcs, and making people hate orcs less is about as much fun for me as getting stabbed in the stomach with a fondue fork. (Side note: yes, I have actually been stabbed in stomach with a fondue fork, and no, I didn't enjoy it, though I do like fondue very much, and still do, though maybe not as much as I once did, and I'll never have fondue in Plorigen ever again.)

It turned out that "first light" for this crew meant just before midday, which was just fine with me, but clearly annoyed Nadi. Whiska was not an early riser, Borg took a solid two hours to eat breakfast (I stopped counting after he ate his thirty-seventh egg, which he claimed was not a record, but was "a pretty...good effort"), and Rummy kept saying he had "forgotten" things from his room, only to make them "magically" appear somewhere. To be fair, it was pretty impressive to watch him pull his mace out from behind Nadi's ear, but she seemed less wowed by the trick than the rest of us—even Whiska, having knocked back a stiff Bloody Lindy, applauded. (A Bloody Lindy, incidentally, is a twist on a Bloody Mary wherein the mixer is not tomato juice and a combination of spicy seasonings but is, instead, clam juice and lime, and it tastes as awful as it sounds.)

Eventually, however, we hit the road, only, unlike in the heroic version the bards sing, we went on foot—gold being in short supply, we were in no position to purchase (not to mention feed) mounts. So, the journey to the orc encampment took almost two weeks, and absolutely nothing of interest happened along the way. You hear about the high points of the adventuring life in songs, but most of it involves walking down a dusty road in the hot sun singing "Ninety-Nine Pints of Ale on the Wagon," or maybe beating whoever in your party keeps singing "Ninety-Nine Pints of Ale on the Wagon" (Rummy) in the kidneys with a bar of soap wrapped in a cloth, in an effort to trick your brain into forgetting how incredibly bored it is.

On the plus side (mostly), I had plenty of time to get to know my new companions.

Despite his relatively undwarf-like appearance, Rummy grew on me quickly. He was unfailingly (and sometimes irritatingly) cheerful—even when something bothered him, he got over it in less time than it takes most dwarves to chug an ale, which is approximately three seconds (not that I've ever timed it). He was clearly both smart and clever (there's a difference), but tended to purposefully obscure that fact behind a stream of inane chatter. He was basically your favorite (if occasionally annoying) uncle, who would alternate stupid, punny jokes with playing the "got your nose" game—only in Rummy's version, instead of tucking his thumb between his fingers to make it look like he was holding a nose, he would use his sleight-of-hand skills to produce a schnoz fruit, which looks remarkably like a human nose, save for the fact that it's purple. He also had a habit of stealing things from you in the midst of all the patter and prestidigitation, though he always gave everything back immediately (he said that it was necessary to "stay sharp" while on the road, though I think he really just enjoyed how much his taking things annoyed Nadi).

Whiska was almost as powerful as she was offensive, which was saying something, because she was easily the most offensive creature I'd ever met. She seemed incapable of making a statement without insulting someone, and her ability to work a slight into a response to even a simple question like "Can I offer you some breakfast?" was truly impressive (example: "You could, but you'd still be a poorly dressed tree humper."). Interestingly, she didn't seem to care one way or the other whether you were offended by what she said, which made her insults seem more like a verbal tic than a genuine attempt to hurt feelings. It quickly became apparent that she was as loyal as she was rude, berating a guardsman in one of the towns we passed through for suggesting that

Borg was, perhaps, not the swiftest rabbit in the warren. When she finished, the man not only apologized profusely, but broke down in tears and sobbed hysterically. When Nadi thanked Whiska for standing up for their companion, she insulted Nadi for suggesting that she would do anything other than defend her friends.

Speaking of Borg, he most certainly was *not* the swiftest rabbit in the warren (to be fair to the now-emasculated town guardsman), but nor was he the dumbest rock in the box—far from it, actually. It was like he lived two minutes in the past and was having conversations with our past selves in what was, for him, real-time. Throw in the fact that the common tongue was his second language and Borg seemed simple, but he was actually fairly intelligent, highly empathetic, and, like Whiska, very loyal to people with whom he hadn't been traveling for all that long. I couldn't help but like him, even if I didn't particularly enjoy his near-constant need to defecate at inconvenient times.

That leaves Nadi. Nadi was clearly competent, strong, and a natural leader. She was quiet and thoughtful, but when she spoke, she spoke with authority. Nadi was more reserved than the others, so I spent a lot of time trying to figure out what made her tick. I figured her father's death at the hands of orc raiders had spurred her desire to become an adventurer, but she said that had little to do with it, though she wouldn't tell me what had. She rarely lowered her guard, though she sometimes loosened up around Rummy, who she clearly adored despite frowning upon his habit of taking things that didn't belong to him. She also had a very bad habit of staring a hole right through your head, though she did it to me more than the others, so maybe she just took a while to get used to new people. And, it's not like I'm not used to being stared at, both as a performer and as a "paragon of ethereal beauty" (again, not my words—that's how Kenneth the Pretty Okay Sometimes Wandering but Usually Sedentary Minstrel once described me; I should note that Kenneth was much better at sweet-talking than he was at marketing himself).

By the time we neared the orc encampment, I had a much better understanding of my new companions and, for the first time, at least a vague sense of hope that they might actually be able to defeat the dragon. I hadn't actually seen them in battle yet, though, so I was reserving judgment until after our encounter with the orcs—assuming we survived it.

"I realize that my job on this journey is to act as a chronicler," I said, "but, just out of curiosity, do we have any sort of plan for when we *actually* encounter the orcs?"

"Besides turning them into orc jelly?" asked Whiska.

"Please tell me that's just a particularly graphic way of describing how violently you'll kill them and not a Ratarian toast topper," I replied.

"Why can't it be both?"

"I need to get a better sense of how the encampment is laid out," interjected Nadi (thankfully). "Do you know how close we are?"

"We're still a few miles away, I think," I replied. "Maybe a little less."

"Let's go another half mile or so—after that, I'll go ahead alone to scout things out."

"Are you sure that's a good idea?" asked Rummy.

"Sending more than one of us would increase the chances that we're seen, and I'm the best choice for this sort of thing, given my ability to move quietly and, ah, not necessarily kill everything I see." Nadi looked at Whiska. "No offense."

"Why would I be offended by the truth? Personally, I think not killing everything you see is a sign of weakness."

"Remind me to remain unseen by Whiska," said Rummy.

We continued on for another ten minutes before taking shelter in a copse of trees well off the main road that would provide cover while Nadi undertook her scouting mission.

With nothing to do but wait, Rummy decided to cook

dinner. Borg lit a fire while Rummy busied himself slicing up vegetables and dropping them into a pot that looked far too large to have come out Rummy's pack. When he started pulling out an array of jars and bottles containing various oils and spices that clearly would not have fit into his bag, at least not without constantly clanking, I raised an eyebrow and gestured toward the absurdly large collection of cooking paraphernalia.

"Oh, this?" Rummy surveyed his implements. "Just because one is traveling doesn't mean that one can't enjoy a good meal." He picked up one of the spice bottles. "I realize that Sunderlen ginger root isn't necessary for all meals— though a little pinch of it will do nicely in this one—but I'd hate to be without it when I need it, you know?"

"I was less questioning your particular spice selections than I was how much room you have in your trunk there." I motioned toward his bag. "Especially for someone with such a small trunk."

He shrugged as he considered his pack. "It was a gift from a former employer, now deceased, sadly."

"Bequest or burglary?"

"Well, he didn't pass until several years after the bag came into my possession."

"Natural or suspicious causes?" I asked.

"He was affected by unfortunate circumstances."

"Excellent use of the passive voice and vague details," I remarked.

"Tools of the trade," replied Rummy.

"Sunderlen ginger root...is very spicy," interjected Borg.

"It does have a little kick," said Rummy with a nod. He pointed toward his pack. "Anyway, I can fit pretty much anything I need to in that thing, and it's as light as some leather."

"Don't you mean *light as a feather*?" I asked.

"Well, it has *some* weight to it, and it's made of leather, so…"

I walked right into that one.

Rummy's vegetable stew was excellent, and we all assumed comfortable positions as we waited for Nadi's return. I confess that mine was somewhat less ladylike than maybe it should have been, but, come on…have you ever tried to relax in tight leggings after eating stew?

Nadi returned a short while later, nodding her thanks to Rummy as he handed her a bowl of stew. "How's it look?" he asked.

Nadi chewed and swallowed a bite before she responded. "That's good." She wiped her lips and idly stirred her stew. "The main entrance is heavily guarded, but no surprise there—I wasn't exactly planning on a full-frontal assault anyway." She took another bite. "About four hundred yards from the main entrance, though, there's a weak point in their perimeter that I think we can get in through. There are some sentries, but if we time it right, we should be able to avoid them."

"And once you—well, we—get inside?" I said.

"The encampment's too big for us to take out entirely, unfortunately. If we go in under cover of darkness, I think we can at least get the chief and the shaman—if I know anything about orcs, that should start some major infighting that, at the very least, should buy everyone in the region a few weeks of peace while they sort things out."

"Don't worry," said Whiska, "we'll kill as many of them as possible. And maybe grind some of them into sparkling wine."

"I don't think that's a thing," I replied.

"That's where you're wrong," she said. "Why do you think people always talk about popping the orc before they open a bottle?"

I waited for Whiska to guffaw, or chuckle, or even just

crack a tiny smile—something, anything to congratulate herself on her terrible pun. Her expression didn't change in the slightest and, after an awkward moment of silence, I realized that she was completely serious. Deadly serious, even.

"I don't think that's exactly what…you know what? Never mind. It's not important." I looked at the sky and noted that the sun had just about dipped below the horizon. "I'd say we've got about four hours or so until midnight, so we might as well get some rest." I laid out my bedroll next to the fire. "Think we're safe here, Nadi?"

"I'll make sure you're safe, Heloise." Nadi's response was strangely intense, and she gave me a look that indicated either fierce conviction or long-term constipation (though I suppose those two things aren't necessarily mutually exclusive).

"Ah…right. Thanks. Guess I'll get some sleep, then." I slid into my bedroll and closed my eyes.

"I will…keep watch," said Borg.

"Aren't you tired?" I murmured without opening my eyes. Around me, I could hear the others bedding down.

A moment passed and silence ensued, broken only by an occasional bird call or buzzing insect. Then, a gravelly voice spoke. "Rock giants…need very little…sleep."

Entirely too short a time passed before Nadi was gently shaking my shoulder to wake me up. I blinked my eyes to find her crouching next to me and looking down at me with a small smile. "It's time," she said, letting her hand linger on my shoulder.

I sat up, stretched, and yawned. Nadi's hand was still on my shoulder. I looked at her quizzically, and she stood up quickly. I couldn't tell for sure, given her tan complexion, but I think she blushed. I decided not to say anything, which is pretty much like a skrindip refusing a latcha leaf (and I've seen skrindips kill badgers to get a latcha leaf). But, every once in a while I like to display some self-control.

We packed up our stuff (with much of it disappearing into Rummy's bag—I really needed to get one of those) and headed down the road toward the encampment. As we walked, Nadi quietly detailed her plan.

"We'll veer off the road in a bit and travel through the woods the rest of the way. Whiska and I will breach the perimeter first and take out any sentries that are nearby. Once we give the all-clear, the rest of you will follow us in. From there, we'll skirt the main thoroughfares within the encampment to get to the shaman's tent and take him down first. If we do that quietly enough, we go for the chief. If we raise any kind of alarm, we get out as quickly as possible. Understood?" Nadi looked at Whiska. "No going off script."

Whiska made a gesture that was simultaneously dismissive and rude. I made a mental note to remember it. It seemed like something I could use frequently.

"All right," whispered Nadi, "let's do it."

Nadi led us off the path and into the deep gloom of the woods. Shimmery stars gave us just enough light that we didn't stumble into every single object that could have bruised sensitive shins—just most of them. After several minutes of Borg loudly crunching through the underbrush and Nadi wincing with each snapped stick, she called a halt. "You three," she said, pointing to Rummy, Borg, and me, "wait here. With any luck, we'll be back within the hour."

"Wait a minute," I replied, holding up my hand very authoritatively. Most things I do are very authoritative, in fact, except dancing the Flamnllewllyn, a traditional elvish dance, which I did very tentatively (but only because "Flamnllewl-lyn" translates as "Dance of the Tentative Feet"). "You hired me to tell your story, right?" I tilted my head from side to side as I considered my phrasing. "Well, more accurately, you promised me a share of theoretical treasure to tell your story. Right?"

Nadi nodded slowly. "Yes…"

"So, it stands to reason that I need to know what your story is so I can tell it properly. Right?"

"I suppose," said Nadi. "But, I don't want you to—"

"Nadi," I interrupted (authoritatively), "I'm a bard. I eat danger for breakfast. And scones. I really like scones. Ideally with chocolate chips. Or cinnamon. But not both at the same time."

"Well," she said, fidgeting...not quite nervously, but maybe uncomfortably. "I wasn't so much worried about the danger as, well...Whiska and I need to move quickly and efficiently, and having an extra person with us might...might..." She trailed off.

"Oh...oh, I see. Yeah. I see how it is. Heloise can't take care of herself. Right. She's certainly never been in a fight before. Not once. She never took down a troll with a knife and a torch. She never disarmed a dark elf with a spoon. She never killed a goblin with a song." (Two out of three of those things are true...I'll let you figure out which two.)

"Please, Heloise," said Nadi, "it's not that I don't have confidence in your ability to handle yourself—I do. And I very much want to see how you handle yourself." She paused, seemed to consider her words, and then blushed, and a light very belatedly went on in my head. "Just...can you just wait here? Please?"

"No," I replied, though I kept my tone soft. "I can't. Not if I'm going to do this group any justice." I smiled. "Don't worry —I'll be fine. Really."

"Wait a second," interjected Whiska, looking from Nadi, still blushing, to me. "You—you like her!" she said to Nadi (somewhat accusingly, I thought).

"No! I'm just...just worried about her. And...and we haven't seen her fight..."

"You like her!" shouted Whiska again.

"Quiet!" said Rummy, somehow using a loud whisper. "You'll give us away, you walking drain clog!"

Everyone braced themselves for Whiska's response. Whiska blinked and looked at Rummy for a full moment before she nodded. "That wasn't bad."

"Thank you. Now, Nadi, whatever your feelings on the subject, I think Heloise is right—she needs to go with you. She needs to be part of the action for our plan to work. Besides, I'm pretty sure she can, um, handle herself. Boy, does that sound awkward now."

"It's funny...that she likes...women because...her name is..." began Borg thoughtfully before Nadi cut him off.

"Enough! Whiska, come on." She motioned to the wizard before turning to look at me. "If you slow us down, you turn back. Understood?"

I nodded. "Let's go."

Rummy and Borg (belatedly) waved as we parted company, and Nadi, Whiska, and I plunged into the under-brush. Frankly, I'm not sure what Nadi was worried about; I can say for a fact that half-elves are much stealthier than Ratarians, and that's just in the general case—in the specific case of me versus Whiska, it was an even more lopsided contest. I glided through the underbrush, skim-ming across the tops of leaves and twigs without making a sound or leaving a trace of my passage, though I wasn't quite as stealthy as Nadi, who might as well have been a ghost.

Whiska, on the other hand...I think she went out of her way to crunch every stick, acorn, and crackbug she could find (crackbugs are small, but when you step on one, it sounds like thunder splitting a thick log; they also glow pink in the dark, so they're not particularly hard to avoid stepping on).

Nadi shushed her several times before giving up and settling for shooting her looks that would have turned a raw chunk of lamb into a fully cooked shish roundabob. Whiska either didn't notice or didn't care (my money was on the latter), though I think she might have regretted her nonchalance at least a little when, a moment later, an orc arrow thunked into a tree trunk two inches away from her snout.

"'Ware the archers!" shouted Nadi.

"'Ware the archers?'" I echoed, incredulous. "Seriously? That's how you talk in the middle of a fight? You revert to high-middle Folarian? Why not, oh I don't know, '*look out!*' or something, you know, less ridiculous?"

"Just fight!" said Nadi.

"See? Was that so hard?"

We scattered, and Whiska immediately began chanting. A few seconds later, she flung a barrage of green energy toward our attackers. Someone yelped, and more arrows whizzed past us (one distressingly close to my nose; thank goodness it's already small (and so cute and button-like), or it would have become (painfully) smaller.)

Nadi had her sword out and was spinning wildly, looking for someone to strike. I took my long knife from its sheathe and did the same, but looked considerably more graceful while doing so.

A moment passed in silence. We looked around; Nadi and I closed in and stood back to back. Whiska moved toward us. "Orcs!" she snarled. "Not only do they smell disgusting and taste terrible, but they're cowards! If I could see one of them right now, I swear I'd rip its intestines out and—"

Whatever creative (and, knowing her, ultimately culinary) fate Whiska had in mind for our opponents was forever lost in a scream of "*Aaaaaaaaaaahhhhhhhh!*" as she was flung up into the air, trapped in a net that had been cleverly concealed along the forest floor.

"That's not good," I observed sagely.

Nadi lowered her sword. "Point your knife down," she whispered. "If they wanted us dead, they'd have taken us with arrows. They've got us covered from an elevated position, and we can't see them. Our only hope is to let them get up close.

Draw them in." She dropped her sword on the ground and raised her hands. "Be ready."

I raised an eyebrow, but did as she asked.

"I hear something," she whispered as she took a step forward, "get ready to—"

For the second time, one of my companion's comments was cut short by a scream. That made two of us hanging helplessly in nets. And, as the famously rotund and campy bard Beef Roast once sang, two out of three ain't great.

The moon, which had been hiding behind the clouds, suddenly broke through, shining through the forest canopy and enabling me to see a group of at least 10 orcs closing in. The first to arrive hefted a spear, pointed it up at Whiska, and said gleefully, "We have lattice roped ourselves some interlopers!" Then he made a choking, hacking sound that I eventually realized was laughter. It was the first time I'd heard an orc laugh. I didn't enjoy the experience.

The other orcs approached. One, apparently the oldest of the group, shook his head. "No, you mean that we have 'netted ourselves some interlopers.' Not 'lattice roped.' That is not a thing people say." He looked at me and shrugged apologetically. "We are very bad at jokes. Especially the kind with words."

"But very good at making lattice ropes!" said the first orc, grinning.

"I see that," I said. "Am I going to get pulled up into one if I step in the wrong spot?"

"Yes," said the old orc.

"Could you, I don't know, tell me where to step so that doesn't happen?"

"No."

"Right, then." I looked up at Nadi, who was furiously trying to saw through her ropes with a dagger (ineffectively, I might add). Whiska was neither moving nor hurling epithets, which worried me. The only thing I could think of that would silence her was unconsciousness, and she was so stubborn that I'm not even sure that would stop her from cursing someone.

"Get them down," said the old orc. "Carefully."

I decided to stay put, waiting for the orcs to come get me. I watched as they lowered Nadi and Whiska, moving quickly to bind their mouths and hands—not, however, before a possum-playing Whiska was able to utter a few syllables and twitch her fingers. Flames erupted from her hands, causing the closest orcs to fall back, shrieking, though others jumped in to gag and bind her before she could do anything else. The orcs she'd hit slapped frantically at themselves in an effort to put out the flames, looking more than a little pained. They growled and gave Whiska dirty looks, but, much to my surprise, didn't move to strike her.

I was next in line for binding and gagging, and while there's an easy joke to make here about them not being nearly as good at it as most dwarves I've known, I'm going to refrain from making it. It wasn't the most comfortable arrangement I'd ever experienced, but neither was it unduly painful, which, again, surprised me. I could only assume that the orcs had plans to eat us or something equally horrible that required our flesh to remain tender and unbruised.

We were marched single file through the woods, stopping to rest after about an hour. Rather than removing our gags, the orcs wet them with water so we could suck the moisture from them—not exactly thirst-quenching, but better than nothing, and, I had to concede, a reasonable approach given what Whiska had attempted when they'd cut her down from the net.

We continued on, reaching the orc encampment just as dawn broke. Turns out that "encampment" didn't do it justice —it warranted "settlement" at the very least. Maybe even "town." I mean, there were fences—not barbed-wire, skewer-the-intruder fences...like, white picket fences. There were little old orc ladies sitting on porches crocheting doilies. I had no idea little old orc ladies were a thing—I assumed that most of them either died in battle or were killed (and maybe eaten) by their mates long before reaching their dotage. I even saw an ice cream shop, though I naturally assumed that the flavor of the month would soon be Neapolitan (elf/half-elf/Ratarian). I shook my head. Something strange was going on.

Our escorts took us to a building that resembled a courthouse—primarily, it turns out, because it was a courthouse (I couldn't decide which was more shocking—the doilies or the fact that the orcs had a courthouse). They hustled us inside and we came to a stop in front of a desk where sat a wizened, but still huge and scary-looking, orc wearing dark robes. White hair flowed down to his shoulders, and he grunted when he saw us. He picked up a knife and pointed it at Nadi. I feared he would throw it, and frantically (yet somehow still coolly and heroically, because "frantic" just isn't a good look for me) looked around for a way to stop him, but instead of hurling it, he used it to pick his nails. "Well, what are you waiting for?" he growled to our captors. "Ungag them."

"This one's a wizard, High Chieftain Gnurk," replied one of the orcs holding Whiska.

"Well, then, stick the point of a knife on the back of her neck and shove it through if she starts to say anything magical," replied the orc at the desk, clearly irritated. "This is not math, Klung. You should be able to do it." I was stunned to realize two things: first, that the orcs were speaking the common tongue, and not ineloquently, most likely for our benefit. Second, that I kind of liked the older guy—and not just because he was feisty. He had a kind of dwarvish handsomeness going on.

The orcs moved quickly to remove our gags. I opened my mouth to stretch my jaw and then glanced over at Nadi. She stared at the High Chieftain, her clenched jaw a pretty clear indicator of what she would do if she could get her sword back. Whiska seemed on the verge of speaking, but a pointed (so to speak) application of the knife on the back of her neck caused her to bite back whatever she had intended to say. I was relieved to see that Whiska did, somewhere in the deepest recesses of her brain, have a pragmatic survival instinct that at least occasionally prevented her from talking.

"What's the charge, Klung?"

"Trespassing, High Chieftain. With intent to commit malice."

"Do you base the second charge on evidence or simply the fact that they are armed and garbed as...adventurers?" He wrinkled his nose in disgust before he said "adventurers."

"We overheard the greasy one say 'I can't wait to melt those possum-screwing orcs into goo and pick my teeth with their bones,' High Chieftain."

"I'm not greasy!" screeched Whiska. "I just have a naturally shiny coat!"

"We'll add slander to the list of charges, then—possums are not native to this area, and so we couldn't possibly have relations with them," said the High Chief. "If the rat creature had suggested that some of our people lie with, say, beavers, the slander charge would not apply."

I started to laugh, but then realized that the old orc wasn't joking. I cleared my throat instead.

"The rat creature does not deny the claim, then?" he asked.

Whiska chortled. "Hardly."

Adept as a wizard, maybe, but not the sharpest cheese in the cold case, and apparently less pragmatic than I'd hoped. "Whiska, it might be best if you let Nadi do the talking," I suggested. Then, I looked at Nadi, whose jaw remained clenched as she stared with naked hatred at our captors. "Or, maybe me."

I fixed my gaze on the old orc. "High Chieftain Yerk..."

"Gnurk. Not 'Yerk.'" The High Chief shook his head. "Humans and elves always make such poor attempts to pronounce Orcish words. Dwarves are better, given the guttural similarities of our languages, but rarely do they care to try."

"High Chieftain Gnurk," I said, rolling the strange word around on my tongue. "My companion, Whiska, has a tendency toward hyperbole. Our intent is not to cause harm to your people, but rather simply to pass through on our way to Skendrick."

"You think me naïve, she-elf?"

"Half-elf, actually."

"Irrelevant."

"I'd say it's been pretty relevant all the times in my life I've been spit on and called 'half-breed' by ignorant morons."

Nadi's look softened for the first time in hours. "Heloise..."

"Irrelevant for this purpose," interrupted Gnurk. "I do not believe for a moment that you intended no harm to the orcs of Bblargnorg."

"Gesundheit," I replied.

"You're not half as funny as you think you are, as I suspect you have a very high opinion of yourself."

"My opinion of myself is in direct proportion to my amazingness," I said sweetly.

"Regardless, there is no way that a half-elf, elf, and whatever that destructive creature there is"—he gestured dismissively toward Whiska—"planned to pass through orcish territory without trying to rack up as high a body count as possible. The enmity between our races is far too great."

"Yes," I replied with a nod, "that may be true. As far as I can tell, though, you only have circumstantial evidence—hardly enough to convict us. So, if there's nothing further, we'll just be on our way, then..."

The old orc laughed, a dry, dusty chuckle that sounded

like what I imagine it would sound like if a cactus lizard burped (though as far as I'm aware, cactus lizards, which only live in the Kordise Desert, don't burp—they expel all excess gas through bags on their knee pits, which makes them sound a little bit like a creaky bellows when they walk; it also makes them look ridiculous). "You foolishly presume that an orcish court functions the same as a human court." His expression grew stern. "I am High Chieftain Gnurk! My word is law."

I got the distinct impression that we were in trouble.

"I cannot release from custody those who I know would plot to murder my people."

"Your notion of '*justice*' is exactly what I'd expect from an orc," spat Nadi.

The High Chieftain smirked. "And the elves would respond differently if they captured a group of orcs planning to slaughter them in their sleep? They would frolic with them and fete them and release them without punishment? Braid their hair with flowers, perhaps?"

Nadi glowered, but lowered her eyes to the floor.

"So, what happens now?" I asked.

"Now? Now we feed you."

"It's about time, you ham-fingered puke stains!" said Whiska.

"And then we execute you," said Gnurk, smiling.

AFTER TASTING the food the orcs served, I kind of wished they had executed us first. Nadi didn't even try it, though Whiska seemed to enjoy it, noisily slurping down every bite of what our captors called "graulich," but which might better be described as "stewed entrails slathered in cow urine." (They didn't actually disclose the recipe—old family secret, they told us—so I'm just guessing about the ingredients based on the one bite I managed to choke down.)

"I should get executed by orcs more often," said Whiska as she finished licking not just her own bowl, but mine and Nadi's as well. She took her time grooming her whiskers and hands (paws?) afterward before letting out a massive, floor-vibrating belch.

"Feel better?" I said.

"Ratarians don't burp to relieve ourselves, straw hair," she replied. "Just to gauge the quality of the food. And that food was exceptional."

I spent a moment debating whether I should take "straw hair" as an insult or just a description of my hair—which, to be fair, was at least the color of straw, if not the consistency (and thank goodness for that, because braiding it would be a nightmare)—but decided to let it go.

"Now then," said Whiska as she stood up, "are we ready to get out of here?"

"Yes," said Nadi as she, too, stood and began to stretch. "I see only one weak point." She gestured broadly to the windowless room in which we found ourselves, which was nicer than some inns I'd stayed in (which, admittedly, wasn't saying much, because I've stayed in some real holes). And it had doilies.

"I see two," replied Whiska.

"Where's the second?"

"There." Whiska pointed at the door.

"How is the door a weak point?" I asked. "It's a foot thick, made of iron, and loves being locked up—it's the portal equivalent of one of my former lovers." I cocked my head. "Okay, maybe two of my former lovers. Fine. More than two. It's like multiple of my former lovers. Point being, that thing is impenetrable." I pointed to the series of seven locks that ran up the right-hand side of the door. "Unlike most of those former lovers," I added quietly.

Whiska scoffed. "You're as bad at sizing up doors as you are picking lovers." She uttered an incantation and pointed at the locks. Each, in turn, unlocked itself, the final bolt sliding open with a resounding click.

"Well then," I said, "that's a trick I need to learn." I turned to Nadi. "Just out of curiosity, where's the other weak point?"

She pointed toward the back right side of the cell. "See that stone? The one right there in the corner? That's not mortar in between it and the other stones."

I looked at the dark gray substance that filled in the gaps between the stone Nadi pointed at and its neighbors and shrugged. "I'm no mason, but that looks like mortar to me."

"Right—that's the point. Smell it, though."

"Seriously?"

"Yes."

I raised an eyebrow, but got down on my hands and knees and leaned my nose close to the floor, taking a deep breath. "Smells like...it smells a little like cinnamon," I said, surprised.

Nadi nodded. "It's chirrup."

"What the hell is chirrup?"

"You ever seen a gigaloo?" asked Whiska.

"They look like cats, right? But a little smaller. And pointier," I said.

"Right. When they puke, they make something that looks and functions like mortar, but is easier to remove."

"And it smells like cinnamon?"

Now Whiska nodded. "You're not quite as dumb as you look."

I chose to let that pass. "Why's it called chirrup?"

"Because that's the sound gigaloos make when they puke."

"Naturally," I said. "So, what, someone dug a tunnel underneath the floor and used gigaloo puke to conceal their escape route?"

"Like I said," replied Whiska, "not quite as dumb as you look."

"If you two are done discussing theoretical exits," broke in Nadi, "I'd suggest we use the one we know is open, find some weapons, and go get Rummy and Borg."

"Excuse me for trying to learn something about exotic animal vomit," I said, probably more defensively than was necessary. Bards have a tendency to display a natural curiosity that can get in the way of things like trying to survive imminent death.

"Whiska—do you have any spells left?" Nadi asked as she pressed her ear against the door.

"One, but it's only a minor cantrip—if you had been paying attention and knew how to count, you'd have been able to figure that out on your own."

"There's no way you're going to hear anything through that," I said to Nadi. "Foot thick, remember?"

"You've got some idea because you're a half-elf, but elven hearing is even more acute."

"So you *can* hear something?"

"Enough to know that there's at least one guard outside the door, and he's hungry."

"How do you know he's hungry?"

"I can hear his stomach growling. Also, guards are almost always hungry."

"Fair point."

"Here's the plan," said Nadi. "The minute we open the door, Whiska will use her cantrip to distract the guard. I'll hit him high. Then we'll—"

"Why are you assuming it's a him? Could be a her," I pointed out. "Seems like kind of a sexist assumption."

"No woman's stomach growls like that."

"Clearly, you haven't been around me that long," I replied.

Nadi looked annoyed. "As I was saying, I'll take out the

guard. Heloise, you go right—you're looking for either an exit or our weapons. Whiska—you get my back."

"Be more fun if we do it the other way around, wouldn't it?" I said teasingly.

Nadi ignored me. "Let's go!" she cried as she ripped open the door.

Whiska began to activate her cantrip, which would create a distraction in the form of sensory overload for her target (strobe lights, explosive noises, terrible smells, and so on), but it fizzled as her voice faltered and trailed off.

Two dozen crossbow-bearing orcs stood outside the door, beads drawn on our heads.

"Huh," I said, "didn't see that coming." I turned to Nadi. "That's some keen hearing you've got—there's an entire grope of orcs hanging around outside our door and all you can pick out is some guy's rumbly tummy."

I could see Nadi struggling—on the one hand, we'd all die within seconds if we decided to fight; on the other, we'd be just as dead within a short time if we didn't fight. It seemed like the only real question was whether we preferred a crossbow bolt through the eye or a rope around the neck. Neither seemed all that appealing to me. Why is a painless poison cupcake never an option?

Before we could make a decision one way or the other, however, our old friend High Chieftain Gnurk took the decision out of our hands. "Boring and predictable," he said, shaking his head. "Subdue them."

The orcs dropped their crossbows and surged forward to restrain us (and none too gently). Instinct took over and the three of us fought like Darkonian mini punching mollusks. We landed some hits, but the orcs wrestled us to the ground, more than earning the grope moniker in the process.

"I was going to allow you to live until tomorrow, but this egregious breach of etiquette makes me think we're better off just killing you now." Gnurk gestured to the orcs to get us up on our feet.

"Breach of etiquette?" said Nadi, angry and incredulous. "You don't expect us to fight for our lives?"

"Yes, of course I expect that—how could a desire to survive possibly be a breach of etiquette, fool?" Gnurk shook his head dismissively. "It seems elves possess far more whimsy than common sense."

"To be fair," I said, "Nadi's probably the least whimsical elf I know." I pursed my lips as I had a thought. "Truth be told, Gnurky, the whimsical thing gets a little oversold. Most of the elves I know are pretty practical."

"Nmromath forbid that I perpetuate an incorrect stereotype about another race," said the High Chieftain, entirely too dryly in my very well-informed opinion.

"Here's one stereotype that's true, you withered husk of a booger," said Whiska (entirely too smugly, also in my very well-informed opinion, given that four orcs held her captive). "Ratarian necks don't break or strangle, so good luck hanging me!"

Gnurk and the other orcs laughed. "Hanging? That's something humans do. It's a terrible means of execution. Often ineffectual and not very much fun."

"What do orcs do?" I asked, dreading the answer.

"We rip you in half—but good!" said the orc holding my right arm.

"Well, that sounds uncomfortable," I replied.

"If it's any consolation, I don't believe it hurts for very long," said Gnurk, not so consolingly.

"So, what exactly *was* our breach of etiquette?" I asked as we were led to what humans would call the gallows, but what orcs call the "krumfishnaw," which translates loosely to "the rippin' place." (Gnurk later told me that "krumfishnaw" is more of a slang term, and that the formal name is "krumfishnel," which translates to "the rippin' location." I suggested that this didn't seem to constitute a significant difference in level of formality, but he got really huffy, so I dropped the subject.)

"You've no respect for, nor understanding of, other cultures. You are a hypocrite of the highest order," he replied coldly.

"Fine, yes, I get it—I also stole chocolate once, occasionally have bad breath in the morning—though I'd appreciate if you wouldn't mention that to anyone else—and sometimes wish bad things would happen to good people who I just don't happen to like. I'm not perfect, even if I look like I am. And sing like I am. And, if we're being honest, make love like I am."

"You unlocked the door."

"What?" I asked, confused.

"Unlocking the door—that was your breach of etiquette."

"I thought you said that you expected us to fight for our lives," Nadi said.

"I do," replied Gnurk. "But, locks are sacred in orc society. If you had, say, used a fireball to destroy the door, that would be one thing. But, undoing the locks..."

"Isn't that a little bit like condemning a person for killing someone with a sword, but shrugging if they do it by running someone down with a horse?" I tried to keep my tone respectful, given that we were being groped (by which I mean held by a lot of orcs), but I'm not sure I successfully kept all traces of incredulity from my voice.

"No."

"No?"

"No."

"Well, all right then." I looked at Nadi and shrugged. She shook her head. Whiska just muttered something about orc cakes.

"Do you know what 'Nmromath' means in your tongue?" The High Chieftain's expression was stern.

"Well, I know I don't want him *on* my tongue, that's for sure," I said in an attempt to lighten the mood (a poor attempt, I admit, but *you* try coming up with a good joke when you've got an orc blade on the verge of severing your neck).

I gained a whole new respect for the elasticity of orcish skin when Gnurk managed to extend his frown to the bottom of his chin. "It means 'Lock Keeper.'"

"I would have guessed 'elf murderer,'" replied Nadi as she tried to shrug away from her captors, who gripped her tighter.

Gnurk smirked. "Orcs murder elves. Elves murder orcs. So it has been, and so it will always be. Do we kill elves because they are elves? Probably less than you slay orcs because they are orcs. But, to learn about orcs, particularly orcs as individuals, about what we believe and how we live and what we stand for, would shake the foundations of your beliefs and engender the crippling pain of guilt, and so you choose to place us in the box in which you believe we belong —a box of your own design. A self-fulfilling prophecy." The High Chieftain shook his head. "Who did you lose, elf woman? A lover? A sibling? A parent." He nodded as Nadi's jaw tightened. "A parent, then. I am almost as sorry for your loss as I am mine, having lost a brother, a nephew, and, most recently, a daughter to elvish arrows."

"While raiding elven lands, no doubt," said Nadi defiantly. I began to worry that she would strain her neck with all the jaw-jutting she was doing.

"Defending this very settlement, actually," replied Gnurk without even a hint of bitterness. He turned to look at me. "You say you are passing through to Skendrick...do you not wonder why the people of Skendrick and the other nearby human settlements have not banded together to oust us from our land? We are not so many in number, after all. We could be defeated with but a little coordinated effort."

"Have you met the people of Skendrick?" I said. "I'm not sure they could band together if you gave them all instruments."

Gnurk looked at me sternly before his lip twitched strangely, more of a spasm, really, and I worried—or maybe hoped—that he was in the throes of some sort of fit. Maybe a stroke. Turns out he was just smiling. Or, at least, trying to smile. "I will enjoy your death the least."

The High Chieftain turned his attention back to Nadi, who looked troubled. "The reason they do not attack us, and the reason we have lived here for years—long enough to have built this community, a rare occurrence for orcs indeed—is that the humans have learned that we present no threat. Yes, it took years—and, ironically, much bloodshed—for us all to come to common understanding about our lack of enmity for each other, but now we coexist more or less peacefully, save for when hot-headed 'adventurers' take it upon themselves to stir up trouble for the sole purpose of making a name for themselves." He spat on the ground. "Fools."

"If I weren't restrained right now, I'd shove that headdress so far up your toilet hole that you'd have to open your mouth to change the feathers," interjected Whiska. "What are those from, anyway? A turdkey?"

(No, dear readers, "turdkey" is not a typographical error—they're an offshoot of the turkey family that have their plumbing in a different spot—namely, right in the middle of their back, which means that, when they void waste, they end up covered with it. They're disgusting. But, I should note, also delicious. Not the feathers—the bird itself, I mean. And their feces are sterile. Or so I've been told, though that may have just been to make me feel better about eating an animal that defecates on itself up to seven times each day.)

"Bold words for a captive rodent," replied the High Chief. He nodded to our captors. "Ring the bells, and take them to the Ripper."

"Practical with naming conventions, these orcs," I said to Nadi as they dragged us away, Nadi and Whiska straining to break free as I walked calmly. It's not that I wanted to die or was any less terrified than they were; I'm just a lot classier and generally more dignified.

A few moments later, we stood on a dais in the center of the settlement next to a very unpleasant rust-colored contraption that featured a flat surface about the size of a bed, chains and manacles, a giant spring mechanism, and a lever. A horizontal line in the middle of the flat section indicated that the device operated by binding the unfortunate victim by the hands and feet and pulling the lever to separate the two sections (and, presumably, the victim as well). That's when I realized that it wasn't rust that gave the device its color, but, rather, a whole lot of dried blood.

There were four poles with bells on top surrounding the square, and our captors pulled vigorously and enthusiastically on the ropes that hung from the bells, creating a deafening clang and clatter. "This might be worse than getting ripped in half!" I yelled, but I don't think anyone could hear me very well, given that the only response I got was from one of my orc captors, who said something to the effect of, "I don't believe in betting *or* math—they're both sinful!"

As the echoes from the bells died down, a crowd formed. I expected a raucous gathering of bloodthirsty onlookers (as is the custom in cultures where criminals, or, at least, alleged criminals, are ripped in half for public enjoyment), but they were generally subdued and, save for some murmuring and occasional pointing and gesturing toward us, quiet and orderly.

"This is the first time I haven't enjoyed being in front of a crowd," I whispered to Nadi. "Well, maybe the second, but I didn't realize I was in front of a crowd the other time, and let's just say it didn't end well for my dwarven companion when I found out that I was." I shook my head. "Who thinks to look for hidden peepholes?"

Nadi ignored me as she looked around desperately for an escape route. It didn't look good—four strong orcs held each of us tightly, and they'd gagged Whiska just to make sure she couldn't conjure up any more trouble (though the gag didn't prevent her from managing to spit semi-intelligible and highly creative insults, most of which, as near as I could decipher, involved not just a suggestion, but an order that the orcs choke on a particular part of their anatomy, and she offered weirdly specific guidance on both the optimal method for that part's removal and preparing it for consumption, which involved roasting, slicing, and adding just a hint of lemon).

High Chieftain Gnurk raised his hands to quiet the crowd and gestured toward the orcs who held Nadi. They dragged her toward the Ripper, though she didn't make it easy, throwing one to the ground and managing to head butt another so hard his nose splayed across his left cheek. The other orcs wrestled her into position, pinning her down and shackling her to the table. Nadi strained against her bonds, but if orcs know anything, apparently, it's how to make a solid shackle—she wasn't going anywhere.

"Silence!" said Gnurk. "We come together today to bear witness to justice." He swept his arm across in a grand gesture, encompassing all three of us. "These three individuals plotted, planned, connived, and conspired to do us harm. To kill us in our sleep. To murder our children in coldest blood." I thought he was playing a little fast and loose with the facts—we had not, in fact, intended to murder any children (in cold blood or even in warm blood)—but I wasn't exactly in a position to protest. "Furthermore, while awaiting the dispensation of justice, they committed an even worse crime." He paused dramatically and the crowd leaned forward. Then, he roared. "They dared to unfasten the locks in their cell!"

At this, the previously well-behaved crowd of onlookers exploded, and a riot nearly broke out. They launched what I took to be old produce at us, though I later learned that, by orcish standards, it was, in fact, exceedingly fresh produce—orcs apparently prefer their fruits and vegetables overripe, as they find the combination of stench and bitterness appetizing. Soft tomatoes, brown bananas, and wilted lettuce sailed through the air and struck home, leaving a distressingly sticky and gooey combination of tomato seeds, mushy banana, and bits of green dribbling down between the heavenly contours of my décolletage.

Gnurk allowed the assault to continue for a few moments before he raised his hands for silence once again. "There are some in this world"—Gnurk glared pointedly at Nadi—"who think us savages, who assume that we are but animals incapable of feeling. Of kindness. Of mercy."

He turned back toward the crowd. "When it comes to punishing those who would do us harm, they are right." The High Chieftain raised his hand. "Prepare to rip her!"

I expected the onlookers to cheer and shout, but, instead, they remained silent, almost, dare I say, respectfully so. The orc holding the lever that would separate the two halves of the Ripper—and Nadi with it—tightened his grip and nodded.

The High Chieftain started to bring his hand down, presumably the signal for the execution to proceed, but before he could complete the gesture, a shout rang out.

"Which would you rather see—a boring old elf ripped in half...or a mysterious stranger make a khurlap disappear?"

As one, the orcs in the crowd turned toward the speaker, who came into view as the crowd parted to allow him to make his way to the dais.

Rummy, with Borg in tow.

He held something high above his head—a small, brownish-black pastry, or khurlap (an orc breakfast treat that tastes like dirt with a hint of cinnamon). Rummy strode up the stairs to the dais without being challenged and stood next to Nadi. Gesturing to the khurlap, he said, "Release her, and you will bear witness to feats of prestidigitation that will astonish your eyes and warm your hearts!" He glanced around slyly, focusing on an orc child. "They might even fill your belly." With that, he held the khurlap in front of his face with his right hand, covered it with his left, wiggled his fingers, and rotated his wrists suddenly, opening up both hands to show that the khurlap had disappeared.

"Ooh!" cried the astonished onlookers in creepy unison.

The orcs standing next to Nadi scrambled to undo her shackles, and she sat up slowly, a look of confusion on her face—one that was mirrored on both Whiska's face and my own.

"Now then," said Rummy, hopping down off the dais and walking among the crowd, which parted like a drunk man's zipper. "I have astonished your eyes. Can I warm your hearts?" He stopped before a young orc couple who were holding hands (orcs hold hands?) and crossed his arms, cupping his chin in his left hand. "Hmmm...I think I can." He gestured to the male orc's oversized ears. "May I?"

The orc nodded eagerly, and Rummy twisted his head from side to side to crack his neck and then locked his fingers together before stretching out his hands and arms. "I believe," he said, looking at the female orc as he reached behind the male's ear, "this is for you." He produced a pale blue rose and handed it to the lady orc, who blushed furiously. The crowd applauded enthusiastically.

Rummy took a modest bow before strolling through the crowd once more, in complete and total control. He paused before the young orc he had smiled at a moment before and knelt down so that he could look him in the eye. The crowd circled around, eager to see what he would do next. "I also said something about filling your bellies, didn't I?" The orc child nodded solemnly. "Are you hungry, my good lad?" The orc nodded again, more vigorously. The crowd laughed. "Do you like khurlap?" asked Rummy. This time, the orc's nod was accompanied by a shy smile. "Well, then, it seems silly to keep it tucked underneath your tunic rather than eating it." The boy looked at Rummy, confused, as Rummy pointed to his stomach. "Isn't that a big hunk of khurlap right there?" He prodded gently at the boy's midsection. The boy shook his head sadly.

"It's not? Hmmm...well, that's too bad," said Rummy. "A nice piece of khurlap would probably taste good right now." The boy nodded, still looking sad. His stomach rumbled, loud enough for those nearby to hear. They laughed, though not mockingly or unkindly, and the boy blushed. I think. It was hard to tell with his green complexion.

"Do you mind if I take a quick look? Just to make sure you didn't miss anything?"

The orc boy shrugged and spreads his hands out wide.

"See, here's the thing," Rummy said, patting the boy on the shoulder with his right hand. "I'm not wrong very often." He looked up toward the dais. "Right, Nadi?"

Nadi, stunned by the sudden turn of events, could only nod.

"I bet that I'm not wrong here. Right?" He clapped the boy on the shoulder. As the boy nodded in response, Rummy brought his left hand up from where it had rested briefly on the boy's stomach to reveal a large piece of khurlap. "Ah, see! Looks like old Rummy is right one more time."

The boy's face lit up as Rummy handed him the khurlap. He stuffed it quickly into his mouth, to the delight of all (myself included, I admit). One satisfied belch and some raucous laughter later, Rummy returned to the dais.

"I know what you're thinking," he said as he stood with us once more. "'You've put a delicious pastry in the belly of that boy, Master Tooltinker, but what about *my* belly?'" He looked out over the crowd, which must have included two hundred orcs. "And what about our High Chieftain?" Rummy turned toward Gnurk, whose expression gave no indication of what he thought of Rummy's performance (note to self: no poker games with Gnurk). "I fear, High Chieftain, that I have violated a rule of etiquette."

He moved to stand before Gnurk, bowing slightly as he did. "By all rights, I should have offered you the first khurlap, for which I apologize. Please note, however, that *this* khurlap"—Rummy seized Gnurk's hand, turned it over, and opened it up to reveal another piece of khurlap nestled in the High Chieftain's palm—"is for you."

A slow smile spread across Gnurk's face. He looked at the khurlap, crammed it into his mouth, and chewed slowly. He swallowed, wiped the back of his hand across his lips, and nodded. Then, he began to clap—slowly at first, but then faster and more enthusiastically. The crowd followed their High Chieftain's lead, resulting in a deafening ovation.

Rummy bowed again, with a flourish this time, and then pointed toward Borg, who held up a large basket. "My friend will make sure that you all can enjoy khurlap."

The orcs swarmed around Borg, hopping up and down as they waited for a piece of pastry. After everyone had gotten theirs, the High Chieftain raised his hands for silence. "Master Tooltinker," he intoned formally, "you have earned a boon by virtue of your fine performance. What will you ask of the Orcs of the Gloom Forest?"

"High Chieftain," replied Rummy, mirroring Gnurk's formal tone, "I ask that you release my friends: the elven warrior Nadinta Ghettinwood, the wizard Whiska Tailiesin, and the famed bard Heloise."

Gnurk turned to regard me. "Just Heloise? No surname?"

"How many 'Heloise the Bards' do you know?"

He nodded sagely. "Touché." He looked at Rummy and tapped his finger against the side of his cheek, considering the request. "Very well. I will grant the release of your companions, with two conditions."

"What might those conditions be, High Chieftain?" Rummy could pull off polite without being obsequious, which made it actually seem genuine. I was going to have to learn that trick from him.

"First: Nadinta Ghettinwood, Whiska Tailiesin, and Heloise the Bard are hereby banned from the Gloom Forest and may never reenter upon pain of death."

Rummy nodded. "That seems reasonable, given their lamentable actions. And second?"

"You will give us another performance after we have feasted."

Rummy grinned. "That seems even more reasonable. Especially the feasting part."

The High Chieftain clapped his hands and the orcs exploded into action, moving with a precision and unity I wouldn't have thought possible. Within minutes, an impromptu feasting area had been erected in the square, plates and silverware were being laid out, and smells wafted through the air (the scents weren't entirely unpleasant, though they smelled less like food than they did something with which you might clean a chamber pot.)

Nadi moved to stand next to me and shook her head as she watched the orcs scurry about. "What just happened?"

I shrugged. "I have no idea, but we haven't been ripped in half and we're apparently going to be fed. I'm going to call it a win."

Whiska sidled in between us. "If I can find a few minutes alone, I can regain enough spell power to immolate at least a score of these green fecal remnants in one go, which should buy us time to escape."

"Uh, Whiska?" I replied in my politest voice (which, I should note, isn't really all that polite). "You do realize that they're letting us go, right? After they had us dead to rights?"

"So?"

"So...turning them into orc flambé is probably a suboptimal tactical decision." I looked at Nadi. "What do you think, boss?"

Nadi let out a long, slow breath. "Heloise is right. Stand down, Whiska—no attacking our...our *hosts*," she said through gritted teeth.

"Seriously?" Whiska looked incredulous.

"First of all, even if we have the element of surprise, there's no way we make it out of here alive, given the odds against us. Second, maybe we were, well...maybe we were wrong. About the orcs. I don't know."

"And maybe Heloise will go an entire day without talking about how hot she thinks her backside is...but I doubt it," replied Whiska. "They're *orcs*."

"I'm not quite sure what to make of all of this," I said, "but, come on—did you ever think orcs could be filled with child-like wonder?" I nodded to where Rummy was dancing a coin across his knuckles, much to the delight of not only the young orcs gathered around him, but more than one grown-up orc as well. "I don't know about you, Whiska, but my primary goal is to get out of this situation alive—though, to be fair, that's pretty much my motivation in any situation, though I don't object if there is also chocolate, wine, and dwarven behinds involved as well." I shrugged. "If making nice with Gnurk and his wide-eyed pack of prestidigitation enthusiasts is going to get me—and, yes, my indescribably hot backside—out of here in one piece, then that's exactly what I'm going to do. If you want to go on a suicide run, leave me out of it."

Whiska responded with something that sounded like "*harrumph*," but I wasn't entirely sure.

"What did you say?" I asked.

"Oh, I said '*harrumph*'," she replied.

"That's what I thought," I said.

The next couple of hours were among the most surreal of my life, and I've visited the barridium dens of Kangadoon. The orcs sang and clapped and danced, and at least some of the dishes they served were edible, even verging on tasty (I recommend the roast roggrat, but would suggest staying far away from the pureed plurant).

I found myself seated next to Gnurk, who presided over the proceedings with complete authority and a no-nonsense surliness that made him feel like everyone's curmudgeonly uncle, albeit one who's secretly a big softie.

At one point late in the meal, Gnurk turned to me, gestured to the happy orcs around us, and said, pointedly, "Exactly how you imagined it, no?"

I shook my head. "Look, I'm part elf, which means I inherited certain...viewpoints. But, I'm also a traveler and someone who approaches new situations with an open mind —well, generally speaking; that philosophy does not extend to Killorian orgies."

"That is an understandable position," replied Gnurk with an understanding nod.

"That notwithstanding, this...well, I don't even know what to say about this. Are all orcs like this, or are the Orcs of the Gloom Forest unique?"

Gnurk looked around at his people, laughing and joking with Rummy and Borg, before responding. "Yes."

"Yes, they're all like this, or yes, the Orcs of the Gloom Forest are unique?"

"No."

"You're really infuriating, you know that?"

The High Chieftain smiled, a genuine, something-gross-I-won't-mention-eating grin. "To be fair, you did try to invade my land and murder my people."

As a general rule, I don't do sheepish, so I aimed for contrite. "Look, about that...well, we got some bad information."

"Informed by your own prejudices?"

"From other...from people who...okay, fine, yes, we assumed, because you were orcs, that you were sitting around eating human babies, despoiling the forest, and leaving toilet seats up, and we thought that a strike on your encampment—"

"Community," interrupted Gnurk.

"Right, your community...we thought that a strike on your community would boost the reputation of this, ah, neophyte adventuring group before we make the case to the town of Skendrick that these are the heroes they need to rid them of the dragon that keeps attacking them."

Gnurk snorted. "Your group of adventurers couldn't fight their way out of a bluhrtach."

"What's a bluhrtach?"

"A wrap we put around babies to help them sleep."

"Well, I assume orc babies are stronger than most babies, so maybe that's not such a condemnation."

"I could crush an orc baby's skull in my hand."

I raised an eyebrow. "Have you?"

Gnurk ignored my question. "I have heard about this dragon."

"Anything useful that would help us?"

"Why would I share such knowledge with you, even if I were to possess it? Recall that you are henceforth banned from my lands. "

I gave him my most winsome smile. "Because I'm Heloise, the famous bard."

He grunted. "You are at that." He scratched his chin. "I find it curious that the dragon hasn't turned its attention to our community. We are not so far as the crow flies."

"Just a matter of time, I'd imagine."

Gnurk shook his head. "I don't think so."

"Why do you think that?"

"I think this dragon's objective is...unusual."

"How so?"

Gnurk shrugged. "Call it High Chieftain's intuition."

"Is that a thing?"

"It is if the High Chieftain says it is."

"Fair enough." I took a bite of food. "So, let me ask you this...why do you think we're so, well, wrong about orcs?"

"Elves hate us, and perhaps not unfairly. We have long been at war."

"It can't be that simple."

Gnurk nodded. "It's not. Our people are, almost to a one, illiterate. Even I, for all my wisdom, can form only the most rudimentary written characters. We can create no written record, nor do we excel at telling stories. But, do you know who does?" He gave me a pointed look.

"Elves. Well, and half-elves. Present company particularly included. Meaning me."

"Correct. Bards, storytellers, poets...elves craft the stories and the histories of our world. Orcs are not the actors; we are acted upon. I cannot speak for all orcs any more than you can speak for all elves, or half-elves, but the Orcs of the Gloom Forest would as soon live in peace as any other state—though we do enjoy a good ripping." Gnurk looked wistfully at the unused Ripper. "But, we have no one to tell our story...or to contradict the unfair stories told about us."

I wanted to say something clever, even flippant, but Gnurk was making too many rational points I couldn't refute...or ignore. Deflecting guilt with insults is a time-honored Heloisian tradition, but it felt suddenly trite, which was really annoying. I hate conversations that make me want to be a better person.

What may or may not have transpired between me and Gnurk later that evening, after numerous glasses of what tasted like wound glue (the very sticky and hard-to-remove stuff some primitive healers use to attempt to staunch the flow of blood on the battlefield), but turned out, by orcish standards, to be considered fine whisky is not a tale that will be told in these pages. Suffice it to say, however, that when we left the Gloom Forest the following morning, intact save for pounding headaches, I had a lot to think about.

Not the least of which was how I was going to sell this ragtag bunch to the people of Skendrick as dragon-killing saviors.

CHAPTER 15

THE HEROES ASCENDANT BRING HOPE TO A BELEAGUERED POPULACE

After besting the foul Orcs of the Gloom Forest and ensuring that they would no longer plague the goodly folk in the surrounding towns, our heroes walked the winding road to Skendrick, intent on embarking on their quest.

Roadworn and dusty but covered in glory after their encounter with the orcs, the heroes strode boldly to the gates of Skendrick and knocked with the authority of those imbued by the gods with the gift of righteous purpose. And so did the gates of the beleaguered town open to receive them and welcome them in, naming them friends and saviors both, their reputation burnished by the presence of the great bard Heloise, whose virtue and integrity were legend, and who vouched for the skill, ability, and character of the heroes.

The town Alderman looked them over and nodded and smiled, for they were an impressive company indeed. Led by the fierce elven warrior Nadinta Ghettinwood, the group, which also included the powerful Ratarian wizard Whiska Tailiesen, the rock giant gladiator Borgunder Gunderbor, and the accomplished rogue

Rumscrabble Tooltinker, was a shining beacon of hope for the beleaguered—but still strong—people of Skendrick.

The town council convened immediately, and their deliberations took only moments. They declared Nadinta and her band of adventurers the official dragon slayers of Skendrick, promising to back their claim to all treasures found in the lair of the dragon, and supplying them with all manner of victuals and equipment as might be needed to aid in the successful completion of their quest.

Three days of feasting ensued, with the good people of Skendrick feting their heroes and sparing no expense to make them feel rested and ready for their mission.

Nadinta and her band showed their gratitude for the citizens of Skendrick by gathering them all in the town square and, as they prepared to set off on their quest, kneeling before the assembled town council and swearing many solemn oaths, not only to defeat the dragon, but to remain evermore defenders and protectors of Skendrick, so great was their loyalty to these honest and hard-working folk who had welcomed them in and whose eyes shone with the reflected glory of deeds soon to be done.

With the hopes of an entire town resting on their broad shoulders, the heroes said goodbye to the good people of Skendrick and, with the great bard Heloise accompanying them to tell their tale, set off to seek the lair of the dragon, knowing that they would first need to pass through the fetid Dukbuter Swamp, home to shambling bog men and dangerously enchanting will o' the wisps...

CHAPTER 16

WELL, MAYBE THE SKENDRICKIANS COULD HAVE SHOWN A LITTLE MORE ENTHUSIASM

It was a pensive adventuring crew that made an uneventful journey to Skendrick.

The only one who seemed unaffected was Whiska, who not only managed to insult a tree root that she tripped over on one particularly rutty path, but to do so using a string of epithets that made even me blush, and I didn't even blink when I accidentally walked in on the legendary Mithral Mine Dwargy of 1027 (Fentenian Reckoning, of course).

Elven pensive moods can literally last for months, during which the pensive elf might not say a single word the entire time, so I pulled Nadi aside late in the afternoon on our third day of walking to try to snap her out of it. "I'd offer a copper for your thoughts," I said as we walked ahead of the group, "but I'm kind of cheap, and I hate to overpay for things."

Nadi frowned. "Is there a point to your being mean, or do you just want to torture me?"

I shrugged. "You just seemed a little distant." I looked

behind us. "Though I guess we're all processing what happened back there in our own way." I gestured toward Whiska, who was cackling about having used an enormous fireball to incinerate a fly. "Some more combustibly than others. Is '*combustibly*' a word?"

Nadi looked at Whiska and shook her head before fixing her eyes on mine. "I suppose."

"So," I said, figuring I'd get right to the heart of the matter, "that whole thing with the orcs didn't really go according to plan, huh?"

"You think?" replied Nadi with a sarcastic edge I'd never heard from her.

I pretended not to notice. "That High Chieftain Gnurk was really something." I knew she would take my comment at face value. Nadi was astute when it came to strategy and tactics, but social nuances were lost on her, so I didn't think she had any idea about what may or may not have taken place after Gnurk and I had disappeared from the festivities within a few minutes of each other.

"I'm not sure I want to talk about this." Her look softened. "At least, not yet."

"I understand," I said.

We walked in silence for a few moments before Nadi spoke again. "It's just...hard when something you've assumed to be true your entire life, something that's informed who you are, turns out to be...well, maybe turns out not be what you thought."

"I felt the same way the first time I saw a dwarf naked. In that case, though, the surprise was a pleasant one."

Nadi gave me a strange look before bursting into laughter. "I'm glad you're here, Heloise."

"So am I," I replied, "though I'm less excited about being there." I nodded up the road, where the outskirts of Skendrick had come into view.

"Why's that?" asked Nadi. "You're the one who convinced us to go to help them."

On the one hand, I wanted to tell Nadi that the Skendrickians were an intellectually stunted group of subhumans whose collective intellect could fit into the hollowed-out body of a gnerfly with room to spare. (Gnerflies, for those unfamiliar, are pint-sized versions of gnats.) On the other hand, I *did* talk them into this ridiculous quest, and I didn't want to undermine their confidence in their chosen path (or their beautiful bardish guide), so I just shrugged. "Let's just say I prefer more cosmopolitan areas."

Nadi shook her head. "Give me the forest canopy over a town anyday."

"Village," I said reflexively.

"What?"

"Never mind."

We continued in silence until we reached the gates of Skendrick, such as they were. The bored guard blanched when he saw Borg and brandished his polearm in a way that suggested he was unused to handling anything larger than a baby carrot. I quickly explained the situation, and the guard heaved a sigh of relief, waving us on but backing up a few steps as Borg walked by. He underestimated Borg's reach, however, and the too-friendly rock giant reached out to pat the man on the shoulder, missed, hit him in the head, and knocked him unconscious. It took several minutes to revive him, and by the time we managed to get him upright and convince him that we were not, in fact, a conquering force sent to destroy the village masquerading as its would-be saviors, the sun had begun to set. Just once, I wish a military commander would recognize the value of putting someone with the faintest semblance of intellect on guard duty; so many unnecessary conflicts could be avoided. Then again, given the general dearth of intellect in Skendrick, I supposed it was possible that our brain-addled friend was the town's best and brightest.

I led our merry band to the only decent inn in Skendrick and proceeded to barter my services for room and board. Even on short notice, the crowd turned out in force, though the inn's promise of half-priced ale (watered down sufficiently to offset the potential lost profits) might have had something to do with it. Skendrickians, never the most enthusiastic supporters of the arts, tend to be even less enthusiastic than normal when they're stressed about potentially being immolated by dragon fire.

Pussies.

(It's come to my attention that in addition to suggesting cowardice, "pussies" is a word used in certain cultures to refer, in quite vulgar fashion, to certain parts of the female anatomy. I'm using it here in the Cervarian sense, which, as everyone knows, is in reference to the seeds of the pusing plant—or pussies—which have the odd ability to float away when confronted with the threat of wildfires. Which means, of course, that I'm not really calling the Skendrickians cowards, but, rather, suggesting that they are behaving sensibly in response to the threat of some domineering asshole trying to do them harm. Like a pussy.)

Toward the end of my performance, I started building the case for my companions, selling my fawning admirers on the notion that these people really could defeat a dragon. After finishing a well-received Heloise original called "In Skendrick the Beer Tastes Like the Seven Heavens," I called Nadi up to stand next to me.

(Confession: when performing that particular song, I just plug in the name of whatever town I happen to be performing in. When I'm in Tollton, then, it's "In Tollton the Beer Tastes Like the Seven Heavens." It only becomes problematic when the city/town/village names get long. I don't tend to perform the song in Norblunderingtonvillburg, for example. Then again, I don't tend to perform in Norblunder-ingtonvillburg at all—they take a pretty racist view toward elves. And anyone who's not a gnome, really.)

"This brave warrior," I said to the adoring crowd, "is Nadinta Ghettinwood."

"Me neither!" slurred a drunk man at the back of the room.

"You're an idiot," I replied. "Nadi is the leader of a band of adventurers who have traveled to Skendrick, braving considerable challenges along the way, including a fierce struggle with the Orcs of the Gloom Forest, to answer the call for aid in slaying the mighty red dragon that threatens your town's very survival."

"Village!" shouted an angry woman in the front row.

"Whatever. Gods. The point is, Nadi and her companions are the heroes you have so desperately sought."

Nadi just stared at the crowd. "Say something," I whispered.

"I...I...right. Yes. We're here to, um, help. With the dragon. The one that's...that's burning things. Here. In your town."

I wouldn't have figured Nadi for the stage-fright type. But there's a reason that not everyone's a bard, beyond not wanting to compete with the likes of yours truly.

"What she means to say," I interjected, "is that her group's experience in fighting—and defeating—creatures of all types will stand them in good stead in their quest to kill the beast. For make no mistake, friends—it is no small thing to slay a dragon, and though this group be mighty, their success is far from guaranteed. The way will be full of peril, a harrowing journey to find a creature so foul and so mighty that only a handful of people in all the world would dare brave its wrath—and even fewer still who could survive the encounter."

Nadi gave me a look. "Don't worry," I whispered, more quietly this time so that only she could hear, "it's all part of the show. If they thought it was easy, you wouldn't get any credit."

"They'll be killed!" yelled an overserved man in the middle of the room, his bushy mustaches quivering. "They haven't a chance!"

"We appreciate your confidence," said Rummy, rising to his feet, a less-than-intimidating physical feat that engendered a hearty round of snickering from the crowd. He walked over to stand next to Nadi. "Fine," said Rummy. "How about if that guy stands up?"

Rummy gestured toward where he had been sitting. A moment passed in silence as the crowd looked around, confused. "Me?" said the mustachioed man, rising to his feet.

"No, not you—him!" Rummy pointed again.

Another moment passed. Old walrus mustaches spoke again. "Is one of your party members invisible?"

Finally, Borg stood, and the crowd gasped. He rolled his shoulders back, his massive biceps rippling and his hard skin glinting in the firelight. He stared down at the man with the mustache, who quailed. "I think...this is actually...a village. Right?" said Borg.

As if having a rock giant towering over him wasn't enough, Whiska jumped to her feet as well and pointed her staff at the quivering Skendrickian and said, "How about we show you what we'll do to the dragon?" Her staff flared. "Or maybe I'll just turn that lip rug into a kavarat!"

(A kavarat, incidentally, is a little bit like a wolverine...if a wolverine were three times larger, five times stronger, and ten times nastier.)

The man, already pale, turned whiter than a Fluvian death mask and stumbled backward, tripping over his seat and landing hard on his backside.

"Whiska!" yelled Nadi, back in control. "Back off! Rummy, help him up."

Rummy was already moving toward the man and

extended his hand. The man gripped it nervously, but allowed Rummy to pull him to his feet. "No hard feelings?" said Rummy. "I'd say yes, because I'm pretty sure the rat lady was serious about that kavarat thing."

The man nodded vigorously, the tips of his ridiculous facial adornment bobbing up and down, his flop sweat having caused the ends, carefully waxed just moments before, to fray. "No, no, no hard feelings at all. You all look very capable, very capable indeed! I'm sure you won't die." He bowed to Whiska, an awkward gesture that almost sent him tumbling to the floor again. "We're lucky to have you!"

I sighed. "I'm glad that's settled." I salvaged the evening with a rousing rendition of "Drink Up Today, For Tomorrow We Die" and sent the crowd home happy, though I noticed more than a few questioning looks directed toward my companions.

It looked like I still had some selling to do.

⌁

THE NEXT DAY, I left Nadi and the others (still sleeping) at the inn and headed to a meeting of the town council.

After my performance the previous night, Alderman Wooddunny had sent an urgent summons asking me to appear bright and early the following morning to answer a few questions the council had regarding their would-be saviors. I was actually relieved that my companions hadn't been included in that summons; it would be much easier to plead their case without them present to undermine everything I said.

It looked like the council had turned out in full force. I couldn't decide if that boded well or not. It's entirely possible they just didn't have anything better to do.

Did I say "possible"? Because I meant "certain".

The council had some business to address before it

turned to the matter of the dragon, so I sat quietly while they heatedly debated a number of essential issues, including whether to allow a rogue group of chickens to continue to nest in the village square (no, but the vote was close, and permission was given to one resident to eat any uncooperative chickens—raw, at his request); which color should be considered "official" for the painting of the weathervane that sat atop the town council building (options included mauve, lilac, lavender, violet, and light purple—consensus was not reached due to a vehement disagreement over whether one displayed shade was, in fact, either lilac or light purple); and whether to approve a tax to raise funds to make improvements to the local school, which seemed like a sensible issue to discuss until it became apparent that the school was, in fact, for chickens, and its falling into disrepair may have been the cause of the first issue discussed.

Once these pressing issues had been eloquently debated and resolved or tabled for further discussion, Alderman Wooddunny asked me to stand. "We now recognize Heloise Thebard, who has come to present us with a band of, ah, brave adventurers who have volunteered themselves to try to rid us of our dragon problem. Do I have that right, Miss, ah, Thebard?"

"The. Bard. Not 'Thebard,'" I replied.

"Beg pardon?" replied the Alderman.

"It's 'Heloise *the* Bard,' not 'Heloise *Thebard.*'"

"Are you sure? I'm quite, ah, certain I was told your name is Heloise Thebard..."

"It's a description of a vocation, not a surname. I mean, is your given name 'Alderman'?"

"Actually, yes, it is. I realize that it's a little bit like a shoemaker whose surname is 'Cobbler,' but, well, the, ah, truth is sometimes stranger than fiction, as they say, right? Prescient parents, I suppose."

"Wait," I said, holding my hands up and looking around

the room. "You are Alderman Alderman Wooddunny?" No one else looked confused or surprised by this revelation.

The Alderman nodded. "Yes, Miss The Bard, I am."

"It's not Miss The...you know what? Skip it. Never mind." I shook my head. "Now, do you mind telling me why I'm here having this barely-a-conversation instead of sleeping?"

"Well, ah, while we are grateful for your help in seeking out a hearty band of adventurers to slay the dragon that plagues our fair village—"

"Town!" shouted someone (I'm not sure who—after a while, all Skendrickians start to look alike.)

"Hang hie yer mongrel mooth, then, an' away wi' yuir blasapheemin'! Alderman Alderman's a' th' purdium, an' hay'll spake et fit and has th' right o' it!" said a gnarly looking older man wearing overalls and a dirty hat. For reasons unexplained and unremarked upon by anyone else, he was holding a baby pig.

"Thank you, Farmer Benton, I, ah, appreciate your enthusiastic support," replied the Alderman. "As I was saying, while we are grateful for your, ah, relatively prompt assistance in locating some would-be dragon slayers, there is some, ah, concern that, perhaps, the group in question, based solely on their appearance, may not be entirely qualified for the task at hand."

"They look like a bunch of knicker-twisting nipple tweakers!" shouted an exceedingly shrill older woman who had the misfortune to have one of those faces that makes her look angry even when she's telling a fluffy puppy that she loves it.

"Now, now, Widow Gershon...let us not be too hasty in our, ah, judgment of these brave adventurers." The Alderman turned toward me. "We just wish to, ah, reassure ourselves that they are indeed likely to achieve success."

"Alderman Alderman," I replied, "not to be disrespectful of your, ah, authority,"—I couldn't resist the verbal tic—"but you do recall that you're not paying them anything, right?"

"Well, yes, I suppose that's technically true..."

"So what does it matter if they fail? Your highly intelligent emissaries"—I pointed toward Goodman Drunkman and Goodman Youngman, both in attendance—"have already paid me the full contents of your coffers, and I'm not only discharging my duty to Skendrick by bringing these brave warriors to you, but have agreed to accompany them on their quest to find and slay the dragon at no additional charge." Save, of course, for a potentially massive quantity of treasure, but I didn't mention that.

"Your logic, Ms. Bard, is impeccable, and you are correct regarding the, ah, disposition of our funds." The Alderman shot Goodman Drunkman and Goodman Youngman a withering glare. Youngman at least had the grace to look down and compel his face to turn the color of a red-bellied knockadoor (I've heard that, in some places, they're called "woodpeckers," but that's just a ridiculous word, so I'll stick with the proper name). Drunkman, however, was focused on trying to pry open a flask and didn't see the look. "But, even you yourself must concede that a group that counts amongst its number what appears to be a sick dwarf and a large, talking vermin doesn't exactly inspire the most confidence as it pertains to, ah, slaying a mighty and powerful wyrm."

"I'm going to call racism on that one," I replied, "on both counts. A Ratarian might just as easily call you a 'nearly hairless wankstick'; would that be a fair and accurate characterization of the value you might contribute to a heroic expedition?" Honestly, the answer to that question was yes, but I decided to proceed as though it had been rhetorical. "As for the dwarf, he's not sick—except maybe for his strange obsession with the *got your nose* game. That's just weird. Anyway, he's half-halfling. That's why he's smaller than you'd expect."

The Alderman, a cannier politician than I'd have given him credit for, immediately walked back his comment without backing off his point. "Ah, yes, well, no one means to suggest that the racial heritage of our good heroes would be in any way an impediment. After all, we here in Skendrick draw great strength from our diversity of, ah, um, well, hairlines, I suppose." He surveyed the all-white, all-human, mostly male, universally stupid assemblage. "But, you must concede that the dragon is an imposing foe, and that, to all appearances, this group may lack the, ah, appearance of battle-hardened adventurers whose experience and success in defeating similarly powerful foes might inspire in us great confidence in their prospects to, ah, rid us of this menace."

I couldn't really argue the point; not with facts or logic, anyway, but I wasn't sure that facts or logic would have been all that effective with this particular audience. So, I opted for the magic of song.

"Gentlemen," I said before turning to the trio of women in attendance, which included the delightfully plain spoken Widow Gershon. "And ladies. I believe I can convince you that this group, despite your misplaced misgivings, is more than capable of saving your fair town." I unslung my lute from my back, gave it a quick strum—perfectly in tune, as always—and said, "But, don't just take my word for it. Music never lies." (That's a lie, incidentally.)

I struck up an up-tempo, rousing tune and played for a moment before I began to sing.

The Legendary Company *of the Broken Statue*

Lean in, friends, and listen close
For I won't repeat myself.
This is the story of a band of adventurers
Led by a heroic and unstoppable elf.

Nadinta is her name, *remember it well*

She comes from a land far away.
Raised in sylvan woods, no stranger to fear
Her wits and her bow keep her foes at bay.

THEN THERE'S RUMSCRABBLE TOOLTINKER,
Prestidigitator extraordinaire.
Able to make objects of all sizes
Disappear into the thinnest of air.

BORGUNDER GUNDERBOR, *tall and strong*
Hails from the hearty race of rock giants.
With powerful hands and bulging biceps
He makes sure enemies are compliant.

FINALLY, *the group needs some magic;*
That's where Whiska Tailiesen comes in.
Her waving wand and scintillating spells
Explode monsters both thick and thin.

ALL IN ALL, *it's a powerful group,*
One who is immune to fear.
Rest easy tonight, fair Skendrick,
For your heroes are, at long last, here!

I STRUMMED the last note of the song and then held my hand high as I soaked in the enthusiastic applause and adoration of my witless audience.

Well, mostly witless.

"Yes, well, while that was an, ah, admittedly catchy tune—quite a gift for melody our Ms. Heloise has—we're really just, ah, taking her word that this group is capable," said Alderman Wooddunny. "Nowhere within that song was there anything approximating a proof point for the, ah, many assertions of the group's ability and deeds."

I crossed my arms and smiled as the townspeople shouted the Alderman down, drowning out his protests with a chorus of boos and, in the case of the Widow Gershon, shouts of "Go pick your strawberries!" (I later learned that the Alderman had a taste for overripe strawberries and would let them linger on the bush long after others would have picked them, a proclivity the Widow apparently didn't approve of.)

"Shall I tell our brave band of heroes they can proceed, then?" I asked innocently when things had quieted down.

The Alderman frowned, but knew when he was beaten. "Very well. Nadinta's band will represent the good people of Skendrick, and we wish them many blessings and the protection of the Gods of Erithea on their quest! We will fete them in the village square this evening and, ah, see them off in the morning."

I nodded. "Good—I'm glad that's settled. Now then, while I hardly need beauty sleep, I do need regular sleep, so I'll see you all tonight." I bowed and departed to another round of applause.

IF I CAN SAY anything about Skendrickians, it's this: they throw terrible parties. Despite my bravura performance and the enthusiasm with which it was received, the turnout for the evening's festivities represented less than half of the village, no one remembered to bring food, and the only liquor available was a barrel of small beer—thankfully, it was an enormous barrel, but given the relative lack of alcohol in small beer (I saw a five-year-old drink four glasses without showing any ill effects), people spent more time peeing than they did shucking clothing or slurring speech (sadly or fortunately, depending on your perspective).

In all fairness, when your village is suffering from post-dragonic stress syndrome, the inability to throw a good party is understandable, and it's tough to prepare hors d'oeuvres when the only surplus food you've got is an endless supply of korgoli. (If you've never had korgoli, don't—at its best, it tastes like rotten broccoli doused in fish guts, and that's when it's prepared by someone who knows that they're doing; in the hands of the unskilled, it tastes more like something Borg would leave in a tavern bathroom (though I'm given to understand that korgoli is highly nutritious, so there's that).)

The next morning's sendoff wasn't much better, though at least there was bacon. Or, at least, what I think was bacon. I didn't see any pigs in or around the village, so it's entirely possible that what we were served simply looked (and tasted) like bacon, but I'd rather not think about where it came from if not pigs.

Alderman Wooddunny said a few unmemorable words in the midst of a drizzly mist, punctuated with numerous pauses and throat clearing, that inspired confidence in no one (least of all our hearty group of adventurers), and we went on our merry way. As we passed through the "gate" and headed out of town, my keen hearing picked up a few final parting comments.

Words of support or encouragement? Hope for our success?

Hardly.

Some enterprising Skendrickian had started a betting pool, not to wager on our success, but to see how long we'd last; he even seemed to have a number of very charming prop bets in mind, ranging from which of us would lose a limb first to whether the dragon would crush anyone's head in its jaws.

With the wind at our backs (in the form of the hot air being generated by the good people of Skendrick), we set off toward Mount Fenneltop, where the dragon purportedly lived.

First, however, we'd need to pass through the Dukbuter Swamp.

I really hate swamps.

CHAPTER 17

CONQUERING THE SHAMBLING BOG MEN OF THE DUKBUTER SWAMP

Through fetid swamp and mucky marsh our brave adventurers strode, their purposeful steps slowed and befouled by the mud and quicksand that sucked greedily at their feet, malignant forces intent on dragging their bodies down beneath the ground to join the corpses of so many heroes left unsung.

But Nadinta and her band would not be deterred. By day, Mount Fenneltop loomed large before them, its imposing bulk magnified by the prospect of encountering the dragon that awaited them there. By night, dancing will o' the wisps sought to lure them off the one tenuous path that threaded through the swamp, so narrow at points that even putting one foot in front of the other was no guarantee of not falling off to the side to be swallowed up by the gaping maw of the sucking mud.

They paused for rest when they could on little islands in the swamp—rocks on which lichen had accumulated in such a way as to provide some cushion, albeit not a comfortable one. Those brief respites were interrupted by the snorking, stentorian breaths of shambling bog men, fearsome nocturnal predators whose ability to move through the swamp in total silence belied the power and ferocity with which they attacked.

Fierce though the bog men were, and though their attacks seemed endless, Nadinta and her mighty warriors repelled them time and time again, with Whiska's bolts of lightning splitting the murky night air, Borgunder's crushing club shattering bog men's skulls, Rumscrabble's mighty mace dealing death disproportionately to his diminutive stature, and Nadinta's sword slicing soundlessly through the stinking flesh of the putrid bog men.

They battled for days on end, and where a lesser troop of warriors would have fallen, Nadinta and her troops emerged triumphant, escaping the last sticky steps of soft, swampy ground just as the sun began to set over the top of Mount Fenneltop.

The battered band of brothers and sisters stood side by side, their breath heavy, but their will strong and their purpose undiminished. Their collective gaze turned toward the mountain, and though they knew the dragon waited for them atop it, they felt prepared to defeat the great wyrm—if they could find their way into its lair.

CHAPTER 18

TURNS OUT WALKING THROUGH A SWAMP IS EXACTLY AS MUCH FUN AS IT SOUNDS

We stood at the edge of the Dukbuter Swamp, the last solid stretch of ground for several miles—miles that stood between us and the mountain the dragon allegedly called home. Despite asking a number of the locals, I'd never been able to determine the origin of the word "Dukbuter," though one old wag I'd met at a pub had jokingly (or so I assumed) suggested that it was an ancient word in a lost tongue that, loosely translated, referred to the stench of sweat that builds up on the, um, undercarriage of a large man on a swelteringly hot day. That's a recurring theme on this quest, apparently.

Standing next to the swamp and smelling the noxious gas that washed over us, I realized the old timer hadn't been trying to be funny. It smelled like a goblin corpse had just popped out the backdoor of a giant with indigestion issues.

"I don't know about the rest of you," said Rummy amiably, "but it's the glamor that attracted me most to the adventuring life."

Whiska scrunched up her face as she looked at each of us. "What's the problem? Why do you all look like you're about to vomit?"

"You don't smell that?" asked Nadi, wrinkling her nose in disgust.

Whiska inhaled deeply. "What? Smells like a swamp. Or a nice bowl of homemade ghomboh."

"What on earth is ghomboh, and how do I avoid ever having to taste, smell, or be in the same room with it?" asked Rummy.

"Smells like...poo," added Borg.

"It's funny," I interjected, "and I don't mean like ha-ha funny, but, like, interesting funny how you never hear about adventurers standing at the edge of a swamp trying to figure out exactly what disgusting smell it most resembles when bards are singing legendary tales."

"What's your point?" asked Whiska huffily.

"My point," I replied (pointedly), "is that we can stand around talking about ghomboh and poo, or we can get on with it."

Silence reigned as everyone realized how unheroic they were being. Or, at least, that's what I assumed everyone was thinking. Turns out not so much.

"It's really an awful smell," said Rummy. "I mean, I've honestly never smelled the like."

"I think I might actually vomit," said Nadi.

"I still think it smells like ghomboh," replied Whiska approvingly.

"And that's a *good* thing?" responded Rummy.

"Yes," said Whiska, matter of factly.

"I don't like...how poo...smells," said Borg.

And so on for another fifteen minutes. After that, finally, we got on with it.

Okay, so the smell was otherworldly, but the real danger was the presence of innumerable sinkholes. Even in the middle of the day, with the sun at its peak, the swamp was only dimly lit. Swamp gas and the light-absorbing shrubs that dotted the few pockets of solid ground combined to absorb much of the sunlight before it could burn off the top layer of fog that perpetually hung over the area. That made seeing the sinkholes almost impossible, and it's not like there was a lighted path with enormous arrows and warning signs featuring funny pictures of people falling off the path and suffering horrific deaths to guide you safely through. Even Nadi, a trained ranger who could track a mouse through a cornfield, couldn't easily navigate the swamp—the constantly shifting landscape made it impossible to walk the same pathway twice, and you had to test every step before you transferred your weight from back foot to front foot if you didn't want to get sucked down to a stinky demise.

While the patient approach suited Borg quite nicely, asking Whiska to take her time and tread carefully was a little bit like asking a bear not to defecate in the woods, and then tying him up in the middle of the woods and force-feeding him Rajami food (which, it goes without saying, even though I'm saying it, is considerably spicier than the average bear's fare). It was only after we had dragged her out of the muck a third time—smelling like Rajami food that had just come out of a tied-up bear—that she finally agreed, albeit grudgingly and with the liberal use of epithets in at least three different languages.

By the time daylight started to fade (not that it made much of a difference), I looked back in an effort to gauge our progress...and proceeded to liberally use epithets in three different languages—the common tongue, elvish, and a few creative orc curses I'd picked up when demonstrating certain Heloisian submission techniques on a very confused (but not unaroused) High Chieftain Gnurk. Unless my eyes deceived me, we'd gone no more than one hundred yards. Maybe not even seventy-five.

"We need to make camp soon," said Nadi as she surveyed our surroundings. "If we try to wander around here in the dark, we're all going to smell like Whiska."

"It would be an improvement in every case!" shouted Whiska.

"Be that as it may," said Rummy, "I'm not entirely sure I've got Ms. Tailiesin's intestinal fortitude, so would prefer to remain, at least insomuch as it's possible in the middle of a multiday trek through a swamp, unsullied by muck."

"It's getting...dark," said Borg.

"There," I said, pointing to our left. "That mound over there. It should be big enough for all of us to spread out. Or, at least, sit down."

Nadi nodded and led the way. Even though the mound was only about 15 yards away, it took us nearly an hour to navigate the smucking pathway ("smucking" is the only word I can think of that accurately describes the combination of sucking and muck; it's also less offensive than how I actually referred to the pathway, though it does rhyme with at least one of the words I used). When we reached the mound, we collapsed, tossing our packs down and not moving for a while. You don't realize how exhausting slow, careful walking is until you stop doing it.

Our respite ended when a loud rumble shook the mound.

"What in the name of flaming cockroach anuses was that?!" yelled Whiska, leaping to her feet.

"Flaming cockroach anuses?" I silently mouthed to Rummy, who shrugged.

"Weapons out," said Nadi, straining to see through the dim light.

"I bet it's bog men," said Rummy.

"It's not bog men," I replied.

"How do you know it's not bog men?" asked Rummy.

"Quiet!" said Nadi.

We stood in silence, looking everywhere but seeing nothing.

"I'm...hungry," said Borg. "My stomach...is rumbling."

Nadi slapped her forehead as Rummy patted Borg on the arm. "Maybe a little warning next time, big guy."

"I just...gave you one," replied the rock giant, nonplussed.

"Warnings are supposed to come before the thing happens," said Rummy helpfully. "Otherwise it's just a recap of what happened."

We set to preparing dinner, pulling rations from our packs. Whiska scraped together a bit of moss and pointed her staff at it, but before she could utter an incantation, Nadi grabbed the staff. Whiska's eyes flared. "*Never* touch my staff, you pointy-eared tree licker!"

"No," replied Nadi, her voice steely. "We've already made too much noise. You want to start a fire? Why not just send up a flare or build a lighthouse to let the bog men know where we are?"

"Bog men—bah!" said Whiska, but she sat back down without setting anything on fire, which was no small thing for her.

We ate in silence, save for Borg's crunching, Whiska's slurping, Rummy's lip smacking, and Nadi's teeth grinding (which, to be fair, was a result of Borg's crunching, Whiska's slurping, and Rummy's lip smacking). When we were done, Nadi looked once more into the fading light, nodded when she was satisfied that no imminent threats presented themselves, and turned to face the group.

"We need to get some rest," she said, "but we also need to stay vigilant. We'll sleep in shifts and double up on watches. I need less sleep, so I'll take the first watch alone. Whiska and Heloise, you're up next. Rummy and Borg, you'll finish things off. We move at first light, or whatever passes for first light around here. With any luck, we'll be through the swamp in a couple of days."

It was a good plan until *a couple of days* turned into two weeks.

There are only so many consecutive days you can slog through a bog, with the ever-present threat of falling into the muck (which not only sullied clothes, but also entailed a not small possibility of death) and without being able to heat the very meager food you've got with you, before you start to go a little crazy. Not surprisingly, Whiska succumbed first to swamp madness, though I'm not entirely sure I could tell the difference between normal Whiska and swamp mad Whiska. It was when Borg started giggling hysterically after an alligator nearly ate Rummy (and injured him quite badly) that I realized the mental state of the party was rapidly deteriorating. (Rock giant giggles, incidentally, sound a little bit like bullfrog hiccups.)

Toward the end of the second week, I pulled Nadi aside. "I'm not quite sure how long we can keep this going," I said, pointing at Rummy, who was using his index finger to blub-blub his lips while Whiska yelled at a snail for moving too fast.

"I'm not sure we have a choice," replied Nadi grimly. "It'll take us just as long to go back as it will to go forward."

I sighed. "At least we haven't seen any bog men yet."

Just then, there was a horrible blorking sound, and a muck-covered head popped out of the swamp. It was dark green and brown, had no discernible facial features beyond a squinty pair of eyes, and, when it fully emerged to the point where only the bottom half of its legs remained obscured by the swamp, it stood about eight feet tall.

"Bog man!" yelled Rummy.

"With incredible timing," I muttered.

"What do we do?" squeaked Rummy as the creature bore down on him.

Borg stepped in front of our diminutive companion and thrust his hand out, striking the monster in the chest. It toppled backward and splashed into the brackish water, uttering what sounded like a long, drawn-out "Ooooowwwwwww!"

Nadi drew her sword, Whiska brought her staff to bear, and I pulled out my dagger. We waited, tense, expecting an army of shambling bog men to descend upon us. Local legends suggested that bog men traveled in packs, and that they were as deadly a creature as could be found in the swampland.

Turns out local legends are sometimes full of it.

The bog man stayed down, and, after five minutes of waiting, I sheathed my dagger and shrugged. "Wasn't such a chore now, was it?"

"No," said Nadi, shaking her head. "No. It has to be a trick. That was too easy."

We waited for a few more minutes, but didn't see or hear anything.

"So," said Rummy slowly as his head continued to swivel in search of a threat, "are there no bog women?"

"What?" replied Nadi, turning a stern gaze on him.

"You always hear about shambling bog *men*, but you never hear about shambling bog women. There must be women, right? Or else how would they make new bog men? Bog people. Whatever the proper term is."

"How do you know that wasn't a bog woman that we just saw?" I said.

"Because it...well, huh. Fair point, Heloise," replied Rummy. "I don't, really. I don't know much about bog person anatomy."

"So maybe they're all women and we've been wrong this whole time," I continued. "Maybe there's not a single bog man."

"But then why call them '*bog men*'?"

I shrugged. "Because people are idiots. And we live in a patriarchal society."

"It had...a penis," interjected Borg.

"What?" asked Nadi, incredulous.

We waited for two minutes before Borg spoke again. "It flopped around...when I pushed...it."

"You pushed his penis?" I asked. "Geez, buy a bog man dinner first, Borg. Or at least a drink."

"I don't think he did that," said Rummy. "I hope he didn't, anyway. Because Borg didn't ask, and it's not okay to touch a bog man's penis if he doesn't say it's okay."

"I'm pretty sure it's not okay to touch anyone's penis without consent," I said.

Rummy tilted his head to concede the point. "I think that's a good general rule. Or maybe just a good genital rule." He paused expectantly.

No one laughed, though Whiska did mutter something to the effect of "rather cut them off than touch them."

Rummy cleared his throat. "Well, at least we've established that."

"I meant...that I pushed...the bog man. And then...his penis flopped...when he fell."

"That makes more sense," said Rummy, looking relieved. "I knew you weren't that kind of rock giant."

"So, we still don't know whether there are bog women," I said.

"Oh, come *on*!" roared Nadi. "Shut up! All of you, shut up! Just stop talking! We're in the middle of a swamp. We were just attacked by a shambling bog man, and—"

"I'd really call it more of a saunter than a shamble, truth be told," said Rummy.

"Can we call them bog people? I'm just really sensitive to gender issues," I added.

Nadi buried her head in her hands. It was another two hours before she said anything.

OVER THE NEXT THREE DAYS, we were attacked by shambling bog men—we made it a point to identify their penises to confirm (though Whiska, displaying a rare and irritating maturity of thought, opined that bog man (person) anatomy might not necessarily mirror our own and, consequently, what we thought were penises (peni?) might, in fact, serve some other purpose, such as allowing them to breathe while submerged, obtaining nutrients from the swamp, or just being something to swing around when they were bored, like a biological toy (though, let's face it, that's basically what a penis is)).

Every single time, a quick shove from Borg sent the creatures sprawling, and not a single one got back up and resumed its assault (or what we assumed would be an assault —in the absence of any of them actually striking any member of the party, I wasn't entirely sure they were really trying to attack us). So, it turns out that the threat posed by shambling bog men is vastly overrated, though I'd have no problem turning them into fierce and deadly killers when I composed my epic song about the quest. I did, however, omit any mention of their peni.

A considerably greater threat was the numerous alligators that lived in the swamp. I mentioned that Rummy almost got eaten by one (and badly bitten in the process), but that wasn't the only instance where we almost met death at the hands of toothy jaws.

Deep into our trek across the swamp, Nadi, leading the party and carefully testing each step with the tip of her sword, stepped onto what, by visual inspection and with the probing of a sword tip, appeared to be solid ground. A second later, she went hurtling through the air, landing face first in deep muck and alerting the rest of us that we might need to watch out.

Rummy was next in line, his right arm in a sling from the previous gator encounter, making him even more ineffectual with his mace (though he spent far more time worrying about how the injury might affect his prestidigitation skills). He stumbled backward into Borg, who propped him up and stepped forward, assuming, perhaps, that it was another shambling bog man (person) that had caused the disturbance.

Not so much. The creature that exploded out of the brackish water was fully fifteen feet long and had jaws the size of a hearty dwarf's legs (and just as strong, too, by the looks of it, and believe me—dwarf legs can do some things). It looked mostly like an alligator, except for the fact that it was missing all of its flesh. In other words, it was a gigantic undead skeleton alligator, because a regular gigantic alligator attacking you in a swamp isn't terrifying enough.

Fortunately, if any member of our party was going to get bitten by a gigantic undead skeleton alligator and survive, Borg had the best chance. The beast locked its jaws on Borg's arm, and though its teeth had a hard time penetrating the rock giant's craggy skin, it was heavy enough to pull him off balance, and both Borg and the beast fell down into the water. It was hard to tell who was winning the fight as they thrashed and struggled beneath the surface, churning water and muck high into the air (and covering all of us with stinky swamp goo in the process).

"Borg!" cried Rummy, helplessly (and ineffectually) brandishing his mace.

"Move, you useless coin diddler!" yelled Whiska, elbowing Rummy aside. She pointed her staff at the roiling water and muttered an incantation. The end of her staff glowed purple, and what appeared to be a lightning bolt sizzled into the water.

"What are you doing?" screamed Nadi, horrified. "Bones don't electrify, but rock giant flesh does!"

"Oh, shut up, you golden-haired goody-goody—it's not a lightning spell," replied Whiska. "Just watch."

A moment later, a huge bubble broke the surface of the water, carrying within it one mildly confused rock giant (I say mildly confused because Borg had yet to evince any particularly strong emotion, save for urgency, and that only happened twice per day when he needed to find a bathroom). The bubble floated over to the little patch of ground on which we stood and popped, depositing a muck-covered Borg right at Nadi's feet. "You're welcome," said Whiska.

"Oh, well...that was, uh, that was well done, Whiska," said Nadi. "Nice work."

"Have to...poop," said Borg urgently and with strong emotion.

"Gonna have to hold it for a bit, big guy—our friend is back," said Rummy, not even bothering to hold his mace up as the creature burst back out of the water.

"Heloise—can you do anything?" asked Nadi, moving to stand in front of me with her sword held in a defensive position.

I shook my head. "Undead creatures aren't affected by my music magic. I mean, I could try to bash the thing with my lute, but I'm pretty sure skelegator's going to win that battle."

"All right—you and Rummy to the rear."

"Whose rear?" I asked innocently.

"Just move, Heloise!" replied a now flustered Nadi.

"Borg—you're the front line." The rock giant grabbed his club and stood up, prepared to swing it at the gator. "Whiska —any spells that might help?"

Borg connected with the creature's head, a solid blow that sent it splashing back into the water, but didn't do any serious damage.

"I've got one thing I can try," replied Whiska. She closed her eyes and whispered words of magic. She pointed to the surface of the water and an amber-colored circle appeared. A few seconds later, the skelegator popped up again, right through the circle, and took on the amber hue of the spell.

"Hit it again, Borg—hard!" Whiska cried.

Borg brought his club around with particular gusto; when it smashed into the beast this time, its bones shattered, floating through the murky light of the swamp like glitter at a Barvindian dressing club. (Fun fact: Barvindians generally wear little to no clothing, so unlike in other cultures with more provocative flesh-based entertainment, they derive excitement from watching attractive dancers put clothing *on*; yes, it's as weird as it sounds, especially by the end of a routine, particularly the ones that conclude with the donning of parkas and snow pants.)

We all looked around anxiously, waiting for another threat to emerge, but silence reigned. Finally, Nadi sheathed her sword. "That was really great teamwork," she said, nodding appreciatively toward Whiska and Borg.

"I...pooped," said Borg, pointing toward his bulging backside.

"Well," said Rummy, "before choosing the exciting life of epic adventure, I always did wonder whether that happened in the middle of a battle. Now I guess I know the answer."

"It's not like the smell's going to get any worse," I noted.

Dangerous words, Heloise. Dangerous, and portentous, words.

HAVE you ever smelled a dead poleranka?

Let me back up: do you have any idea what a poleranka is? It's probably the ugliest thing in existence—if a deformed gopher had revenge sex with a particularly fertile giant spider...well, their offspring would be about one hundred times prettier to look at than a poleranka.

And it turns out dead polerankas smell even worse than they look.

We stumbled across the corpse on what turned out to be

our last morning in the swamp. It was sprawled on top of a mossy group of rocks, half-submerged in the water and partially ripped open, though whether that ghastly wound caused its death or was a result of swamp creatures trying to eat its insides afterward is a mystery I couldn't care less about finding the answer to.

Regardless of how it met its untimely demise, passing within ten feet of the creature caused each and every one of us to vomit. Multiple times. Well, there was one exception: rock giant physiology doesn't allow them to vomit. Instead, they get explosive diarrhea (the smell of which, I might add, resulted in at least two additional rounds of heaving for most of us).

I hate swamps.

FINALLY—*FINALLY*—WE emerged from the swamp, with our lives, but none of our dignity, intact. And, thankfully, blessedly, within an hour of clearing the last of the marshy ground, not only did the air begin to clear and the glorious scents of flowers and things that *didn't* smell like decaying skunks restore some semblance of joy to the act of breathing, but we found a small, pristine spring in which we submerged ourselves completely. We burned every article of clothing, modesty be damned, and sat around naked for about an hour afterward (incidentally, it is *not* true what they say about rock giants, at least based on the single specimen I happen to have seen in the buff...they do only have one butt).

It occurred to me somewhat belatedly that in burning all of our clothes, we had, you know, burned all of our clothes. Look, you can sit there in your warm house with your mulled wine and your fluffy robe and judge us for making a decision that showed maybe just a slight lack of foresight. Until you've spent multiple weeks wandering a swamp that smells like a dying ogre's taint and fending off everything from shambling bog men (people) to undead alligators, you can just choke on your wine.

Nonetheless, I decided that one of us needed to broach the issue. "So," I began nonchalantly, "not that any of you are hard on the eyes sans clothing, but I'm wondering if maybe—just maybe—we might have considered washing at least one set of clothes instead of burning them all, given our need to wear clothing for the next step of our journey. And everything that will come after." I looked at the smoldering fire pit where scraps of fabric still burned. "I'm thinking that ship has probably sailed, and, as far as I'm aware, there are no clothing stores, reputable or otherwise, in the area—if there are, those shambling bog people would apparently rather be naked than shop there, which doesn't suggest a particularly great selection of garments." I shrugged. "Any thoughts on how we deal with this little problem?"

"Well," said Nadi, looking around in an effort to not look at anything in particular, and blushing when she looked at me, "I'm hoping that Whiska might have a magical solution. Whiska?"

"What?" snapped Whiska defensively as she popped a rather large beetle into her mouth.

"Can you help?" asked Nadi.

"No! I saw it first!" Whiska crunched loudly on the bug. "Get your own."

"I meant with clothes," said Nadi, exasperated.

"Who needs 'em?" countered our furry friend. "Human weakness, if you ask me."

"None of us is actually human," interjected Rummy.

"Well, I'm half-human," I replied.

"Fine," said Whiska. "Bipedal weakness."

"You're bipedal," I noted.

"*Fine*," growled Whiska. "Weakness of those who don't have tails or fur."

"That may be true," said Nadi, "but the fact remains that we still need clothes."

Whiska mumbled something that sounded a little bit like "snucking gorons," but I didn't quite catch it. (Snucking gorons are gentle, frog-like creatures found in lakes and rivers around Norindia, named for the cute, snuffling "snuck" sound they make when they get excited. Given that I didn't think Whiska was comparing us to adorable, runny-nosed amphibians, I might have misheard her.) "I can do it. But, I need time to rest and study my spells."

And so we sat around naked for the next eight hours. It got cold, which was obvious when you looked at any of us. We got hungry, so we caught some fish (incidentally, bent over holding a wriggling fish is not a good look for a naked half-dwarf/half-halfling) and cooked them (note to self: fire is especially hot when you're naked). We got bored, so we played rhyming games (Borg was surprisingly good at them, notwithstanding his tendency to rhyme with lines from which we'd moved on several minutes before).

Finally, Whiska declared that she was ready. We stood in a line facing her, all trace of self-consciousness gone (except maybe for Nadi, who continued to try to avoid looking directly at anyone). Whiska walked up and down the line, hands behind her back, for a moment before pausing in front of Rummy. "Now," said Whiska, "I do have a spell that will clothe you."

"Great!" responded Rummy. "This cold air is really not good for my already limited sense of self-worth."

Whiska resumed walking, coming to a stop in front of me. "But, I can only create a single outfit for each of you, and the spell is limited in what it can do."

"So, muumuus for all of us?" I asked jokingly (or so I hoped).

"Yes," replied Whiska.

"You're not good at being funny," I said. "Which means… you're serious, aren't you?"

"Why would you think I'm not serious, you thick-headed bibblebop?" (Whiska's insult was sort of redundant—bibble-bops are known for their immense heads, so calling them "thick-headed" is a little bit like calling something a "smelly skunk" or a "winged bird.")

I sighed. "No reason." I looked at the others, none of whom seemed particularly distressed. "You guys know what a muumuu is, right?"

"We're not really in a position to be picky," said Nadi. "Whatever Whiska can do will have to suffice."

"I'm with the elf—well, the full elf—on this one, Heloise. I'm all in favor of whatever's going to minimize the obvious effect the cold is having on me."

"Is it like…a shirt for…cows?" asked Borg.

"No, Borg, it's a—" My response was cut off when Whiska waved her magic wand and, in a flash of light and a puff of smoke, clad us all in…long, white, loose-fitted dresses patterned with black blotches.

"More like a cow dress than a shirt, apparently," said Rummy, admiring his new garment.

Sometimes I hate my life.

At least we'd made it out of the swamp. Now, we just had to get into the mountain the dragon called home, which I figured would be the easy part, and then battle it dressed in cow costumes, which I figured would be the hard part.

It turns out I'm not very good at figuring.

CHAPTER 19

THE BRAVE HEROES PROVE THEIR BRAINS ARE EQUAL TO THEIR BRAWN

At the foot of Mount Fenneltop our doughty warriors stood, battle scars fresh from their victories in the Dukbuter Swamp. With renewed vigor they began their climb, scaling the nearly sheer face of the mount. Hand over hand, clawed foot over clawed foot...it was a grueling and torturous climb, but the difficulty did not deter the band of heroes, so intent were they on finding the dragon and bringing to a close their quest to save the good people of Skendrick from further agony and destruction at the beast's fire, jaws, and talons.

At last, they reached the summit, and stood for a moment gathering their breath and stretching weary muscles. They knew that an epic confrontation awaited them, and began to steel their nerves for the coming battle. First, however, they had to gain entrance into the dragon's mountain lair, which was blocked by a massive, round stone that none of them, not even the mighty Borgunder Gunderbor, could so much as budge, no matter how hard they pushed.

It was the quick-thinking mage Whiska who first noticed the

spidery text above the door, written in the language of magic, and she summoned her companions together and read the words aloud.

"Ye who enter here," she said slowly, translating as she spoke, "take heed, for only those who can solve this riddle may gain the safety of the mountain." Whiska looked at her companions, who nodded, ready to take up the intellectual challenge. "Name for me these ideas three: you can't begin before it happens; it gets shorter the longer it lasts; and it ends its opposite."

The heroes pondered long and hard, calling upon the prodigious powers of their collective intellect to consider any number of possible answers, knowing that to answer incorrectly would prevent them from having the chance they so desperately sought to defeat the dragon. Finally, Nadi looked up and said, with confidence, "Birth. You can't begin life before you're born."

Rummy's eyes widened, and he took up the thread, adding, "And birth begins life, which gets shorter the longer it lasts."

Whiska smiled and nodded, adding the final piece: "And what ends life? Death—its opposite."

With Whiska's words, the grating sound of rock grinding against rock reverberated through the air, bouncing off the mountain and amplifying to a deafening degree as a passageway opened before them. The dark tunnel appeared to head straight into the heart of the mountain, though the companions had heard rumors that a dangerous creature guarded the maze of tunnels that led to the dragon's lair, and so they steeled themselves for one final challenge before the time came to take on the foul and mighty wyrm itself.

CHAPTER 20

SHUT UP...YOU WOULD HAVE BEEN STUMPED, TOO

Riddles are for smart people what sexy underthings are for attractive people—a way to flaunt what they've got, to tease the possibility of something greater, and to generally frustrate the hell out of you.

As you can probably guess, I hate both riddles and sexy underthings.

After a long and arduous climb, we reached a plateau on the mountain that, we believed, presented the entry point that would lead us to the dragon. Unfortunately, standing between us and that goal was a boulder the size of a Harvingian wedding cake. "There's a rock...in our way," said Borg succinctly after we had all stood staring silently at the impediment for a good five minutes.

"Sure is, big guy," said Rummy, "any chance you can roll it out of the way?"

Five more minutes passed before Borg said, "I will...try." Our muscular friend braced himself against the side of the boulder and began to push. After about a minute of pushing and no result, Borg stepped languidly back from the boulder, staring at it thoughtfully.

"Whiska," said Nadi, "any ideas?"

"Short of blowing it up? No."

"Can you do that?" asked Rummy.

"I'm not sure," replied Whiska doubtfully.

"The rock is...too heavy...to move," added Borg.

"Thanks for trying," said Rummy, patting the giant on the arm.

"Want to give it a go, Whiska?" asked Nadi.

The wizard shrugged and lifted up her staff. "I'm always up for blowing things to smithereens. Might want to stand back, you brainless half-twits."

"I think you mean 'half-wits,'" I corrected.

"No, I mean half-twits," said Whiska.

"That doesn't make any sense," I replied (stupidly, given who I was talking to).

"None of you is smart enough to be a full twit—you're all half a twit. Half-twit."

"That's not a...never mind. Let's just get out of the way." I motioned to the others as I took refuge behind a rocky outcropping that looked solid enough to withstand the blow-back from whatever Whiska had in mind.

Whiska closed her eyes and concentrated for a moment before pointing her staff at the door, uttering arcane syllables, and unleashing an absurdly large and insanely bright energy bolt.

We'd all been staring at Whiska when she cast her spell, which meant that none of us could see for several minutes. When the spots finally cleared from our vision, there stood the rock, utterly untouched. If it's possible for a rock to laugh mockingly, this one was doing just that.

"Did you hear that?" asked Nadi, sword at the ready as she looked around.

"Hear what? The rock laughing at us?" asked Rummy.

"I thought I heard it too," I said.

"Don't be ridiculous, you refuse-refusing rejects!" For some reason, Whiska enjoyed chiding us for not wanting to eat garbage. I was okay with accepting that insult. "Rocks can't laugh!"

"Some of them can," said a gravelly voice that seemed to come from everywhere and nowhere at once.

When something unexpected happens, most people freeze. There are two reasons, as near as I can tell, for that reaction: one is to give your brain time to process what is happening, and the other is to stay put so that you don't put yourself in harm's way. That's exactly what we did, though Whiska also belched.

"Some of them can do more than just laugh—they can talk, too," continued the voice. "Obviously."

I was staring directly at the massive boulder that blocked the entrance to the mountain and saw a very slight movement on the rock face. "Wait—was that a mouth?"

"What do you mean?" asked Nadi.

I pointed. "There—I'm pretty sure I just saw a mouth. On the rock. Great. It's a talking rock. An immovable talking rock."

"So is Borg," said Rummy.

"You," I said, addressing the giant rock, "what's the deal? How do we get past you?"

"But you only just got here," replied the rock, its mouth now even more visible. Two craggy eyes appeared above the mouth, and an outcropping in the form of a nose pushed its way out as well. Far more disturbing were the caterpillar-like eyebrows that popped out. "Why are you in such a hurry to leave?"

We drew together closely so we could confer without the rock hearing us, though we indicated to Borg that he could remain where he stood astride his mess. "Anyone ever seen one of these things before?" I asked.

"Nope," replied Rummy jovially. "But, we do have a rock giant with us. I think we should ask him."

I ignored Rummy. "Whiska?"

"Nope."

"Nadi?"

She shook her head. "This is new for me, too."

"Let's ask Borg," said Rummy.

"What do we do?" I asked.

"I think Rummy thinks we should ask Borg," said Nadi.

"I'm right here, you know," said Rummy.

"Might not be the worst idea," I replied.

"I also...look like...a rock," called Borg, stepping away from his pile at last.

"Hey, giant rock," I yelled—I'm not sure why I yelled; I mean, we were right next to the thing—"do you know our friend Borg? Over there? His full name is Borgunder Gunderbor. He's a rock giant."

"I am a magical talking rock," replied the rock in its gravelly voice. "It's ridiculous that you'd assume, because we share superficially craggy features, we might know each other." The rock's gaze slid over to Borg. "He is very handsome, though."

"We meant no offense," said Nadi.

"Some of us did," interjected Whiska.

"Not helping," said Nadi. "We seek passage, um, through you. Around you?"

"You are...handsome too," said Borg, coming to stand behind Nadi.

"I've never actually seen myself," replied the rock, "but I appreciate that. No one's ever told me that before."

"Borg's right," I said, "you're probably the handsomest rock I've ever seen."

"But not the stupidest," replied the rock. "Flattery will not get you past me."

"Then how do we get past you?" asked Nadi.

"By answering my riddle," said the rock.

Nadi looked at me and shrugged. "Tell us your riddle, then."

"It's nothing personal, you know," said the rock.

"What do you mean?" asked Rummy.

"Not letting you pass—it's an enchantment. No matter how much I might want to, I can't roll aside unless someone solves my riddle."

"Who created the enchantment?" Rummy seemed genuinely curious.

"I don't know," replied the rock.

"Seriously?" I asked. "I feel like I'd pay attention to anyone who was enchanting me." I looked around. "Which none of you are, incidentally." Sometimes you have to take the easy shots. "Except maybe Rocky here." I winked at the rock.

It didn't seem to notice as it raised its eyebrows in what was the visual equivalent of a shrug. "I was not always conscious. I spent eons weathering the storms in silence before I gained sentience...well, I think I spent eons. Given that I wasn't aware, I suppose it could have been longer. Or shorter."

"The riddle?" prompted Nadi.

"Yes, yes," said the rock. "I forget that creatures with such short lifespans are always in a hurry. It would be nice to make some small talk once in a while, you know. I don't often get company."

"The riddle," said Nadi again, more forcefully.

The rock's eyes slid over to look at Borg. "She's a tough one, isn't she? Not to mention very impatient. Is she mean, too?"

"Please?" asked Nadi, her tone softening slightly.

"Very well," rumbled the rock. "I will present you with my riddle."

"Yes, she...is," said Borg.

"What?" asked the rock.

"He's a little slow," said Rummy. He turned to Borg. "Try to keep up, big guy."

"I'm not mean!" said Nadi.

"Tough, but not...mean," said Borg, almost at the same time.

"If you all don't shut up and let the giant talking rock speak, I'm going to stab each and every one of you in the throat." The comment, perhaps surprisingly (even to me), came from me and not Whiska.

"That's the first intelligent thing you've ever said," replied Whiska with an approving nod.

"She's kind of mean," offered Rummy, gesturing toward yours truly. One glare shut down further comment.

"Please," I said sweetly to the rock, "continue."

Before it could answer, a crack and a rumble broke the silence. We looked around in alarm and grabbed for weapons before we realized that the rock was laughing.

"It's been some time since I've conversed with a group of adventurers like yourselves," said the rock.

"Brave and intrepid?" asked Rummy.

"Dysfunctional and in over their heads," replied the rock.

"Also accurate," said Rummy.

"Now then: to business." The rock moved its eyes to take in each of us before fixing them on Nadi. "Before you can pass on through you must answer first these questions two."

"Isn't it supposed to be three questions, you crack-faced, oversized pebble?" asked Whiska.

"What do you mean?" asked the rock.

"Questions always come in threes. Everyone knows that!" She looked at each of us as she gestured dismissively toward the rock with one of her weird, ratty thumbs.

Everyone shrugged except for Borg, who said, "We are not...dysfunctional. We are a...good team."

"Right on!" said Rummy as he saluted our giant companion.

"The first riddle is this," said the rock. "Bob leaves the stronghold of Canarvon on a gold dragon at four o'clock FSM (Fanting Standard Time) and flies eastward. Lavinia leaves the elven forests of Gloraria at five o'clock FSM, flying west on a silver dragon. What time do they meet in Borokia?"

Nadi's eyebrows rose in confusion, and she turned to me. "What?"

"It's a story problem," I replied before looking at the rock. "A story problem? Seriously?"

The rock raised its eyebrows and then lowered them, its version of a shrug. "I didn't make up the riddle," it replied. "I just say what I'm enchanted to say."

"Whiska," said Nadi, "if the rock is enchanted, can you dispel the magic that controls it? Would that get us into the mountain?"

Whiska shook her head. "If I do that, the stupid rock will just become inert, and then we'll have no way to open it and get in."

"Not to mention the fact that you'd lose out on the opportunity to converse with me, and I feel like that would be sad for everyone," said the rock.

"Does anyone know anything about how fast dragons fly?" asked Nadi.

"Faster than I can," I replied helpfully.

"Why would we know that, you golden-haired mungieblat?" (Mungieblats are a particularly ugly toad-like creature that secretes a toxin that smells like wet dog fur. They're not pleasant.)

"Are we allowed to ask questions?" Rummy looked hopefully at the rock.

"You are...though I can't guarantee I can answer them all," replied the rock. "Though I do know a lot of things. Probably more than a talking rock should."

"Dragons are...also faster...than I am," said Borg to no one in particular.

"How fast does a gold dragon fly?" asked Rummy.

"A northern gold or a southern gold?"

"There are no northern dragons, you idiot," said Whiska. "They only live in the south."

"Very good," said the rock approvingly. "You're a sharp one." He turned his eyes toward Borg. "She's a sharp one."

"So...can you tell us how fast?" asked Rummy.

"Gold dragons fly twelve kelms per hour." (A kelm is the standard unit of distance in Erithea; it's approximately equal to the distance a man named Hornadar Kelm, formerly a general of some renown in the kingdom of Halifar, was able to run in an hour as he sought to warn the capital of the kingdom of, ironically enough, a pending dragon attack. He made it just in time, and many people lived, though the good general himself was immolated in a spectacular blast of flame. It's an arbitrary and utterly moronic unit of measurement.)

"Okay," said Rummy. "Now we're getting somewhere. How fast is a silver?"

"They fly at about ten kelms per hour," replied the rock with a smile.

"Heloise," said Nadi, "you've traveled everywhere—do you know where Canarvon is? Or Borokia?"

I shook my head. "I know a lot of things, including the fact that I should not have unrestricted access to chocolate at night, but I don't know that. I've heard of Canarvon, but never been there, and it's not on any of the maps I've seen. I have no idea where Borokia is."

"You've been to Gloraria, I take it?" she asked.

A rush of memories trampled me like a doughty dwarven fire brigade. I'd been young, especially by elven standards, and the memories were more scenes and fragments than wholly formed recollections, but I remembered the most vividly green trees I'd ever seen, ethereal music that I felt as much as heard, the most delicious roast dryad, and one old elf who thought it was funny to pretend to be an orc saying racist things about elves. (I'm kidding, by the way—the roast dryad was terrible; they're small, tough, and bitter...sort of like a member of a doughty dwarven fire brigade.) "Once," I said at last, "a long time ago. But, that doesn't help me figure out how far it is from somewhere I've never heard of."

"That's why we're going to ask the handsomest talking rock we've ever seen, right?" said Rummy.

"Am I really the handsomest?" replied the rock, sounding bashful.

"I can say unequivocally that you are," said Rummy.

"Wait a second," said the rock suspiciously, "am I the only talking rock you've ever met?"

Rummy shuffled his feet uncomfortably. "Well, that depends...does Borg count?"

"No," replied the rock flatly. "He is a rock giant. Not a giant rock."

"Right," said Rummy. "Well, then, I suppose that you are the only talking rock I've ever met."

"So I'm also the ugliest," said the rock mournfully.

"Hey, maybe learn how to tell a lie to spare a feeling once in a while, eh?" I said pointedly to Rummy.

"Are you saying...that I'm not...handsome?" asked Borg. He didn't sound upset; just curious.

"No, no—not at all," replied Rummy hastily. "You're a good-looking guy, Borgy. Honest."

"See?" I said. "It's not hard, is it?"

"But that wasn't a—"

"Save it, Rummy," said Nadi, cutting him off.

"Look, Rocky," I said, trying to smooth things over in my own inimitable way, "this is a first for all of us. But, I'll say this —you've got features that look like they were carved out of granite, and a man with strong features is generally considered a handsome man."

"They looked carved out of granite because they are carved out of granite," replied the rock.

"Makes sense," I said, sagely.

"I think that…I am handsome," Borg interjected.

"No question!" said Rummy enthusiastically.

"I'm not really a man, you know," said the rock.

"No?" I raised an eyebrow.

"You people are nuts," muttered Whiska.

"No—not in any conventional sense, anyway. I mean, I'm just a face—no genitals. No distinguishing gender characteristics."

"Fair point," I conceded. "I guess your voice just makes you sound like a man."

"Because it's deep?"

I nodded. "You don't meet a lot of ladies who sound like that."

"But you've never met any other talking rocks, so you have no basis for comparison—maybe my voice is very high compared to others of my kind," said the rock with an annoying degree of logic.

"Are there any others of your kind?" asked Nadi.

"Not that I know of," replied the rock.

"Then this whole conversation is kind of pointless, no?" I said.

"Is it ever pointless to try to understand who someone truly is?" replied the rock.

"Oh, sure—make me look like the kramlin's gaping waste hole," I said, exasperated. (Kramlins are huge, elephant-like creatures that produce significantly larger discharges of excrement than any other animal in the world. It's pretty disgusting. On the plus side, their waste smells like peppermint, so that's not a bad deal.)

"Maybe we should get back to the riddle..." prompted Rummy.

"Yes, please," said Nadi. She looked at the rock. "Where is Borokia?"

"You don't want me to tell you *everything*, do you?"

"Actually, yes," replied Nadi. "Is there any reason you can't? Other than the answer, I mean."

"Nothing in the enchantment prevents me," said the rock, seeming surprised. "It's strange—no one has ever asked me for objective facts to help solve the riddle before. In fact, no one has ever solved the first one. People generally just wander off and disappear after I give it to them."

"Well, then, we'll be the first!" said Rummy.

I looked at Nadi and whispered, "Something seems off."

She nodded. "Agreed. But, as long as the rock is forthcoming with facts that will help us answer the question, let's keep going."

I shrugged. "You're the boss."

Nadi turned back to the rock. "Let me ask that again—where is Borokia relative to Gloraria and Canarvon?"

"It's one hundred and twenty-five kelms to the east of Canarvon and five hundred kelms to the west of Gloraria." The rock pursed its lips. "I mean, approximately. No one expects an *exact* answer."

"Wait—you mean to say that there's a range of possible answers to the riddle?" asked Whiska curiously.

"Yes," replied the rock. "Well, within reason—a range of a few minutes, depending on how precise your measurements are."

"So, the enchantment allows for more than one answer?" Whiska looked at us. "Do you hairless skin rags know what that means?"

"That we've got a little margin for error?" ventured Rummy.

"Obviously, you addle-brained ale slurper! What it really

means is that whoever cast this enchantment is incredibly powerful."

"So we probably don't want to bump up against them in a dark alleyway," I replied before looking at the peak looming before us. "Or a mountain."

"I seriously doubt that whoever created the enchantment is still around," replied Whiska, managing to utter an entire sentence without insulting someone for maybe the third time since I'd met her. "This is ancient magic! Thousands of years old."

"Be that as it may," said Nadi, ever practical, "we still have a riddle to solve."

"My skin is...hard. You couldn't...use it to...make rags," said Borg, looking at Whiska.

"Here's what we know," said Nadi, ignoring our largest and smallest party members. "We know how far Borokia is from both locations. We know how fast each dragon travels. Now we just need to calculate how long it takes them to get to the same point, right?"

"Well," said Rummy, "the riddle is kind of a trick question." He looked at the rock. "You asked us what time the two travelers meet in Borokia, right?"

"Yes," replied the rock, wiggling its rocky eyebrows.

"Well, then, the answer to that is just how long it takes the slower traveler to get there, accounting for their different start times; they're not meeting at some indeterminate midpoint based on their speed of travel...they're meeting at a fixed location, and they can only meet up once they're both there. Right?"

Nadi nodded. "Makes sense." She looked sheepish. "Does anyone actually know how to figure that out? I never really... well, no one ever taught me how to do that sort of thing."

"Not me," said Whiska. "Math is for clerks and crotch grabbers."

"Crotch grabbers?" I said, my tone intentionally neutral.

"Well, everyone I've known who had a head for numbers liked to stick their hands down their pants."

"How many people have you known who had a head for numbers?" I asked.

"One," answered Whiska.

"And that person liked to grab his—or her; I'm not sexist—crotch because he—or she—liked to do math...?" I prompted.

"No, you witless tree climber! He—it's always a he when it comes to crotch grabbing—just liked grabbing his crotch. And he was good at math," said Whiska huffily.

"I'm so confused," said Rummy.

"That makes all of us," I said.

"So, none of us knows figures?" asked Nadi, looking worried.

"Assuming they...do not stop...to sleep...Bob will take... ten hours and...twenty-five minutes...to reach Borokia. Lavinia will take...fifty hours. Lavinia is...an elven name. She will only...need four hours...of sleep. It would be...hard to sleep...on a dragon's...back. Gold dragons...must rest...for two hours...for every...ten hours they...fly. Assuming the gold...is rested at...the start, and assuming...Lavinia sleeps when... the dragon rests...it will take fifty-eight...hours of travel. So...she would arrive...at three in the morning ...Fanting Standard Time ...two and...a half days...later." Borg paused as we all stared at him in wonder, but before anyone could say anything, he continued. "But 'Bob'...is a title...reserved for a... high priest...of Kandar. They...won't enter...Borokia because it...allows citizens to...wear open-toed...shoes." He looked at the rock. "So the answer...is that they...never meet...in Borokia."

"Holy balls," breathed Whiska.

"Borg, are you sure that you're right about—" began Nadi before the rock cut her off.

"That's...that's correct," said the rock. It let out a low whistle. "You're as smart as you are handsome!" It seemed delighted.

Five minutes of high-fiving and celebration ensued, with Borg smiling awkwardly; I don't think he enjoyed being the center of attention as much as other members of our party.

After we finished slapping Borg on the back—which I don't recommend, incidentally, both because it's a strain to reach up that high and because making contact with a rock giant's skin is a painful experience—we turned our attention back to the rock and asked for the second riddle.

"I'll need a moment to think," replied the rock. "I've never issued the second riddle before, and it's been so long since I was enchanted..."

"Join the club, Rocky," I sighed. Everyone looked at me. "What? It's almost impossible to find your equal when you're simultaneously uniquely gifted and impossibly beautiful."

The rock heaved a heavy sigh, too. "She's right," it said ruefully.

"Once we've cracked that pesky second riddle, I'll buy you a drink and we'll talk," I said.

"Sure, sure," said the rock, concentrating. "Now...I think I remember the second riddle." The rock cleared its throat, which was weird, because it didn't look like it actually had a throat. "I arrive at dawn when the sun appears, and stay 'til lunch to spread some cheer. By afternoon, my time is done and then I leave, which is no fun. When stars come up, I'm tucked in tight to make sure no one takes a bite. I rest, not sleep, all night through and begin again to start anew. What am I?"

Rummy blew out a long, loud sigh. "Well, I'm stumped. Let's go home!"

"Nervous about the fact that we're pretty much on the verge of fighting a dragon?" I replied, eyebrow appropriately arched.

Rummy nodded vigorously. "Yup."

"We can figure this out," said Nadi. She looked at Whiska. "Right?"

The Ratarian was uncharacteristically silent, her lips pursed. At last, after a nearly Borg-like pause, she replied, but directed her response to the rock. "Are you sure you got it right, or is your head as full of rocks as the rest of you?"

"My head *is* rock," replied the rock amiably. "But, yes, I'm pretty sure I got it right."

"It's just that *'begin again to start anew'* is so redundant...it must be the key to the riddle," said Whiska pensively.

"I'm stumped...too," said Borg.

"Damn. Thought you were our ace in the hole," I said.

"What are you thinking?" Nadi said to Whiska, who was muttering unintelligibly under her breath.

"Please never ask Whiska what she's thinking," I pleaded.

"Well, it depends," Whiska said, ignoring me.

"On what?" said Nadi.

"On how you interpret certain words. This creepy thing has been here for a long time, right?"

"I'm not creepy," said the rock (who was, in fact, kind of creepy). "If you're going to judge me like that, I might just have to hit you with my gravel." The rock paused as we all looked at each other. Nadi shrugged at me; I returned the gesture. "I think that was a funny joke. Someone told me that once. Something about how judges like to hit people with gravel...which I always thought was strange, because my understanding is that judges are generally supposed to throw the book at people, though I don't know which book. Maybe it's any book. Or maybe it's a special book."

"I think," said Rummy diplomatically, "you're thinking of a gavel. It's like a tiny hammer. That's why it's, um, funny. Well, sort of funny, anyway, depending on your standard for funny. Judges pound gavels when they hand out a sentence to a criminal. Gravel sounds like gavel, right? And you're made of rock, or gravel, if you will…so, yeah, it's a pun." He chuckled. "I guess it is a little bit funny, actually."

"Yes—yes!" said the rock excitedly. "That's why it's funny!" It pursed its lips. "I should write that down so I don't forget and can explain it better the next time it comes up."

"You can write?" asked Nadi.

"No."

"Oh."

Whiska cleared her throat. "As I was saying—or *trying* to say before pointless and objectively *not* funny digressions—this riddle was made up a long time ago. Depending on how old it is, and I'd be willing to bet Rummy's balls that it's at least a couple thousand years old, the meaning of a few of the words in the riddle has changed."

"Not willing to wager much, are you?" said Rummy good naturedly.

"No—because I'm not an idiot," replied Whiska. "Now, take 'dawn' for example. That word means the time of day when the sun rises, obviously, or the beginning of something, but it also used to refer to the northern part of the Aberrinian province, before it was conquered by the Calipar horde."

"You really know your history," said Rummy admiringly. "And your etymology."

"Yes, I do," snapped Whiska, though she was clearly pleased with the compliment. "Given that saying 'arrive at dawn when the sun appears,' is redundant—just like the last line of the riddle—which suggests it means something different. I think it's referring to a place, not a time of day."

"Do you really think so?" said the rock. "Fascinating!"

"You know the answer, you ignorant igneous!" yelled Whiska.

"Actually, I don't," replied the rock. "I only know whether the answer you give is correct or incorrect when you say it, and then I forget it immediately. If someone were to ask me to answer the riddle, I wouldn't be able to answer it."

"That is a very weird enchantment," I opined.

"It really is," agreed the rock.

"What happens if we get the answer wrong?" asked Nadi.

"I smite you with lightning bolts," replied the rock, very matter-of-factly. We all took a step back. The rock laughed. "I'm only kidding. The only thing that happens is I don't open. And you have to wait a year to try again."

"Your very weird enchantment gave you a very weird sense of humor," I said (not happily, I might add).

"It really did," said the rock.

"So, dawn is a place—what does that tell us about the answer, Whiska?" asked Nadi.

"I don't know, you yellow-tressed flower sniffer!" Whiska shot back. (It's a commonly held belief that elves love to smell flowers, but that's not true—I mean, some do, just like humans, but it's not a racial characteristic. I have no clue why the idea got traction, and even less of an idea why Whiska thought that was an effective insult.)

"Let's think through this," I said. "If dawn is a place, then the speaker in the riddle arrives there when the sun comes up and stays until the midday meal to 'spread some cheer.' That suggests that the speaker is a physical being and not a concept like love or death or some nonsense like that, right?"

"The sun...comes up early," added Borg.

"The part about taking a bite is throwing me off," said Rummy. "I agree with Heloise that it sounds like the speaker has a physical form, but I'm not sure it's a being. It could be food, right?" He looked around for support for his theory. "What kind of food do you tuck in at night? A pie? Maybe salad, because it's on a bed of lettuce?"

"But you can also 'tuck in' to a meal, which means to sit down to eat it," mused Nadi. "Though the riddle seems to indicate that the tucking in happens so whatever it is *doesn't* get eaten." She shook her head. "This is so confusing."

"Well, if it was easy to solve, everyone could get into the mountain, right?" said the rock.

"Why don't you want people to get into the mountain?" I asked. "I mean, what do you care if people want to go get barbecued by a dragon?"

"I don't care at all," said the rock. "In fact, I'd be delighted if you get what you want—you all seem nice. But, it's not up to me—it's up to whoever enchanted me."

"If this enchantment is as old as we think it is," said Whiska, "there's no way the dragon lived in the mountain when it was enacted."

"So, why did he, or she, or it—whoever created the enchantment, I mean—want to keep people out?" asked Nadi.

Whiska shrugged. "What do I look like, the Oracle at Vanataw?"

"Not really," said Rummy. "You don't have the head of a lion. And, well, let's just say the vicinity around your décolletage isn't quite as robustly proportioned."

"If this enchantment predates the dragon, it means two things," I said before Whiska, who looked on the verge of unleashing a tirade on Rummy, could respond. "One: there's something in the mountain someone wants—or, at least, wanted—to protect. Two: there's another way in and out, unless the dragon solves the riddle every time it comes and goes."

"Does the dragon solve the riddle every time it comes and goes?" asked Rummy.

"I've never seen the dragon," replied the rock.

"So, all we need to do is find the other way in!" I concluded (brilliantly).

"It's possible that there's another way in," said Nadi slowly, thinking out loud, "but it's also likely that the way the dragon goes in and out requires you to be able to fly."

"Whiska—got any flying spells?" I asked.

"Go to Pemblach!" Whiska shouted before storming off, not that she could go too terribly far, given that the precipice we stood on wasn't all that big. (It turns out that Whiska is particularly sensitive about the fact that she can't cast flying spells, which, unbeknownst to me at that time, is a major limitation of Ratarian schools of magic. Apparently, the structure of Ratarian hands makes it almost impossible to form the particularly intricate gestures required to enact a flying spell—though I can tell you they work exceedingly well for non-magical gestures meant to suggest anatomically challenging acts. It's rumored that one Ratarian mage, known by his stage name, The Great Tailini, once managed the feat...but, given that he was never seen again after that, it's hard to say whether that's true or simply a fanciful story meant to cover up the tainted cheese-related disappearance of yet another Ratarian wizard.)

(Pemblach, incidentally, is a town on the outskirts of the largest Ratarian kingdom that does not allow cheese to be made or served—what humans might call a "dry" town. Given cheese's intoxicating effect on them, Ratarians really, really hate the place unless they belong to a particularly ascetic sect of Flomanism, which is the primary religion practiced by Ratarians (though not Whiska, who is such an atheist that she doesn't even believe in atheism). I'm pretty indifferent about cheese as a general rule, so I'm not sure Whiska's curse had the potent effect that she had hoped; she was really off her game today.)

"Well, then, I suppose we need to solve the riddle," said Nadi.

"The Oracle at...Vanataw has the...head of an...eagle. Not...a lion," said Borg.

"Ah, right!" said Rummy. "Thanks. I was thinking of the Oracle at Jargone."

"Focus!" snapped Nadi.

"Sorry," said Rummy. He squinted at the rock and rubbed

his beard before turning toward me. "What do you think the 'rest, not sleep' part means? Is there anything that doesn't need to sleep, but needs to rest?"

"There was this dwarven gigolo I used to know..." I started to reply before Nadi cut me off.

"Not helpful. Come on, think! We need to solve this." She looked pointedly at me. "What rests but doesn't sleep? There can't be that many things. What about something that comes to rest? Like, something that moves, but then stops moving? Like...like a rolling stone."

"I think you're mixing your metaphors," said Rummy. "But," he hastily added in response to a death glare from Nadi, "maybe you're onto something. It would have to be something that's not alive if it doesn't sleep. Unless it only doesn't sleep during the one night in question in the riddle." He shook his head and smiled. "This is a real humdinger, isn't it?"

⌖

So it went for three straight days.

We attacked the riddle from every possible angle, but none of us could come up with a response we were confident enough to risk offering to the rock lest we lose our ability to enter the mountain for a year. (Borg suggested "grumpel," which is apparently a rock giant delicacy made from live eels that don't need to sleep, but none of us wanted to give that one a try—in any manner of speaking.) Just as I started to worry that Whiska might begin to electrocute various members of our party out of boredom and frustration, a small, high-pitched voice sang out, "Why are you trying to solve the riddle?"

I wouldn't say I jumped in terror so much as I leapt into combat position. Everyone else jumped in terror. We spun around, weapons at the ready, to confront our foe, only to discover that the threat was…

A seven-year-old orc girl with a giant yellow flower woven into her hair and armed not with an elf-sticking dagger, but an empty basket.

The girl giggled. "You are good jumpers."

"No," I said (possibly huffily). "We're good at instant combat positioning."

"Oh," said the girl, sounding unconvinced. I couldn't help feeling that she seemed familiar somehow.

"Who are you?" asked Nadi as she looked around warily for other orcs.

"Etty Loo Betterken," replied the girl. "Who are *you*?"

"That's not important," I said. "Well, no, that's not true—it's mostly not important. I'm Heloise the Bard."

The girl shrugged. "Okay."

"What's more important," I said, possibly through gritted teeth, "is whether there are any more of you."

"Don't worry—there's only one Etty in our whole village."

"Thank goodness for that," I muttered perhaps too loudly. "There aren't any grown-up orcs wandering around here with you? What are you doing here?"

"Adult orcs don't go mushroom picking," replied little Etty in her best know-it-all voice. "So why would they be with me?"

"That's what you're doing then?" interjected Rummy, clearly in an attempt to forestall what was going to be a curse-filled retort from yours truly. "Picking mushrooms?" He sounded genuinely curious.

The girl nodded enthusiastically, taking an immediate shine to our most diminutive party member. "Yes—I'm the best in the village! I'm the only one who knows where the rarest, tastiest mushrooms are."

"Where are they?" asked Rummy.

"Inside the mountain," replied the girl, sotto voce. She

winked.

"You know the answer to the riddle?" asked Nadi, excitement in her voice.

"No," giggled the girl.

"Then how do you get in, you green-skinned doorstop?" said Whiska.

"Through the door," replied the (obnoxious) child.

"What door?" demanded Whiska.

"The one that's right around the other side of that rock, genius." The girl pointed to a particularly large outcropping of stone.

Nadi raced over, peered behind the stone, and slapped her hand over her face. "This leads into the mountain?" she asked without turning back toward us.

"Yeah," said the girl. "That's where the mushrooms are. Unless you can fly like the dragon, it's the only way in."

"Unless you can answer the riddle," said Rummy.

The girl giggled. "The riddle is impossible. My da says that it was made that way to keep the morons away from the mushrooms."

"I'll show you a moron," muttered Whiska as she whipped out her wand and prepared to rain electric death down on the tiny orc.

"Whiska!" shouted Nadi, holding her hand up.

Whiska grumbled something that sounded suspiciously like, "Hang you from a tree and pull out your innards and have a contest among buzzards to determine which is the strongest and most worthy of consuming your intestines, which it will share with me before I then pan fry and eat the buzzard so that I can consume all of you and the most evolutionarily desirable buzzard in the process," but I might have misheard. Nonetheless, she lowered her wand.

"Well, rock?" said Nadi, turning back to our riddlemaster. "Is this true? Does this door lead into the same part of the mountain as the one you guard?"

"As near as I can tell. I've never actually been inside, but I trust Etty Loo—she is nice to me, and always brings me a mushroom, even though I can't eat them."

"And why, exactly, didn't you tell us about this door?" replied Nadi.

"Not part of my enchantment. Where would be the fun in solving the riddles if you knew you didn't need to?"

"I think we might have different ideas of what constitutes fun," noted Rummy with equanimity.

"Can I blast him yet?" asked Whiska.

"Rummy? No, I kind of like him," I replied.

"No, you singing bag of fecal wind! The rock! Can I blast the rock?"

Nadi looked at me. I shrugged. She sighed. "Go ahead."

Whiska cackled with glee as she brandished her wand. "Suck molten eldritch energy, you crag-faced pain in my rancid hairy—" The rest of Whiska's taunt was lost in an explosion of flame, as her wand blew up like a volcano, knocking us all—our new little orc friend included—off our feet. Smoke billowed, and Whiska laughed again. "How does that taste?" she said to no one in particular.

"I don't have taste buds," said a familiar, rocky voice as the smoke dissipated, revealing an utterly unaffected rock wall. "But I don't imagine I would be a big fan of spicy food, and that fireball seemed a little hot." The rock looked from Whiska to Nadi to me. "Spicy? Hot? No?" It frowned. "I thought that was at least a little funny."

"Hey, Whiska, the rock seems pretty unaffected," said Rummy.

"Yes, the enchantment makes me invulnerable, especially to magic. Otherwise, people would just blast their way through me." The rock pursed its lips. "Did I not mention that?"

"Hey, Whiska, the rock can't really be affected by magic," said Rummy affably.

"I will murder you on your wedding day," replied Whiska.

"Good thing I'm not even engaged," replied Rummy.

"You shouldn't...blast the rock," said Borg.

"Well," said Nadi, "I guess we're done here. At least we found a way into the mountain, and, if nothing else, hanging out here for a few days was way better than going through that swamp."

The orc girl giggled. "You went through the swamp?"

"Yes," said Nadi, scowling at the orc. "Why?"

"Right through the middle of it?"

"Yes, that's where the path led," said Rummy.

"Only diiinnnggg-dooonnngggsss use the path!" sang the girl. "If you go about three grope ropes north, there's a log bridge that goes over the top of the swamp. It takes about two hours to cross, and you don't get stinky and smelly. And bog men can't walk on logs. Not that those are hard to beat—I just push 'em over with a stick. They make funny sounds when they splash back into the swamp."

"Three grope ropes?" asked Rummy.

Etty Loo nodded. "A grope rope is the distance one grope of orcs would cover if they stood in a line holding hands. I thought everyone knew that."

"I was never formally educated," said Rummy.

"You should go back to school," said Etty solemnly. "Education is really important."

"How deep into the caves are the mushrooms?" I asked.

"They're right inside the entrance—I'm not supposed to go in deeper. There's a minotaur in there, and minotaurs like to eat orc children."

"I don't think that's true," I said.

Etty nodded vigorously. "Oh, yes—it is. I learned it in my Certainties class."

"I know I'm going to regret this," I replied, "but...'Certainties' class?"

"That's school again," she said knowingly, then shook her head. "You really all ought to be better educated."

"I know what school is," I said through gritted teeth, "but I'm not sure 'Certainties' is a staple of curricula everywhere."

"Certainties is where we learn about things that are factually true. Factually means they're real."

"Yes, as opposed to unfactually true," I replied, sarcasm present in, though hopefully not dripping from, my voice.

"Right," replied Etty, missing the subtext entirely. "You don't always have to have facts to say true things."

"I'd say they're pretty necessary," grumbled Whiska.

"No, that's not true," said the girl. "The President of our tribe says so, and that everyone who says anything different is just saying fake things."

"But how do you distinguish fake from truth without facts?" asked Nadi.

"Truth is just stuff you know is right. Facts are little bits of information you can use if they fit the truth you want to say is not fake. That's where we learned about like how minotaurs eat orc children, bears will attack your campsite if you don't bury your poo, and half-elven lady bards are always sassy—things like that."

"Seems like a pretty good class," I said, sagely.

"Yeah, it was my second favorite."

"What was your favorite?" asked Rummy.

"Jim class."

"Exercising, playing games—things of that sort?" said Rummy.

Etty Loo shook her head. "A '*Jim*' is what we call someone who always says fake things, like humans are smart or vegetables are important. We get to throw rocks at a new Jim each day in Jim class."

"Oh," said Rummy, summing up what I imagined was our collective response.

"I also liked math, though."

"Liked doing your sums, did you?" said Rummy, clearly eager to move the conversation in a new direction.

Etty gave him a strange look. "No, silly—math is where you stab small animals and learn how to cook them."

"I think that word loses something in the translation," Rummy responded.

"I guess," said Etty.

"So, is there actually a minotaur?" asked Nadi, looking from Etty to the rock and back.

"I've never been inside the mountain," the rock reminded us, its eyes flicking down to look at itself.

"I don't know," shrugged Etty.

"Why not?" asked Whiska.

"Look, I'm seven—you're a grown-up. Figure it out your-self." With that, she skipped her way into the mountain, leaving us staring awkwardly at each other in our magically created and extraordinarily unfashionable clothes.

"Well, this has been fun," said the rock at last. "Let's do it again sometime, eh?"

"Um...I'm not sure that's necessary," replied Nadi.

"Though it's been delightful," added Rummy.

"Let's get our gear together and get moving—we're burning daylight," said Nadi.

"That won't really matter inside the mountain," I said sweetly.

"You know what I mean."

"This was...fun," said Borg. "Goodbye...rock."

"Goodbye, you handsome devil," replied the rock.

"Nadi, what are we going to do if there actually is a mino-taur in there?" asked Rummy.

"We'll figure it out," replied Nadi confidently.

"Or just blow it up," said Whiska.

"I'm not...a devil," said Borg. "I'm a...rock giant."

"I know," said the rock.

We gathered our things and headed into the mountain.

CHAPTER 21

A MINOTAUR AND HIS MAZE ARE NO MATCH FOR OUR MATCHLESS HEROES

Having proven their mental mettle by solving the riddle that gained them entrance to the mountain, our brave heroes entered the dark and twisting corridors that led to the dragon's lair with renewed vigor, resolved to end once and for all the threat to the good people of Skendrick. Of course, it is never the case that an adventurer travels the shortest distance between two points, for epic quests and heroic deeds occur not on a straight line, but just around the blind bend ahead.

So it was for Nadinta and her band in Mount Fenneltop, where they soon became lost in the maze of winding passageways that honeycombed the mountain. Even Rumscrabble Tooltinker's innate dwarven sense of direction failed him as they wound their way through the mountain, turning left and right and doubling back so many times that they soon became hopelessly confused. Sensing weakness, the denizens of the mountain maze pounced, attacking our tired heroes at their lowest ebb. Feral mountain cats whose sense of smell was so keen they could sniff out the fear of a wounded gazelle a mile distant snarled and clawed at them, tunnel goblins brandished crude pikes and swords, and sentient slime slithered across their boots, leaving explosive, acid trails of sludge in their wake.

Battered and bruised but never beaten, our heroes fought off every attack, turning blade and magic alike on their foes. Borgunder Gunderbor struggled in the tight quarters, but used his massive bulk to shield his companions, withstanding a rain of blows as his fellow heroes sought opportunities to counterattack their vicious foes. Eventually, the mighty band began to get its bearings, and as they worked their way through the maze, a gradually growing source of light led them to a cavernous chamber where they found the maze's master, a massive minotaur named Mastrato, the ancient Kolethi word for "bloody axe."

The minotaur snarled and brandished the weapon for which he was named, which dripped crimson ichor in the flickering torchlight that lit the cavern. He roared a challenge to the heroes and rushed to meet them head on, flanked by a dozen cave trolls, each armed with a spiked club and a thirst for blood nearly the equal of their bovine master.

Nadinta met him head on, her sword parrying a mighty blow of the axe before she launched into a dazzling display of martial skill, scything her way through the ranks of the trolls while fending off the minotaur. Borgunder strode boldly into the fray, drawing the attention of the trolls while mighty Whiska hurled eldritch death from the end of her crystal-tipped staff. The cave trolls soon succumbed to their combined assault, and not even the minotaur, a legend among its own kind for its size and ferocity, could withstand Nadinta's deft swordplay, Borg's peerless strength, Rumscrabble's precision strikes, and Whiska's magical acid arrows. The beast soon fell, crying out in pain and rage as it toppled. Its breathing soon ceased, and the heroes stood shoulder to shoulder, surveying the carnage around them.

They quickly found the minotaur's treasure room, though they knew that even its loaded chests of gold, jewels, and other baubles paled in comparison to the hoard they would find in the dragon's lair.

They paused for but a brief rest and to take nourishment, steeling themselves to continue on to the final step of their quest.

Their thirst quenched and hunger sated, the heroic band set off with steely determination, intent on finding the dragon and meting out the same justice they had on the minotaur.

Soon, they swore, the good people of Skendrick would rest easy.

CHAPTER 22

MIGRAINE-INDUCING MAZES AND MUSHROOM-MUNCHING MORONS DO NOT AN EXCITING TALE MAKE

I've catalogued a number of things I hate over the course of this chronicle, including, but not limited to, cackleroaches, orcs (though maybe I'm evolving on that issue), things that make me want to be a better person, sexy underthings (by which I mean lingerie, not attractive creatures found in underground caverns, toward which I'm generally indifferent), swamps (which I *really* hate), and riddles.

You can go ahead and add mazes to that list.

We left the rock behind and made our way into the mountain, where Etty Loo was kind enough to share some mushrooms with us. They really were pretty good, too, which was surprising—I wouldn't have thought cave mushrooms could hold a candle to forest mushrooms (especially mushrooms from the elven forests of Llamolarolan, which everyone who's not a Catamite or an idiot knows are the best), but they fried up nicely and made a perfect complement to roasted rock spider (which, incidentally, is a lot tastier than it sounds, though I still wouldn't recommend them if you have other options, such as pretty much anything, including dirt).

I guess I should explain that shot I took at the Catamites—the Catamite region is known in some circles for being a producer of fine mushrooms, but really they're just mass producers of mushrooms that taste like tree bark who are really good at marketing. Don't buy them. Ever. Go find Llamo brand mushrooms—you'll thank me.

The fact that I'm a paid endorser for Llamo has nothing to do with that recommendation; they really are just better. (Am I proud of the fact that I'm a paid endorser of anything? You better believe it—I worked hard to gain the kind of influence over people that would enable me to hock fungus for money. Albeit not that much money.)

The orc girl left shortly after we'd finished our snack, so we turned our attention to the pathway before us. Unfortunately, about ten yards in, the path forked, forcing us to make a decision before we'd even really begun to work our way through.

"Well," said Rummy, "I'm left-handed, so arbitrarily, I choose left."

"You're left-handed?" I replied. "I'd never have guessed—you seem to use your right hand more when you prestidigitate."

Rummy grinned. "Ah, only for the stuff you see, Heloise—the easy, obvious stuff." He waved his right hand back and forth in a grand, broad gesture. "That means people aren't looking at my left hand, which is doing the hard stuff. Most prestidigitators are pretty ambidextrous." He held out his left hand, which gripped my coin purse. "Did you want this back?"

I snatched it away and shot him a look, torn, once again, between being annoyed and being impressed. I smacked him on the shoulder for good measure, a gesture meant to simultaneously punish him and show respect. By the way he yelped and rubbed his shoulder, though, I'm guessing it was more of the former.

Nadi, who had been (sensibly) ignoring us, was studying both passageways, listening intently, and licking her finger and holding it up before her. After a moment of brow-furrowed concentration, she nodded. "Sorry, Rummy—we need to go right."

Whiska snorted. "Based on what? Long-eared intuition?"

"Well, we know the dragon isn't coming and going through this entrance," replied Nadi. "It stands to reason that if it flies in and out of its lair, there must be a fairly large opening up high somewhere. Air must come in through that opening, which means that it should filter down through whichever passageway ultimately leads to the dragon's lair. As long as we can detect any hint of an air current, we should be moving in the right direction." She frowned. "Notwithstanding the possibility of having to get through a minotaur before we can deal with the dragon."

"Anyone ever fought a minotaur?" asked Rummy. "Or even seen one?"

We all shook our heads. "I know they're strong, though," said Whiska. "Unlike the lot of you. But, not too smart, apparently, except for when it comes to navigating mazes. Still, they're fierce fighters, and they usually have lesser beasts as bodyguards."

"Like rock spiders?" I asked hopefully.

"More like goblins, or troglodytes. Maybe trolls."

"Well, that's annoying."

"Rock spiders are...delicious," said Borg. "But it feels...like I'm a...cannibal when...I eat them."

"I feel the same way when I snack on elf babies," I replied.

Everyone looked at each other before taking a step back from me.

"I'm kidding. You know that."

"Let's just get going, okay?" said Nadi, who didn't wait for us to respond before setting off down the right-hand passageway.

"Seriously! That was a joke."

Borg stopped and laid a heavy hand on my shoulder. He looked at me and said, after a moment of contemplation, "I was...kidding too."

That Borg is all right.

The passageway curved around to the right before winding back to the left and dumping us into another cavern, this one much smaller than the one in which Etty had found the mushrooms. The walls glowed faintly with lichen, but the cavern appeared otherwise empty. Two doorways, one to our right and one straight ahead, meant we had to make another choice.

"Is someone making a map as we go?" I asked in an attempt to gently share my adventuring wisdom that we should make a map as we go, even though I hated making maps and had no desire to do it myself.

"I don't, um...I don't have a quill," muttered Nadi, embarrassed, I think, that she hadn't suggested the idea.

"I don't even know how to read," said Rummy happily.

"What is...a quill?" asked Borg.

"I'll do it, you hopeless fence sitters!" snarled Whiska as she dug in her pack to find quill and parchment.

("Fence sitters," incidentally, is a slang term for a particularly lazy—and populous—type of squirrel indigenous to the Cantora region. They really like sitting on fences, but they don't like to do much else.)

"Which way now?" asked Rummy as Whiska sketched a diagram of our path so far.

"I'm not entirely sure how far we wound around," said Nadi, "but it's possible that, if we take the doorway straight ahead, we'll work our way over toward where the other path in the first cavern led. Maybe."

"Not so sure of ourselves when we're underground, are we, sugarlips?" said Whiska.

"Sugarlips?" I asked.

Whiska shrugged. "Bet she likes kissing."

"Nadi, do you like kissing?" I asked.

She blushed. "Let's keep moving. We'll take the route straight ahead, unless anyone objects."

No one did, so we followed Nadi, who had her sword drawn and moved forward cautiously. Whiska followed with Rummy behind her, and I trailed behind Rummy. Borg brought up the rear. As we stepped into the cramped passageway—particularly cramped for Borg—he leaned forward and whispered. "I know...what a quill...is. I...have one. I just...hate making...maps, too." I couldn't see him, but could practically feel his grin.

"I think you're my new favorite," I whispered back.

We continued on without incident for an hour, winding our way through passageway after passageway and becoming hopelessly lost as each new cavern we entered presented multiple exit options. Finally, we reached one that had an absurd seven exit and entry points and Nadi called a halt. "Whiska, please show us the map."

The Ratarian held up her parchment, which was a criss-crossing mess of lines, passageways, arrows showing where we had to retrace our steps, and numerous unexplored paths. It also had a few curse words scrawled on it. As we reviewed our progress and the design of the labyrinth inside the mountain, one thing became abundantly clear: whoever had designed this maze had either been insane or drunk, and probably both.

"How long have we been going?" asked Nadi.

Rummy consulted his pocket watch. "A little over three hours, not counting when we stopped so Heloise could take the scorpion out of her boot, the five minutes she spent cursing afterward, the ten subsequent minutes Whiska spent laughing, and the seven minutes Heloise spent chasing her around the cavern trying to beat her with the corpse of the scorpion after Borg stepped on it."

I glared at Whiska, who snickered.

"I'm not sure it's the wisest course of action," said Nadi, "but we may need to consider splitting up. At the rate we're going, it's going to take us days to explore the whole mountain, and we don't have enough food to last that long. If we stay together, we might get lucky and find the path to the dragon's lair in the next half hour, but we also might be stumbling around in the dark for another three days. I'm think we need to separate so we can cover ground faster."

"I'll play Damnation's barrister," I said. "If we split up, we don't really have a good way to contact each other unless Giggles McRatface over there has something up her disgustingly greasy sleeves other than scrawny arms."

"Scrawny arms? I'll shove one of these scrawny arms right up your plump elven—"

"Save it, Whiska," said Nadi sharply. She narrowed her eyes at me, and I had the good grace to look at least mildly chastened. "Go on, preferably without the editorial commentary."

"We're going to have a hard time beating a dragon as it stands—if it's only two or three of us, it's going to be impossible. Even if one group finds the dragon and manages to avoid detection, they're going to have a hard time doubling back to find the other group—so, even if they can mark the path clearly, it may not do much good." I shook my head. "Together, we might get out alive, or we might die. Separated, we'll definitely die."

"That's a sunny way of thinking about it," said Rummy.

I shrugged. "Adventuring's a rough business, kid."

Nadi looked thoughtful. "Heloise is right—we stick together. Let's keep going for another couple of hours and then we'll...wait—what was that?" She cocked her head, listening intently.

"What was what?" I replied.

"We should...stick together," said Borg.

"Shhh!" hissed Nadi. "Listen!"

It took a moment, but then I heard it too—a hollow pinging sound that seemed to come from inside the walls. I looked at Nadi and raised an eyebrow. She shook her head, looking grim.

"Is that what I think it is?" said Whiska to no one in particular.

"What do you think it—" Rummy started to ask before being rudely interrupted by the wall exploding and three huge, bug-like creatures emerging from the hole.

They had hard shells and pincers, and an array of arms and legs, some of which were insectoid, some of which were more humanoid. Two of those arms/legs had nasty, serrated edges along the sides and ended in a point as sharp as any sword. Their pincers clicked and clacked as they hovered over us, looking menacing.

"Chitinoids!" shouted Whiska, raising her staff.

"What are chitinoids?" asked Rummy, brandishing his mace.

"Those things, you sightless hair muffin!" replied Whiska, gesturing toward the creatures.

"How do we beat them?" I asked, looking doubtfully at my knife.

"They're vulnerable to cold," replied Whiska as she started to whip her hands around in preparation for casting a spell.

"Whiska—hit them with whatever you've got," called Nadi. "Borg—take point. Rummy and Heloise—form up behind me." She raised her sword in a defensive stance.

"I say," said the tallest of the creatures, raising its most humanoid arm up to do something that looked an awful lot like scratching its head in confusion. "Do any of you blokes know where we might find the mushrooms?" It spoke the common tongue with an impossibly posh accent.

"What?" asked Nadi, her sword tip dropping in confusion.

"Hmmm...perhaps I'm not saying that word correctly—I've only recently learned it." Its pincers twitched in consternation. "Mosh-rooms?" it tried. "Moosh-rums?" It looked at its companions. "Help me out, lads."

The creature to the speaker's right stepped forward. "The fungus, you know? We want the fungus." It gave us a sly look and lowered its voice to a loud whisper. "We eats 'em, you know." It laid a finger, or something that looked like a finger, on the side of its nose and said, "Shhhhh."

"Um...right," replied Nadi at her eloquent best.

"So, you're just looking for mushrooms?" I asked.

"Is that not how I said it?" said the first speaker, looking toward his companions. "I'm quite certain I had the right of it the first time."

"You said it right," said Rummy agreeably. "We just weren't prepared for you to speak a language we understand. Or, to ask us about mushrooms." He held his hands out to the side. "Honestly, we kind of thought you were going to try to eat *us*."

The chitinoids looked at each other and then exploded with laughter. "'e thought we was gunna eat 'em, 'e did! Right gorky, innit?" said the creature who had not yet spoken.

"It certainly is—highly gorky indeed," said the first chitinoid patronizingly as he patted the other creature on the shoulder. "Now then, any chance you can point us toward those delectable goodies?"

Nadi looked at Whiska. "Show them the map."

"What? Why should we share our map with these shell-faced fungus lickers?"

"Our faces ain't shells, you know?" said the second chitinoid. (I'd like to distinguish them in some way other than the order in which they spoke, but, well...they really did all look the same.) "You know what they is?" He looked around and then leaned in, lowering his voice as though disclosing his greatest secret, which seemed to be a habit with him. "They's faces." He apparently found this hilarious, as he spent the next two minutes laughing so hard that he began to choke. The third chitinoid slapped him hard on the back, which seemed to straighten out the issue.

"Gorky," said the third chitinoid solemnly once the laughing fit had come to an end.

"Whiska," said Nadi impatiently. "The map. Now."

Whiska looked as though she wanted to immolate Nadi, but gritted her teeth and did as Nadi requested. "There," she said, pointing to a spot on the map. "That's where you'll find your stupid mushrooms, if the orc brat left any behind."

"Orc brat?" asked the first chitinoid, making the word "brat" sound more like a delicious sausage than an annoying kid.

"Never mind," said Nadi. "It's nothing to worry about." She looked to the creature we assumed was the chitinoids' leader. "Now that we've helped you, maybe you can help us."

"I don't know...what gorky...means," interjected Borg.

"Get a load of it, eh wot? 'e don't know from gorky," said the third chitinoid, shaking his head incredulously. "And 'im a talking rock, ain't 'e?"

"I'm not entirely sure I know either," I volunteered, "though I can infer something from context."

"Gorky," said the third one. "It's mental, right? Like, someone ain't got no sense."

"That's what I figured," I replied before shaking my head. "You boys are an interesting bunch."

"We're not all lads," said the first chitinoid, offended.

"You're not?" asked Nadi.

"Good heavens no!" replied the first. "I'm a female of our

species, and deeply into the mating cycle as well, I might add, so the characteristics of my sex should be quite apparent."

Nadi looked at me and shrugged. I returned the gesture.

"Well, we're really sorry about that," said Rummy, reaching out to pat the creature on the arm. "This is our first encounter with chitinoids."

The creature drew back quickly. "Don't touch me when I'm in the midst of mating! You might disrupt the seminal transfer."

As you might imagine, this comment precipitated a few moments of silence as we all struggled to find an appropriate response. Rummy looked at his hand with distaste. Sensing that no one else was willing to do it, I decided to take the plunge. "Seminal transfer?"

"Yes. My mate there," she said, indicating the third chitinoid ("Gorky," as I had come to think of him). "He's currently transferring his seminal material into my fertile womb."

"Currently as in...as in right now?" asked Nadi tentatively.

"Yes."

"But you're not...you're not, ah, actually touching. That I can see, anyway. Not that I'm, um, looking."

"That's not how it works."

"I see," said Nadi, nonplussed.

"Well," said Rummy cheerfully, "I'll be sure not to touch him, either." He winked at the third chitinoid, who gave him one of those "just doing my duty" nods men excel at.

"So, this is awkward," I said.

"Why?" responded the second chitinoid.

"Because those two are...well, you know...they're..."

"Gettin' buggy?" replied the second chitinoid.

"Um, yes," I said.

The chitinoid shrugged. "Not our fault the rest of yous is awkward about the baby making bits, you know?"

"So," interjected Nadi, "what can you tell us about the minotaur?"

"Minotaur?" asked the female chitinoid.

"We were told a minotaur lived down here somewhere," replied Nadi. "Where does it dwell?"

The chitinoids looked at each other. "You don't want to mess with the minotaur, you know?" said the second chitinoid.

"'E'll carve you up for supper an' leave nuffink but your stockings, 'e will, won't 'e, eh wot?" said Gorky. "Don't like to eat stockings then, do 'e?"

"You've seen it?" asked Rummy.

The female chitinoid shook her head. "No. My companions are just having a bit of a jest at your expense. We've never laid eyes on the creature, though we, too, have heard that it rules these tunnels."

"We hain't laid eyes on it, me lovey? What about when we was wiv it the other day and—"

Gorky ended his thought abruptly with a sharp exhalation when his mate elbowed him hard in what I assume was the general vicinity of his abdomen. "You'd do best to steer clear of the minotaur, if one indeed rules this maze. They are powerful foes, and even a hearty band of adventurers such as yourselves would be hard pressed to defeat one in its prime."

Nadi looked at me and I nodded; clearly, these three knew more than they were letting on. "Have you ever fought one?" I asked. "Another one, I mean."

"We should be going," said the female chitinoid. "We must find the mushrooms. We thank you very much for your assistance, and wish you the best of luck in your adventures."

"Why we in such a hurry, lovey?" asked Gorky. "Let's 'ave a spot o' fun and watch these wippets get ripped in 'alf by the—"

Gorky once again stopped mid-sentence, though this time it wasn't due to a sharp blow to the solar plexus, but, rather, the sound of an inhuman roar reverberating through the tunnels.

Gorky shrugged and smiled. "Ah, well—fun to be had wiv the rippin,' sure, but not 'alf as much as livin' to eat another mushroom, eh wot? Ta!" With that, the three chitinoids withdrew into the wall, disappearing as quickly as they'd arrived.

"What just happened?" asked a bewildered Rummy.

"I'm more concerned with what's about to happen," replied Nadi. "Defensive positions—now! Borg, up front. Whiska, behind me. Rummy and Heloise—flank Whiska." She drew her sword and eyed the tunnel from which the terrible roar had come. She risked a quick glance behind her. "Whiska—any idea what might have made that sound?"

"Something hungry or angry, you brainless forest frolicker," Whiska shot back.

We waited, tense, but didn't hear any more roars, or anything else for that matter. It was completely silent.

Completely silent, that is, until three massive ape-like creatures burst into the room, shrieking and slamming their hands on the ground.

"Gormalons!" shouted Whiska as she rapped her staff on the ground and swirled it in a circular motion.

"What?" cried Nadi as she moved closer to Borg.

"Cave-dwellers. They're not very smart, but they're strong and fast, and they don't stop fighting until they're dead." Whiska uttered a sharp syllable that sounded like "*Hurk!*" and the tip of her staff flared with light, causing the gormalons to screech in anger.

Nadi darted around Borg and lashed out with her sword, scoring a solid strike on one of the creatures, but its countering swing, which Nadi just barely managed to dodge, suggested that she didn't do much damage to it.

"Rummy!" shouted Whiska as she reached into her pouches, searching for spell components. "They love shiny objects!"

"Shiny objects...shiny...right, right," said Rummy, patting his own pockets absently as he tried to muster up his courage. A few seconds later, his hand slipped inside a pocket and his face lit up. "Got it!"

As Borg weathered a series of blows from one of the creatures (without apparent ill effect, I might add, as I heard him singing something that almost sounded like it rhymed "oops" with "poops" while the creature pummeled him), Rummy stepped forward and, taking advantage of the light from Whiska's staff that still filled the chamber, held up what appeared to be a multifaceted—and absurdly huge —diamond.

"No way that's real," I said.

"Focus, Heloise!" shouted Nadi, dodging another blow and slashing at her opponent.

"Come on—that thing would be worth, like, a thousand gold pieces! It's fake, right, Rummy?"

"Not right now, Heloise," said Rummy through gritted teeth, a forced smile fixed on his face. "Gentlemen!" he began, then shook his head. "Uh, creatures? Gormalons! Yes, let's go with that—hey, gormalons!" He began to wave the stone above his head, causing it to refract and reflect the light from Whiska's staff across the chamber in a very eye-catching display.

"Hrrrmmm?" said one of the creatures, ceasing its assault of Borg to look at the jewel.

"Ooohh aahhh oo oi!" shouted the creature attacking Nadi, backing away from her and turning its attention to Rummy.

"Aaaahhh aah aaaaaaa!" wailed the third creature, advancing slowly on Rummy and sniffing the air.

"That's it," said Rummy gently. "All eyes on this magnificent diamond." He shot me a look that said something along the lines of, "Don't say anything about whether or not this is a real diamond or I will murder you with a hacksaw," so I elected to remain silent, though I kept my knife at the ready (both to defend against the gormalons and in case Rummy's look was in earnest).

"It's beautiful, isn't it?" he continued, slowly spinning the gem between his fingers. The gormalons shuffled in closer, heads simultaneously tilting as their eyes flicked back and forth frantically in an attempt to capture each reflected facet of light. "Good lads, good lads," murmured Rummy. "Now then," he continued, raising his eyebrows and glancing quickly at Nadi, who nodded. "Who wants to see this beautiful gem disappear?"

The gormalons hooted and hollered; apparently, they didn't think too highly of that idea. Nadi caught my eye and pantomimed a stabbing motion as she slowly circled around behind our opponents. Borg, moving at his natural speed, did the same.

I tried to act nonchalant as I followed suit, oohing a little as Rummy continued his patter. "On the count of three, then, boys—you are all boys, aren't you? So it would appear from your plumbing, anyway. Regardless, on the count of three, I'm going to throw this gem up in the air, and whichever one of you can tell me where it lands gets it. Deal?"

The gormalons continued to stare at the gem with slack-jawed wonder. "One," said Rummy, looking up to lock eyes with Nadi, who nodded again as she took up a position behind the gormalon in the middle. Borg stood behind the one on the right, and I had managed to get behind the one on the left. "Two," said Rummy. "Watch closely now—you won't want to miss this. Three!" Rummy flicked his hand up into the air and the gem disappeared; at the same moment, Whiska extinguished the light in her staff, plunging the cavern into darkness.

Before the gormalons could react, Nadi shouted, "Now!" and I could hear her sword hit its target even as I plunged my knife into the back of the gormalon in front of me. Borg's strike followed a few seconds later, though there was no mistaking the resounding thud of his club smashing a gormalon skull.

Nadi and Borg successfully felled their opponents with a single strike; I wasn't so lucky. The gormalon I had stabbed roared in pain (and presumably rage; I know I'd be pretty peeved if someone stabbed me in the back) and thrashed about, knocking me over in the process. "Watch out!" I called as I fell painfully on my backside.

To my surprise, it was Rummy who stepped in, driving his little mace into the creature's face and dropping it cold. Nadi rushed in and plunged her sword into it for good measure, or maybe just because she likes stabbing things. (Oh, wait— that's actually me.)

"That was almost competent," said Whiska approvingly.

"Quiet!" hissed Nadi. She held up her hand to forestall any further comments as she listened intently. A moment later, apparently satisfied that no other threats loomed, she sheathed her sword. "Agreed—that was well done."

"If we're not careful, we might get good at this," said Rummy.

"You won't live long enough to get good at it," I said.

"Thanks for the vote of support," replied Rummy sunnily.

"Well, there is an encounter with a minotaur looming... and, you know, that whole dragon thing you still have to deal with."

"Whiska—secure the perimeter," said Nadi. "Borg—stand guard on that entrance in case any more gormalons come in. Rummy—watch the back side of the cavern." The three adventurers moved to do as Nadi bid without question. "Heloise," she said, turning to me. "A word."

Nadi pulled me aside. "Look, I know we still have a long way to go, and I know we still need to face a dragon."

"An incredibly deadly dragon. Not to mention a minotaur," I said helpfully.

"And a minotaur," she added, glaring at me. "But, that was

a solid win. Right now, more than anything, we need confidence. It's been a long road—"

"A much, much longer road than necessary due to occasional fits of incompetence and a series of poor decisions, and that ill-advised trek through a really stinky swamp," I interjected.

Nadi glared at me again, and I had the good sense to shut up. "It's been a long road, and we haven't had a lot of moments where it felt like we knew what we were doing. Everyone needs to feel like that's happening, like things are coming together. I need you to reinforce that—not undermine it." She shook her head. "We brought you with us to lift us up, Heloise—not tear us down. If you can't do that, then maybe it would be better to part company here and take our chances on our own."

She walked away to check in with Rummy to see if he'd heard anything, leaving me to stand there with what I assume was a very abashed look on my face.

Being the hero of the story is easy. You say and do what you want, and people adore you. You can be sassy and clever and sarcastic and impossibly beautiful and everyone cheers you on. I'm good at being the hero of the story, even when there's not much of a story, and even when I haven't, in reality, been much of a hero—and I'm really good at telling those stories.

Turns out though, that for a world-renowned storyteller, I'm not very good at telling other people's stories.

It occurred to me then that I'd never really told someone else's story. I mean, not really—I'd told stories about other people, sure, but they were heroes of myth and legend, or they were bit players in stories in which one Heloise the Bard, adventurer nonpareil, was the star. I hadn't told a story in which I'd played a supporting (and not very supportive) role.

It's not that I have a big ego, mind you—after all, I was once named "Miss Modesty" in the famed Florcester

Centarian Beauty Pageant (which I also won, incidentally, but that's neither here nor there (though you should know that the Pageant only happens once every hundred years and features only the most beautiful humanoids in Erithea))—but, well, I'll concede that I might enjoy being the center of attention. I mean, at least a little. Not a lot. I'm very modest, after all, having, as just noted, won an award for that very quality. But...

Nadi was right. My job wasn't to make clever quips (though all good stories need someone who makes clever quips) and drop devastating bon mots; it was to tell the story of her adventuring band, and they really *were* starting to work together better, to function as a team. And, in their own way, to become heroes. I still didn't think they had much of a chance against the dragon (and I didn't particularly relish the thought of smelling Ratarian jerky flambé), but I was starting to have some faith in them. And, with a sense of duty and commitment that worried me a little because it made me think I might be maturing, I wanted to see it through to the end.

Which, of course, meant that I needed to do the thing I hate above almost all others: apologize.

"Nadi," I said quietly. She didn't hear me. I sighed. "Nadi," I said, louder.

She turned toward me. "Yes, Heloise?"

"Can I talk to you for a moment?"

She shook her head. "I think that anything you have to say can be said to the group."

I sighed again, louder. She was right, though. I was beginning to hate that about her.

Everyone gathered around me, save for Borg, who continued to keep watch on the tunnel (though it's possible he just hadn't started moving yet). "All right," I began, "in an effort to be funny a few minutes ago—"

"A very poor effort," interjected Nadi.

This time, it was my turn to glare, but she just shrugged. "Fine. In a very poor effort to be funny a few minutes ago, I suggested that the challenges that remain ahead of us—namely, the minotaur and the dragon—will be tough...which is true." I looked pointedly at Nadi, who tilted her head slightly to concede the point. "I also suggested that this hearty group had made some less-than-excellent decisions along the way that resulted in a longer road than was necessary." Nadi started to speak, but I held up my hand. "Let me finish. Sure, we probably could have done things better—but, hey, that's true for all of us in life generally."

"Speak for yourself, lute licker!" retorted Whiska.

"I've never once licked my lute."

"That's not what I heard," muttered Whiska.

"From who?" I asked, arching an eyebrow.

Whiska looked away and said something under her breath that sounded suspiciously like "your mom," but I didn't press her on it.

"What I'm trying to say is that, well, look—I've been around." Whiska's eyes lit up. "Not like that," I said before she could say anything. Then, I shrugged. "Maybe a little like that. The point is, I've met a lot of adventurers—some of them were successful, but most of them failed spectacularly. Why? Because adventuring is hard. *Really* hard, and it's kind of insane. I mean, who honestly thinks it's a good idea to walk into a dragon's lair for kicks?"

"Not for kicks," said Whiska solemnly. "For treasure. A fecal ton of treasure."

"Even for that reason, it's an absurd thing to do," I replied.

"If this is your big, inspirational speech, you might want to kick it up a notch," said Rummy politely.

"I'm getting there. I need to set the stage. I'm a storyteller, remember?"

"You're the professional," replied Rummy amiably. "Continue."

"Absurd though it may be, someone has to do it, or else good folks suffer and die. So, anyone who decides to take up the adventuring mantle is a hero from the start in my book. Even if they get killed by goblimites their first time out."

"What are goblimites?" asked Nadi.

"Really tiny goblins that are about the size of a squirrel," said Whiska, "and about half as dangerous as one."

"Yet, I know an adventuring group that was killed by some," I said.

"Really?" asked Rummy. "Like, knew them personally?"

"I know *of* an adventuring group that was killed by some," I amended.

"Think that really happened?" asked Rummy, looking around at the group. "I bet that's just a story."

"Fine. Whatever. The point is, adventuring takes courage, and you've all got that in spades. And, now that you've been through some scraps, you're starting to show more than just courage—you're showing competence. And chemistry. And charisma. And all sorts of other qualities that start with 'C.'"

"Coitus?" asked Whiska.

"Not a quality," I replied.

"Maybe not the way you do it," she said.

"I'm not sure you want to challenge me on that one."

"Goblimites are...delicious," said Borg over his shoulder.

"Wrap it up, maybe, Heloise? We've got a minotaur to find," interjected Nadi.

"Right. Look, I'm a little bit self-absorbed and I like to make fun of people. But, do you really think I'd be here with you now, hanging in on this crazy adventure, if I didn't believe in you? If I didn't believe you have the chance to do something special? The fact of the matter is that most adventurers don't do anything great—they either quit or get killed before they do anything noteworthy. Actual epic, legendary quests are few and far between. So, to be on a quest to fight a dragon—and a minotaur to boot—alongside a group that I think is actually capable of defeating both of those creatures? That's pretty much a bard's dream." I took a deep breath and blew it out slowly. "I guess what I'm trying to say is thank you for letting me be here with you, and for the chance to tell your story. I know it's going to be a great one—in some ways, it already is."

Much murmuring ensued, the cacophony of polite noises people make when they want to say thank you but don't really want to get into specifics or create any particularly emotional moments, which suited me just fine—emotions that aren't rapture, joy, or derision make me uncomfortable.

After a few minutes, we gathered up our gear and set off down the tunnel we thought might lead us to the minotaur—and, after that, the dragon.

CHAPTER 23

TURNS OUT MINOTAURS HAVE A FLATULENCE PROBLEM (ONE OF THEM, ANYWAY)

After a while, Whiska's map started to look like someone had plopped a bowl of spaghetti on top of a bowl of linguini. There were so many choices to make that we stopped trying to double back and apply any logic to our passage through the maze and started making directional choices based on who had the longest middle finger (Whiska, surprisingly—not Borg), the smallest feet (Rummy), or the silkiest, most beautiful hair anyone had ever seen (yours truly, naturally). We'd moved so far beyond hopelessly lost that hopeless would have been a welcome upgrade.

Rummy, of course, remained annoyingly cheerful, causing at least one of us to want to shove a long-heeled boot up his rectum (though all of us refrained from acting on that impulse, even if one of us surreptitiously sharpened the heel of one such boot just in case one of us decided to change her mind about not doing it). The rest of us alternated between grumbling and whining, and even even-keeled Nadi began scowling every time someone questioned our progress.

Telling time underground is a little bit like shaving a Borillian wiggle yak—difficult under even the best circumstances, but impossible without the right tools (and, frankly, not really worth the effort in either case—in the former situation, it doesn't really matter; in the latter, wiggle yak fur is coarse and you can never really get the smell of the beasts—which is like pine tree mixed with milk vomit—out of it). It's hard to say how long we stumbled around, but, based on consumption of our limited foodstuffs, at least a day and a half passed before our next notable encounter.

Tunnel goblins aren't the most intimidating or skilled of foes, but they are fast, numerous, and persistent. It turns out they also happily throw themselves into confrontations even where they're at an extreme disadvantage, as we discovered when a pack of them—around a dozen—ambushed us when we entered a small, low-ceilinged chamber somewhere around the time we finished the last of the dried cherries, which had saddened me (I love those things). Their shrill voices sang out gleefully as they rushed in, but their little swords and tiny clubs didn't do much to Borg, who stood closest to where they entered the chamber. He paused, swatted two of them out of the way with one giant fist, and then reported, "I think we...are under...attack." Pause. "By something...very small."

Nadi leaped into action, her sword slashing, cutting, and thrusting, sending four of the goblins to an early grave (or, at least, incapacitating them to the point where they could no longer ineffectually punch Borg). Whiska shouted something in the language of magic and shot spectral, acid-tipped arrows into three more of the creatures, and even Rummy and I got into the act, mace smashing and dagger stabbing our way through a few more. Borg squished the last one with his foot and then laughed. "Feels like...stepping on...jelly."

"Tunnel goblins," noted Whiska as she inspected the

corpse of one of the creatures Nadi had taken down. "We're close."

"What do you mean?" asked Rummy.

"Tunnel goblins always serve a stronger, more powerful master—often a minotaur. They're utterly useless in a fight—sort of like you—and they're morons—also sort of like you—but they're fast and good scouts—unlike you. They also breed so fast they make rabbits look like the Ascetics of Bava." (Ascetics of Bava, it should be noted, are not only not allowed to engage in conjugal relations, but need to chop off their means of engaging in said relations prior to joining the sect. I guess you could say that's the only sects they get after that point.)

(If anyone wants to hit a snare drum for me right now, I'd appreciate it.)

"So there will be more?" asked Nadi.

"Tons more," replied Whiska, lifting her nose to sniff the air. "That way." She pointed toward one of the tunnels that led out of the chamber. "They smell like something the garbage wouldn't let in. I should be able to track them by scent from here on in."

We formed up behind Whiska, Nadi right behind her, then me and Rummy, and Borg (slowly) bringing up the rear. Two rights and a jog to the left brought us into contact with another half dozen tunnel goblins, which we quickly dispatched. Several more scraps ensued, and though everyone managed to avoid major injury, the cumulative effect of nicks and scratches began to take a toll, as did the need for constant vigilance. Whiska had very nearly depleted her store of spells.

We entered a small cavern devoid of tunnel goblins and gratefully collapsed—most of us, anyway. Borg stayed on his feet to stand guard, and Nadi stalked a circuitous route around the cavern, sizing up the most defensible positions.

"Slurry?" asked Rummy, holding out a water skin that we

had filled with a pureed mix of salmon, water bugs, crayfish, and crackleshell worms. Highly nutritious, easy to carry, and tastes like shark vomit.

"No thanks," I said, pushing the skin away before the scent hit me and I promptly refunded everything I'd eaten over the past ten years.

Rummy shrugged and took a long pull before smacking his lips and sighing appreciatively. "Just like great Aunt Bubblekettle used to make."

"Bubblekettle?" I raised an eyebrow.

"My mother's maiden name. Auntie Bubs was a Master Chef, and a trailblazer—the first woman to hold the title in the settlement where my mom grew up. Kind of a family legend. And, bar none, the greatest slurry maker who ever lived."

"I think that's a low bar," I said.

Rummy shrugged. "Come to the Danar Slurryfest with me some year and you'll change your tune." He winked.

"Is that supposed to be a bard joke?"

"Only if you thought it was funny."

"So, it wasn't a bard joke."

"I guess not."

"If you two are done with the lack of comedy routine, maybe we can come up with a plan for what we do now," interjected Nadi.

"Sure thing, Nadi," chirped Rummy. "Slurry?" He held up the skin.

She deliberated for a moment before reluctantly nodding. "We need to keep up our strength." She shuddered only a little as she swallowed a big mouthful of the lukewarm liquid. "We need some rest." She nodded toward Whiska.

"This cavern seems...defensible," said Borg, turning his head slowly to survey the small room. "I am...not tired. I... will stand guard."

Nadi nodded her thanks before turning to Whiska. "Is

three hours enough time for you to recover and study your spells?"

"How in the name of Lapidius's poop tunnel are you going to know when three hours have passed down here in the dark?" returned Whiska, who, for once, wasn't being needlessly vulgar, but was simply using a common Ratarian colloquialism. Lapidius is a key god in the Ratarian pantheon, and his poop tunnel is the passageway through which Ratarians who have lived a good life gain access to their version of heaven. I should note that "poop" in the Ratarian tongue means "heaven" (which should tell you something about Ratarians), and those who lived a "good life" are those souls who, by virtue of their bluntness, cleverness, and intestinal fortitude, managed to amass considerable treasure hoards. I will, for once, refrain from editorializing, but only because Ratarians make it too easy.

Nadi bit back a retort. "How long do you need to rest?"

"I'll tell you when I'm done." With that, Whiska sank to the ground, grabbed a nearby rock for a pillow, and started snoring in less than three seconds.

"Let me know when you need a rest," Nadi said to Borg, patting him on the arm. She sat down, cross-legged, and fell into the elven state of reverie—a state somewhere between sleep and wakefulness. Sort of like smoking the hashish pipe, though Nadi doesn't particularly like it when I compare the sacred elven ritual of communing with the inner-self to toking a Cantarian spliff.

I looked at Rummy, who shrugged and laid out his bedroll. I took my own bedroll from my pack and did the same. Half-elves can't engage in reverie; only full-blooded elves have the ability to do that, which is unfortunate, because a few hours spent in reverie is like getting a full eight hours of sleep. Think of how much more I could get done without having to sleep. So many shoes to try on, not to mention so much wit and wisdom to dispense.

Sleeping while adventuring is a strange thing. Obviously, you need sleep while you're questing about to kill this dragon or find that treasure, and sometimes you need to do it when you're surrounded by things that want to kill you (or, at least, eat your liver, even if they are generally indifferent to the prospect of your continued respiration), but those aren't exactly ideal conditions for closing your eyes and falling into a peaceful slumber, you know? You have to learn to trick your brain. That guttural growling coming from the kobold encampment nearby? That's the sound of gentle thunder rolling through the sky, presaging the soothing pitter patter of a soft spring rain. The raucous roiling of an active volcano that could explode at any minute? Just the hungry stomach of a fellow adventurer. The ear-splitting snoring of a Ratarian wizard? Simply the sweet, final symphony of a companion soon to be murdered in her sleep by a beautiful half-elf.

Beyond being able to block out the sounds of impending death, you also need to place incredible trust in your companions, whom you're relying on to literally guard your life. It can take a while to build that trust, so you end up spending a long sequence of nights only half-sleeping, which means you're exhausted (and half-sleeping) during the day, too. The only advantage to that state of being is that it can be confusing for zombies, who aren't sure whether to eat your brains or make zombie small talk with you ("Grrrr frrrmmm urrggblat?" "Grumph. Hrrrmmm." "Craaaaa.").

(Incidentally, that all loosely translates as, "Don't you think elven brains are the best?" "I prefer human." "You're cray-cray.")

Fortunately, by this point, we had developed enough trust in each other that I felt comfortable closing my eyes. Check that—I had developed enough confidence in Borg as a sentry to close my eyes (sure, he wasn't the swiftest thinker or mover, but he had surprisingly good hearing and a deep, booming voice, so I trusted him to not only raise the alarm in time, but to do so at a volume that would wake even those of us who have a tendency toward particularly deep states of repose (I like to think it's because I'm tapping into some small piece of reverie...but I'm probably just a really heavy sleeper)).

Nadi shook my shoulder gently a while later. "Breakfast?" I said hopefully.

"Only if you want slurry cakes."

"I'd rather starve."

"You may get your chance."

I sighed. "Time to move?"

Nadi nodded. "Whiska just needs a few more minutes to finish studying her spells."

"Speaking of starving...what *are* we going to do if we don't find the minotaur—or a way out of here—sometime soon?" I asked casually, not even a little bit worried (she said, convincingly).

"Think tunnel goblins are edible?"

"Maybe for Whiska."

"I don't know, Heloise." Nadi sighed. "We're so far underground, and so lost...I just don't know." She had big circles under her eyes. Clearly, reverie wasn't all it was cracked up to be. Or maybe the stress made it hard for her to do it properly.

I put a hand on her arm and squeezed. "We'll figure this out. This is a pretty resourceful group." A few feet away, Whiska belched. Borg tittered. "Not classy, mind you, but resourceful."

"Thanks." She looked away as her eyes teared up. She cleared her throat. "Finish packing your gear—we move out in five."

A few minutes later, we were on the move, making our way cautiously down yet another tunnel.

THEY SAY that sometimes it's better to be lucky than good, but I find that "they" say a lot of things, and I kind of think "they" are smug, know-it-all assholes.

Still, there's something to be said for a stroke of good fortune when you're in a tight spot, and, after another day of wandering, we were in desperate need of exactly that. Fortunately, it turns out that Rummy's supply of luck corresponds with his annoyingly high levels of optimism. Just as we (or, at least, the most attractive member of our group) were about to mutiny, Rummy, in an effort to intercede and play peacemaker, took a step forward, tripped on a rock, windmilled his arms like a drunk hummingbird, and stumbled headfirst into a wall that turned out not to be a wall, based on the fact that there was no painful thud when he hit it and the fact that we could no longer see him.

"Rummy!" called Nadi, eyes wide. "What just happened?"

"Did he fall in a hole?" I asked. From where I stood, I hadn't gotten a good look at what had happened. "Kind of looked like he fell in a hole. He's not that tall, you know, or even that bright, though I'll grant that he's pretty street smart and is really good at—"

"He didn't fall into a hole—I saw him hit the wall, and pretty hard," replied Nadi. "Rummy? Rummy!"

"I'm all right!" came Rummy's voice from the wall.

"Ah, crap on a cracker!" said Whiska. "Did you get turned into a wall? Because we're leaving you here if you did. I'm done talking to rocks!"

"I didn't get turned into a wall," said Rummy. "I just fell through one. Actually, I don't think it's a wall at all." Suddenly, he reappeared, having apparently stepped *through* the wall.

"It's an illusion!" cried Whiska.

"Certainly seems that way," said Rummy, nodding. "There's a passageway on the other side."

"Way to sniff that one out, wizard," I said, slow clapping in Whiska's general direction.

"I will turn you into a glorphid," she responded, narrowing her eyes dangerously.

"I have no idea what that is," I returned.

"An insect that, when pregnant, must crawl up a yak's anus to lay its eggs or else it dies a horrible, painful, bloated death."

"I'd rather not be one of those."

"Don't insult me again."

"Duly noted."

"Perhaps we should check out my discovery?" interjected Rummy.

"'*Discovery*' might be giving you a bit more credit than you deserve," I noted.

"Not now, Heloise," said Nadi through clenched teeth. "Rummy—lead the way."

We plunged through the illusory wall and found ourselves in a well-lit stone passageway.

"Dwarves worked this tunnel or I'm a glorphid," said Rummy as he ran his hand along the wall.

"Does that mean this is a dwarven complex?" asked Nadi.

Rummy shrugged. "Probably was originally. I doubt it is now—dwarves don't tend to get on too well with dragons and minotaurs. I'd guess that the dwarves are long gone. Someone's been using this tunnel recently, though." He gestured toward the torches that lined the wall.

Whiska muttered something and then held up her staff, which glowed orange. She shook her head. "Maybe not—those are magic torches. There's an enchantment on them to make them stay permanently lit."

"That seems like a pretty handy spell. Can any old wizard cast that sort of thing?" I asked Whiska. "Not that you're old, I mean. That wasn't an insult."

"No—you'd need a pretty powerful wizard for that kind of magic."

"Do minotaurs do spells?" asked Rummy.

Whiska shook her head again. "'*Do*' spells? You don't '*do*' spells, you five-toed waste of hair surface! You cast them. You *cast* spells."

"How many toes do you have?" asked Rummy curiously.

"Four—the optimal number. Unlike you overbalanced flatfoots."

"I had no idea that was the optimal number. Learned something new today, I guess." Rummy shook his head with what looked like...was that wonder? Sometimes I hate that guy and his wide-eyed innocence. "Okay, so do minotaurs *cast* spells?"

"No—not that I'm aware of, anyway."

"Who do you think enchanted the torches, then?" asked Nadi. "The dwarves who built the tunnel?"

Whiska looked ready to unleash a rant, but Rummy held up a hand. "I've got this." He turned toward Nadi. "Dwarves do—er, cast—some magic, it's true, but it's not the same as what a wizard like Whiska might, um, cast. Lots of healing spells, spells to make barley grow underground—for ale, you know—and other things that might be practical in battle or for strengthening weapons and armor. Accent lighting—well, that's unlikely to be a dwarven magic user's forte."

"You said that too nicely, but you're right," confirmed Whiska.

"Doesn't really matter," said Nadi. "Let's just see where this tunnel leads. Weapons ready. I've got point—fall in line behind. Borg, cover the rear."

We did as Nadi bid and began slowly working our way down the passageway. A moment later, I heard Borg chuckling softly. I glanced over my shoulder and saw that he had placed his hand over his (fairly gargantuan) backside. I raised an eyebrow.

"Covering...the rear," he whispered. He winked the kind of wink an actor in a pantomime might use to let the entire audience know he had just told a major lie, except that he closed the wrong eye, so he ended up blinking with the eye he hadn't widened, which made the gesture seem mildly spastic.

"Do you not know how to wink?" I whispered in response.

"No," he said softly.

The tunnel twisted and turned but, thankfully, didn't branch off at any point. Eventually, Nadi slowed, and then held up her hand, signaling us all to stop. She gestured for us to stay put while she crept forward silently and disappeared around a bend up ahead. A few minutes later, she came back, making less than a whisper of sound. She was good.

She motioned for us to walk back down the tunnel a ways, which we did, albeit not quite as quietly. Whiska belching didn't help matters, nor did Borg loudly pulverizing a rock by accidentally stepping on it. Once we had moved far enough to satisfy her, she leaned in, motioning for us all to do the same.

"Tunnel goblins up ahead," she whispered. "A lot of them, from the sounds of it."

"How far?" I asked.

"Hard to say—sound travels strangely down here, and I didn't want to risk getting too far down the passageway without you. They're close, though."

"What's the plan?" asked Rummy.

"I would say we go in fast and hard behind the brightest spell Whiska has, but tunnel goblins weren't the only thing I heard," replied Nadi. She looked back over her shoulder before turning back to us. "I heard something else—another voice, much deeper and more guttural."

I raised a perfectly sculpted eyebrow. I'd taken a moment during our last rest to ensure that it remained immaculate and artfully formed; good grooming is important even in the face of imminent death. "Minotaur?"

Nadi shrugged. "I've never heard one talk before. If I was a betting woman, though..."

"Five gold!" shouted Whiska. Nadi frantically shushed her. Voice lower, but with undiminished enthusiasm, she continued. "No, no—ten gold! *Twenty!*"

"Quiet!" Nadi silently screamed (by which I mean she mouthed the word with animated vigor). "What in the name of Tenelor's Mourning Ballad are you talking about?"

"I love Tenelor's Mourning Ballad!" I replied. "It was one of the first songs I learned. The best part about it is how you can vary the key every time you—"

"Not now, Heloise," said Nadi, pointedly but not unkindly. She turned back to Whiska. "Now then...what?"

"You wanted to bet. I'm betting you. I want to bet you so much gold that it'll be pouring out of my powerful hindquarters."

"Now there's an image that might scare away a minotaur," said Rummy amiably, "and a half-dwarf, half-halfling."

"It was a figure of speech!" replied an exasperated Nadi.

"Oh." Whiska's face fell for a moment before brightening again. "Well, at least we're getting closer to the gold, right? If we're close to the minotaur, we must be getting close to the dragon." Her eyes glinted and she cackled as she rubbed her hands together, blue tendrils of energy crackling gently across her fingertips.

I looked at Nadi and said, in elvish (which, admittedly, was not my strongest language, albeit better than my orcish), "The one who appears as if to be made from the sexy times of two giant rats and smells in the manner of a horse's fragrant after-meal leavings may punch-face friendly friends when close to all of the shiny stuff you can use to buy ham."

"Ham?" repeated Nadi, also in elvish (obviously), and slightly bewildered.

I nodded, reasonably confident that I'd used the right word. "Ham."

Nadi's brow furrowed as she parsed what I thought had been a reasonably coherent statement. "Wait—do you mean *lurcschus* or *lurcschut*?"

I raised an eyebrow.

"*Lurcschus* means things."

I frowned. "What did I say?"

"*Lurcschut.*"

"What does that mean?"

"Ham."

"I didn't mean to say 'ham.' I definitely meant 'things.'"

"That's what I thought."

"You got everything else, though, right?"

Nadi half shrugged and half nodded. "More or less. I think." She looked at Whiska, who was, inexplicably, still cackling. "We'll keep an eye on her."

"So," said Rummy, sticking his face in between us. "I think it would probably be better to share the details of your brilliant plan in the common tongue."

"Right," said Nadi. "I think we need to assume the minotaur is in there, along with a significant number of tunnel goblins—which means we need to go in more carefully."

"Why?" said Whiska. "That's stupid. You had it right the first time—we go in hard and fast."

"It's not like orcish lovemaking," I replied. "We need to be cautious and feel things out slowly because we don't know what's going on or what we're doing and if we're not careful we're going to be in a real mess." I paused. "Like human lovemaking."

"I agree," said Nadi.

"How do you know how humans make love?" asked Rummy.

Nadi blushed. "I meant about the approach."

"Oh." Rummy looked at me. "I was hoping there was a story there."

"We should...divide our forces," said Borg. "Nadi and I... go first. Distract them. While...they fight us...Heloise and Rummy...work around...the edges." He took a breath—this was a lot of talking for him. "Whiska comes...in last. She... hits hard while...attention is elsewhere."

Nadi chewed her lower lip, then nodded. "It's a good plan. Good thinking, Borg. Any objections?"

Nods all around, except from Whiska, who shrugged. "I still think I should just fling a fireball in there."

"You may still get that chance, so keep it ready," replied Nadi.

"That's like telling a flaccidon to hang loose," scoffed Whiska. (Flaccidons are small lizards that spend most of their days sprawling limply in the sunlight.)

"All right, then." Nadi drew her sword and pointed it down the hallway. "Let's do this."

✦

You'd be surprised how many tunnel goblins even a rock giant who's not that good of a fighter can take down with a single swing of a club. (It's seven, incidentally.) With Borg and Nadi leading the way, we blitzed our way into the cavern, scattering tunnel goblins left and right. Nadi scythed her way through a half dozen in short order, and even Rummy and I managed to cut down a significant quantity. (Two, incidentally, is a significant quantity in my book.)

It wasn't the tunnel goblins that presented the problem, however—it was the two ogres and the exceedingly large minotaur that also occupied the cavern, and none of the three looked all that happy to see us (though who can tell with ogres; they always look like they just sat on a pinecone). Fortunately, Whiska, following hard on our heels, was more than ready to unleash magical destruction, bombarding the trio with a massive fireball the moment she entered the room.

Based on the way they started rolling around on the ground and screaming, the fire caused the ogres some pretty serious pain. Funny thing about minotaurs, though, and something that none of us had known before we walked into the room that day: they're immune to fire. Hitting one with a fireball is pretty much the same as tossing a fluffy kitten who really loves to lick people onto its back. So, it wasn't the most effective opening salvo.

One of the ogres tried to climb to its feet, but Nadi slashed it across the face. The beast collapsed, grabbing at its nose and roaring. At least a dozen tunnel goblins screeched and ran around the room, caroming off the walls like popping corn, but didn't move to attack us. The overwhelming scent of what I assumed was burned ogre flesh hung heavy in the air, and it was all I could do not to vomit. I quickly tied my hair behind my head, just in case—getting puke smell out of luxurious hair like mine takes forever.

The minotaur, however, did make a move to attack, as did the other ogre, who was not as badly burned as his companion. Rummy valiantly tried to strike the ogre, but ended up getting clobbered by its club and fell straight backward, his head hitting the ground hard and his legs flopping up into the air. The way his legs remained up in the air, twitching slightly, would have been comical had he been on the stage overacting a dramatic death; given that he was, however, in the midst of a life-or-death fight and no longer appeared to be conscious, it was terrifying.

Nadi moved to help, but the minotaur cut her off, snorting and holding a huge, double-bladed axe in its right hand. It slapped the middle part of the handle into its left hand and then swung with both hands, a violent swing that, had it connected, would have not only separated her head from her body, but likely pulverized it in the process. Fortunately, it didn't, Nadi having deftly ducked under the swing and rolled through the minotaur's legs, coming up behind it. She raised her sword to swing, but blanched and fell back, coughing. I wondered if the scent of barbecued ogre had overcome her.

Borg stepped closer to the minotaur, though I wasn't sure even his rocky skin would protect him much if the minotaur hit him full force. Borg seemed a little uncertain, too, judging by the way he held his club up in a defensive posture.

I could hear Whiska muttering behind me, preparing another spell, though she had to break off to shout, "Get out of the way, you pebble-brained paperweight!" in what for Whiska was a very kind effort to suggest that her companion remove himself from the line of fire.

Borg nodded, but had to stand in and deflect, at least partially, two blows from the minotaur's axe before he could move. Both strikes grazed Borg's skin, with the second shaving off a thin slice that clattered to the floor. I winced, though Borg didn't show any outward sign of pain.

He stepped to the side and Whiska, who had resumed her muttering, stepped forward and yelled, "Eat hot lightning, burger lips!" as she unleashed a bolt of energy from her staff.

The minotaur's muscles seized and he stiffened, making him look like a giant stuffed statue. The effect didn't last long, though. In a matter of seconds, the great beast shook its gargantuan head, its massive lips flapping like an angry donkey's. The minotaur snarled and raised its axe over its head, muscles rippling, and I stepped backward, over-whelmed by two thoughts: the first being that we were prob-ably screwed, and the second that minotaurs are sort of hot in a scary and gross kind of way.

Nadi had managed to work her way around to Rummy, but the remaining ogre had turned its attention to her. I drew my knife and moved to intercept the big ugly brute, but stum-bled to my knees as I passed by the minotaur, overcome with an odor that can only be described as flaming feces mated with rancid dead possum flesh. I covered my nose and kept going, surprised that Whiska's energy bolt had so badly singed the minotaur as to create such an ungodly stench.

The ogre's reaction to my valiant attempt to prevent it from getting to Nadi was about the same as my reaction to most guys hitting on me after a performance: a derisive snort, a dismissive wave of the hand, and then an immediate focus on what's for dinner (I could only hope that, in this case, I wasn't on the menu). It didn't even feel the need to turn its club on me, choosing instead to raise its hand to backhand me into the wall—and in all likelihood, unconsciousness.

Fortunately, I'm as quick as I am skilled at singing, and I managed to duck underneath the blow, though it passed by so closely that the hair on the left side of my head streamed behind me like it had been hit with a stiff breeze. I countered with a knife strike to the knee, one of my two primary go-to moves (my secondary move, really, which I had to go with because the ogre's pelvis was turned at an angle that precluded my primary and preferred target).

In the next ten seconds, I learned two important facts: one, even relatively small blades like mine can cause ogres some serious pain, and two, ogres get really mad when you cause them serious pain. The creature reached down, grabbed me by the shoulders, and tossed me toward the wall; only my uncanny agility saved me (well, that, and my unbelievable luck, given that the ogre threw me into a section of the wall covered by spongy lichen, which cushioned the impact). Fortunately, I managed to hold onto my knife in the process, though I did accidentally nick my thigh when I landed. It was embarrassing to have first blood drawn by myself.

As I recovered from a wound that, in my later recounting of the event, was both considerably more serious and inflicted by a demon from the fourth level of

Halazar, Nadi knelt next to Rummy and shook him gently. His legs fell back down, making him look slightly less ridiculous (he still looked a little ridiculous, because half-dwarves, half-halflings are just generally ridiculous-looking beings). He was out cold, though, so Nadi rolled him out of the way the best she could and sprang back to her feet, just in time to see the minotaur bring his axe down on Borg's club.

So much for that club. I didn't think it was possible for wood to explode, but I can now say with certainty that it can, and splinters in the eyes are about as much fun as hookworms in the urethra (don't ask how I know that). Fortunately, the club absorbed the brunt of the shock and Borg seemed none the worse for wear, though he did look a little stunned and, for the first time since I'd known him, worried. He staggered back as Whiska circled around the perimeter and seemed unsure exactly how to attack the monster.

"Whiska!" I yelled, hoping to snap her out of it and at least narrow her focus. "The ogre!"

She looked confused for a moment, but then nodded vigorously and raised her staff. After a few magical words, a steady stream of magical darts sprang forth, striking the ogre in the chest and knocking it backward.

Nadi waded in and seized the opportunity to strike, driving her sword into the creature's neck as it swatted frantically at its chest in an attempt to soothe the stinging pain from the darts. The ogre became considerably, and rightly, more concerned with the giant blade that had just severed its jugular, lunging weakly at Nadi as she drew the blade back. Blood spurted like fireworks from the beast's neck and it collapsed to its knees before falling face-down on the floor, feet flopping up in the air one time before coming to rest on the stony floor.

The ogre's death seemed to terrify the tunnel goblins, who streamed past us and fled the chamber, leaving the four conscious (but weakened) members of our band to face one very angry minotaur.

"Drop your weapon and surrender and we won't kill you," said Nadi boldly.

The minotaur stared at Nadi and grunted. A low rumbling filled the cavern.

Whiska, now standing next to the unarmed Borg, gagged and hacked. She looked up at the giant, lips curled. "Gods, man! What did you eat—a sick baby's diaper?"

So overpowering was the stench that even Rummy, still unconscious, coughed.

"Was that really you, Borg?" I asked, eyes watering.

"Drop it, minotaur!" yelled Nadi, somehow still focused, despite the fact that she was clearly swallowing hard and repeatedly in an attempt to choke back the vomit.

"It wasn't...me," said Borg solemnly. "I've been...framed."

The minotaur growled and swung its axe at Nadi, who ducked and danced deftly backward.

"It's not like him to not own it, Whiska," I called, moving around behind the minotaur in an effort to try to figure out a way to help Nadi.

"Smell my...butt," said Borg. "It's...clean. Or...not that gross...anyway."

Naturally, the Ratarian did exactly that, leaning in close to our rocky companion's enormous backside and inhaling deeply. Her eyes widened, and I thought maybe Borg had been lying after all.

"He's right!" said Whiska, shocked. "It wasn't him!" She looked at me, eyes narrowed. "I should have known that something that smelled like someone smeared monkey dung on a sweaty ogre's taint could only have some from a 'dainty' woman who never lets these things out!"

"You think that was me??" I called, outraged, as Nadi danced back in to test the minotaur's defenses with a few tentative strikes, which the beast easily parried.

"Whoever smelt it…" sang Whiska.

"*You* smelled it, you plague-carrying sewer swimmer!"

"We all smelled it!" yelled Nadi, stabbing at the minotaur again. "Focus!"

"Yeah, but that smelled like an old person threw up yogurt all over a dead skunk!" answered Whiska. "We need to figure out where that came from."

The minotaur, moving with an agility that belied its bulk, spun around and hacked at a surprised Whiska, who only barely managed to dodge, sparks flying from her staff as it slammed into the ground to keep her upright. The beast's back was to Nadi now, and that same angry, low rumbling sound returned.

"Argh!" screamed Nadi, dropping her sword and covering her mouth with both hands. "It smells like a hill giant's morning breath after it ate three dirty dwarves!" She spat, trying to somehow get the taste out of her nose and mouth.

"Dwarves don't smell any worse than anyone else, you know," I felt compelled to add, just before the stench washed over me and I had to turn my attention to preventing the mushrooms I'd snacked on earlier from working their way violently back up and out.

"It's him!" shrieked Whiska, pointing at the minotaur. "He's the source! Gods! It's like some horrible creature died inside his colon and is being blown out of his ass by a cyclone!"

"You owe me an apology!" I choked out as I circled around, not for the purpose of gaining a tactical advantage, but in an attempt to find a pocket of fresh air. Unfortunately, when you're miles underground, there's not much airflow, and the cavern had quickly turned into a miasma of stink, like someone had dropped an orc's foot into a pig waller after the pig, who'd been on a steady diet of spicy, rotten lamb, had shat in it.

"I'll apologize over my dead body!" retorted Whiska, raising her staff for another magical strike on the minotaur.

"Gods willing you'll get killed right now," I shot back. "Your festering corpse might actually make the room smell better." Sometimes adventuring is really, really not glamorous.

"*Focus!*" roared Nadi again, picking up her sword.

Whiska responded by loosing a purple bolt of energy at the minotaur, who grunted when it hit him in the chest, but it didn't seem to do much damage. He did, however, glare at Nadi and, in a thick, heavily accented voice that sounded like pebbles slowly rolling down a hill, said, "I have irritable bowels—it's nothing to be ashamed of!" He raised his axe and hurled it.

Whiska tried to dive out of the way, but the broad side of the axe clipped her on the shoulder. She screamed and tumbled onto her back.

"Bad move, swamp cheeks!" I shouted, hurling my own knife at the minotaur's back. He turned his glare on me as the knife bounced off his tough hide. He looked kind of mad.

"I was talking about your butt cheeks, by the way," I said quietly. "Not the cheeks on your face. Which are, um, just lovely." I smiled sweetly, but even though that same smile has brought emperors to their knees, saved (and destroyed) kingdoms, and gotten me a ten percent discount on coffee, the minotaur didn't seem even a little bit impressed. Maybe he was blind in addition to being flatulent—that would explain all the squint-glaring.

The minotaur took an intimidating step toward me. I backed away slowly. Okay, well, not that slowly—pretty fast, actually. Unfortunately, I quickly ran out of real estate and had my back literally up against the wall. "Flatulence is cool!" I said, desperately. "I mean, it's pretty hot! The ladies love it! Wait—are there lady minotaurs? There are, right? Because they must love the smell of rotting fish mixed with severed, gangrenous fingers! It's nature's aphrodisiac!"

Look, I'm generally pretty good under pressure. I once did my nails while sitting on the rim of the Palador Volcano, which is the most active volcano in all of Erithea (it actually erupted three times before I finished my pedicure). But, I had a little breakdown as that minotaur bore down on me. I'm not proud of what I did or said. For the record, I really don't think farts that smell like burnt sloth vomit are even a little arousing. There are a lot of heroes who refuse to compromise their values to survive. Most of them are dead. If I need to tell some hairy cow that his rectal halitosis gets me all hot and bothered in order to make him pause just long enough before he cuts my head off to give the weird rat wizard in my adventuring party an extra minute to hit him with an ice storm so I can escape, I'll do it every time. *Every. Single. Time.*

Thankfully, that's exactly what happened—the axe came up but paused as the minotaur considered my incoherently steady stream of fawning praise recognizing the glory of his gassiness (I can really sling it—and sell it—when I need to; it's all part of being a performer). At that moment, Whiska hit him with a cone of ice, which, it turns out, minotaurs are highly susceptible to. The beast fell backwards and, mercifully, the cold snap managed to blunt, albeit not eradicate, the stench. Nothing short of an exorcism by the world's most powerful cleric might manage that, and, even then, my money was on the stink.

The minotaur stumbled and fell hard onto its backside, though the hard landing produced both a grunt and yet another cloud of noxious gas, which quickly overpowered the cold air around the minotaur and raged around the chamber, turning the simple act of respiration into an endurance test the likes of which would leave even the most hardened of mountathoners gasping and crying and begging for the sweet release of painful evisceration. (Mountathoners, incidentally, are those questionably sane health enthusiasts who routinely run—at full speed—up, over, and down mountains that are at least five miles high for no reason other than that it allegedly makes them feel good; not a single one of them is any fun at parties.)

Nadi, however, didn't hesitate, proving her courage a dozen times over by bursting through the green haze of gut-watering stench, mouth unwisely open in a battle cry, and raising her sword over her head before bringing it crashing down on the minotaur's neck. At the same moment, Borg sprang into action (I say "sprang" for dramatic effect, "deliberately sauntered" being a more accurate descriptor), grabbing a massive rock from the cavern floor and bringing it down hard on the beast's face.

From its prone position, arms splayed out wide, the minotaur couldn't defend itself, and both blows struck home at the same time. Nadi's blade plunged into the creature's neck while Borg's bash blew the beast's nose to bits, splaying it across its hairy, and now painfully contorted, face.

Nadi didn't relent, pulling her blade out and plunging it right back in a few inches to the left. Blood spurted, and though the beast roared in rage, it was an impotent rage, like when a raving old misogynist who loses his town council seat to an eminently more capable young woman can't stop decrying the dissolution of family values (in that instance, I suppose it's redundant to say "eminently more capable" when I'm saying "woman"; I apologize for the unnecessary, if correct, words). The minotaur shuddered and twitched, hands flailing, and managed to clip Nadi in the left thigh, which sent her stumbling backward. The damage was done, though, and the foul cow stopped moving a moment later, blood still slowly pooling beneath it. A stray tunnel goblin, the last one in the cavern, shrieked and doffed its cap (why it was wearing a cap, I have no idea) before racing down the tunnel from which we'd entered the room, leaving four conscious but very tired and one unconscious but presumably better rested adventuring companions and one minotaur corpse alone with our thoughts.

Whiska reached Rummy first, reaching into one of her pouches and producing a small vial filled with bright blue liquid. She popped the stopper off and poured the contents into Rummy's mouth. She tipped his head back and plugged his nose, forcing him to swallow. He coughed and sputtered and, miraculously, sat up a moment later, eyes wide. "That stuff tastes like...well, like the air in here smells." He wrinkled his nose. "What in the name of Goolydar's dangled digit *is* that?"

(Goolydar is a halfling god who...you know what? It's not that interesting of a story. It's a stupid colloquialism that's meaningless. Trust me.)

"That," said Nadi with a satisfied smile, "is the smell of victory."

Rummy's face soured. "I hate to be so crass, especially when we apparently won, but, well...victory smells like minotaur diarrhea."

We made a unanimous decision to relocate to another chamber that smelled slightly less fragrant. We found one not too far away. Unfortunately, the mobility and endurance of minotaur farts is ungodly, so it took a few tries to find a spot where the air was at least moderately fresher. Of course, then we realized that the stench had permeated our jury-rigged clothing, which made burning it a necessity, beyond the obvious crime against fashion we committed each additional moment we spent in them. Unfortunately, that would have to wait.

Once we'd found a spot we could sort of breathe, we brought Rummy up to speed and kicked around options for what to do next. We still didn't have much in the way of food, and we still didn't know where to find the dragon. Fortunately, adventurers have a high incidence of fate intervening to help them, if only because fate so often wants to kill them.

Just as we began to debate which way to go, a tunnel goblin wandered in, nonchalantly gnawing on a strip of jerky (I shuddered to think what animal that jerky came from; my guesses included pony, giant spider, human, and, most disgustingly of all, cow). We jumped to our feet and grabbed for our weapons, but the goblin seemed in no hurry to engage. It took another bite of jerky, swallowed hard, and said, "You go left," pointing to the right.

We traded confused (and, in Whiska's case, murderous) looks. "Excuse me?" replied Nadi.

"Left," the goblin said again, pointing more emphatically to the right.

"Always struggled with that too," said Rummy cheerfully. "I think you mean 'right,' friend," said Rummy, pointing helpfully in the same direction.

The goblin shook its head vigorously. "No! Left! You need to left this place and go that way!"

"Ah, so more of a tense issue than a directional one," said Rummy with a nod. "Makes sense."

"No it doesn't, you goat-touching half-brain!" said Whiska.

"I've never actually touched a goat," mused Rummy. "I bet they're not very soft. Well, maybe the babies are. They're cute, at least."

"Why would we go that way?" said Nadi before Whiska could unleash another stream of invective.

"Find dragon! Go left. Secret passage." The goblin paused to bite, chew, and swallow again. Then he made a gesture that either meant "find a secret passage" or "I have incredible constipation."

"Why would you help us?" asked Nadi.

"Want you get dragon eaten! Then goblins rule tunnels with stinky minotaur dead." It laughed, a shrill bark that sounded like a hyena on laughing gas getting goosed by a candlestick.

"Points for honesty," said Rummy, nodding amiably at the goblin, who returned the gesture in kind before sauntering off on its way in the direction opposite where it said the dragon waited.

Nadi shook her head as she watched it go, then reached out to stay Whiska's hand before she could raise her staff to blast the goblin in the back. "Let it go," she said. Then, she looked at me. "Do we trust it?"

I shrugged. "What else do we have to go on?"

"The goblin's laugh…hurts my ears," said Borg.

"Heloise is right," said Rummy. "We've got nothing to lose by trusting it."

"Unless it's sending us into a trap," replied Nadi.

"Do you really think it's smart enough to do that?" I countered. "And, even if it is, we have no idea where to go, and I am *not* staying down here long enough to be eaten by Whiska —or to have to eat Whiska, which is an even more distressing thought."

"Agreed," said Whiska.

"All right," said Nadi. "Let's go find that dragon."

"And some new clothes," I added. "I really don't want to die in something that looks like haute couture in an insane asylum and smells like a butcher's block in a restaurant that only serves obese cats."

CHAPTER 24

THROUGH BLOOD AND FIRE OUR HEROES EMERGE TRIUMPHANT

After coercing an evil goblin, a foul servant of the mighty dragon, into giving them directions that were straight and true, our brave band of heroes soon found themselves at the entrance of the mighty wyrm's lair. Heat permeated the heavy air in the surrounding tunnels, residual warmth from the sleeping dragon's flaming snores—a reminder that, even slumbering, this was a creature to be feared and awed. The heroes hoped—prayed, even, to all the gods of Erithea—that they might take the beast unawares, but the dragon's hearing was so acute that even Nadinta's soft footfalls alerted it to danger and caused it to growl and stir. It bolted upright and attacked immediately, sparing not even a fraction of its awesome power as it blasted the entrance to the grand cave, melting rock and treasure alike in its terrible wrath.

"No one dares to enter my lair!" roared the great and powerful red, its thunderous voice shaking the walls and bringing a rain of stones and dust down upon our heroes' heads—heads that

remained unmelted only through the timely and powerful magic of Whiska, whose eldritch ice shield withstood the beast's great blast.

Nadinta wasted little time in rallying her mighty band, running headlong into battle with her sword poised to strike and the battle song of Cordalain, the ancient elven sect of indomitable warriors, on her lips. She struck hard and fast, her keen-edged blade slipping between the scaly, armored hide of the dragon.

The beast roared in pain, whipping its head around and thrashing its tail, which connected with Borgunder Gunderbor and sent him flying into the wall with a sickening crunch, the force of the blow so powerful that even the rock giant's nigh-unbreakable bones cracked and shattered.

"No!" screamed Whiska, whose tears streamed freely down the long contours of her face as she considered the prone form of her dear friend sprawled across the cavern floor, his arms and legs bent at impossible angles. She channeled her pain into rage and then into magic, waving her hands in arcane, intricate gestures while she invoked words in the language of magic.

Powerful bolts of energy leapt from her outstretched fingers and sped toward the dragon's chest, striking with explosive force. The dragon's head snapped up and it roared; the echoes of its rage could be heard for miles and miles, as far as away as the nearest village, whose residents suffered violent nightmares that night, with visions of fire and blood causing them to sit bolt upright in their beds.

The great wyrm turned its attention on Whiska and unleashed its mighty breath, intent on destroying the creature that had dared to cause it pain. Whiska moved quickly, diving away from the blast, though she did not escape harm entirely. Her tail was caught within the blistering flames, and she howled in pain.

Nadinta continued her assault, striking the dragon again and again, but despite the might of her blade, she could inflict only limited damage. Rumscrabble Tooltinker fared even worse, his little mace bouncing off the dragon's tough hide as though it were made of rubber.

Things looked grim for our heroes. The beast was simply too powerful, too large, too vicious; what could they do against such awesome might?

The beast inhaled deeply, preparing one final blast of fire to immolate the irritating interlopers who had dared to intrude upon his domain.

Suddenly, Nadinta paused. A voice sang out, calling her. Without thinking, she turned and dove into the nearest pile of treasure, pawing at it frantically. She sifted gold to the side, flung bejeweled chalices behind her, and paused only briefly as she hefted a heavy metal candlestick before tossing it aside as well. For beneath that mound of nearly incalculable wealth lay the source of the song, a sword that sang so sweetly that it succored her in her time of stress.

She wrapped her hand around the hilt and it hummed all the louder and, vibrating in her hand, all but forced her to turn back toward the dragon. The beast had completed its mighty inhalation and opened its maw. As the first black belch of smoke issued forth, the prelude to a withering torrent of fire, Nadinta knew she was too late, that she and her companions were doomed to shortly become smoking lumps of charred flesh.

She did all that she could do in that moment, which was to hold the sword aloft and pray to all the gods of Erithea to spare the lives of her companions. Her life flashed before her eyes as the fire washed over her, the heat of the flame so intense that she felt her eyelashes melting.

The dragon finished its blast, the smoke from its attack obscuring everything in the cavern. The great wyrm coughed once, clearing its throat of the last of the steam, which then puffed out through its cavernous nostrils. It gave a satisfied nod and turned its thoughts toward sleep, intent on resuming its nap.

Those thoughts were interrupted, however, by a sharp stab of pain in its gut. For there stood Nadinta, unharmed by the great gout of flame, undaunted by the size of the beast, unbowed by the challenges and trials that had come before. She thrust her sword forward with all of her might, and the magic blade—a legendary blade, in fact, the very sword once borne by Uthremegar the Rager, the mightiest warrior of the northern Camerian tribes, and the weapon with which he slew the terrible green dragon Porthaxatus —caused great pain to Dragonia.

The beast roared and thrashed, trying desperately to escape the sting of that blade, but Nadinta held fast to the pommel and drove it in deeper, knowing that the lives of her companions—who had been spared a fiery death by the sword's protective nimbus— depended on her to strike hard, strike quickly, and strike decisively.

And strike she did, over and over, until the great Dragonia, the scourge of Skendrick and the surrounding territories, the terrible tyrant responsible for so much pain, suffering, and death, gasped one last gout of flame and fell backward, stone dead, on a pile of treasure so large it dwarfed the royal treasury of the ancient kingdom of Celenia, one of the wealthiest kingdoms that had ever existed.

Nadinta waited a moment before she withdrew the sword. She turned to her companions and nodded, and, as one, they let forth a triumphant yell—for, at long last, the brave band of heroes had vanquished the mighty dragon, and never again would the good citizens of Skendrick feel the pain of its fury.

CHAPTER 25

NOPE—IT WAS ABSOLUTELY (MOSTLY) NOTHING LIKE THAT

It turns out that the tunnel goblin's directions were good, and we found the dragon in pretty short order.

You know by this point that one of my main goals in telling this story is to show that the adventuring life isn't all it's thought to be. It's mostly boring, frustrating, dangerous (though not excitingly dangerous), smelly (dear gods, so smelly), and not particularly lucrative. Occasionally, however, it's exactly how the songs make it sound, and in those moments, it's easy to see why people—even smart, capable people like Nadi—would devote their lives to doing something so irrational. Let the record show that entering a dragon's lair for the first time is one of those moments, and it's fair to say that each member of our intrepid band experienced more than a frisson of excitement as we crept across that threshold.

Side note: "frisson" is one of those fancy words that I normally eschew (not unlike "eschew"), but, in this case, it's really the only word that accurately captures the feeling. I'm all in favor of using the people's vernacular, but sometimes the people should get a bigger vernacular and know what words mean. Also, the people should tip more, and maybe bathe a little bit more frequently. I should stop there. I have a lot more recommendations for the people that they probably won't like, but I'd like them to buy the book, so...you know.

We knew we were getting close when we heard the low rumbles of the dragon's snores echoing through the narrow corridor that led to its lair. Nadi silently called a halt and then did her scout-ahead thing, returning a few moments later looking pale but resolute. She nodded her head and then spread her arms like wings and pantomimed breathing fire. Or, maybe having eaten something spicy.

Rummy assumed the latter, and gestured to his water canteen. Nadi shook her head, but Rummy silently insisted. Nadi gritted her teeth and flapped her arms more emphatically. This confused Whiska, who grew concerned that Nadi had seen an owl (Ratarians hate owls, whom they view as blood enemies and try to kill at every possible opportunity). She growled softly and twisted her hands in opposite directions to suggest strangling an owl. Nadi shook her head again and tried her fire breathing bit one more time, but this just caused Rummy to reach into his pack for a little bit of bread he had squirreled away at some point and push it into her hands in the hopes that it would alleviate what he assumed was a burning sensation in her mouth from eating a hot pepper.

Whiska, of course, misinterpreted this to mean that Rummy hoped to lure in the owls with the bread and wagged her finger at him before pantomiming a little mouse crawling across her hand, which would prove much more effective in luring the owl in close so she could strangle it. Rummy thought that perhaps Whiska was suggesting they could dance their way past the dragon, so he pointed to his left foot and held up one finger and then a second to suggest that he had two left feet and that his effectiveness would be limited if the group chose that approach. Whiska, in turn, assumed that Rummy wanted to stomp on the mice (not once, but twice to make sure they were dead), which caused her to shake her head in vigorous disagreement, as she knew that owls would not take as great an interest in dead mice as they would live ones. She pointed at Rummy's foot, shook her head again, and then made her mice crawling motion again, the fingers on her right hand skittering across the palm of her left hand even more excitedly than before.

At that moment, Borg stepped forward and held us his hand to stop the silent dialogue between Whiska and Rummy. Nadi nodded, relieved that someone else had stepped in to end the confusion. Borg looked slowly and deliberately at everyone in turn before pointing to his stomach and then rubbing it vigorously. He then mimed shoveling food into his mouth before patting his stomach contentedly.

Apparently, Borg was hungry, and the moral of the story is that hand gestures can be confusing.

Nadi somehow managed to slap her hand over her eyes without making a sound.

She pointed down the tunnel and motioned for everyone to move. After about a hundred yards, she pulled everyone in close (none too gently, I might add) and whispered, "The entrance to the dragon's cavern is just up ahead. It's sleeping, as you might have guessed from the snores. We go in hard and we go in fast." She looked at Whiska. "What's the strongest thing you've got?"

"Fireball," replied Whiska far too loudly, causing Nadi to flap her arms and start hissing. "But, I don't think that's going to do much good against the dragon."

"What's the strongest thing you've got that might hurt the dragon?" Nadi asked pointedly.

Whiska scratched her chin. "Probably a lightning bolt.

Yeah, I bet that'll light that oversized iguana up like a St. Chaffin's day kindlesparker."

"Good." Nadi turned to Borg. "Can you get out in front so that, when the dragon wakes up, you're in position to give it a good whack?"

Borg nodded (eventually).

"What about me, Nadi?" asked Rummy, looking nervous.

"You should...hmmm. Good question. Whiska—do you have any of those healing potions left?"

Whiska looked sidelong at Nadi. "One."

"Good—give it to Rummy." She looked at Rummy. "Stay on the perimeter of the battle and jump in to give it to whoever might need it the most. It's likely that we're all going to get hurt, so use your best judgment."

Whiska nodded as though Nadi had just confirmed her deepest, darkest suspicion. "I knew it—I knew it! You want me out of the way! You want my cut of the treasure for yourself, you honey-tressed trollop! Well, you won't get it—it's mine. *Mine*! I'll kill the dragon myself if I have to! Why, I'll—"

"Are you done yet?" asked Nadi coolly.

"No one's trying to take your share of the treasure, you festering, flea-ridden farce," I said, deciding it was high time someone put Whiska in her place. "Though if you want to kill the dragon by yourself, I think we're all in favor of that."

"If you mention fleas one more time..."

"You'll do what?" I got right up in Whiska's face.

"Turn you into cockroach jelly." Whiska sounded deadly serious.

"Okay, fine—I won't mention fl...those things again," I replied. I really didn't like the idea of becoming any more gelatinous than I already was. "But, come on—if you don't trust everyone in this group by now, you're not going to, and you might as well leave. This is it, Whiska—the end of the grand adventure. When you walk into that cavern, you're either walking into legend or into a coffin."

"That's a rather less cheery view of it than I'd like to take," said Rummy.

"Quiet," I said before turning back to Whiska. "You need to make a choice right here and right now—you either trust that no matter what happens in there, Nadi, Rummy, Borg, and I have your back, or else you walk away and find your own way out. Because we're all in this together, and I can tell you that no matter what danger you're in, I'll put myself in harm's way to try to get you out of it—even if your mangy carcass is infested with tiny bugs that suck your blood and make you itch." Well, at least I obeyed the letter of the law.

Nadi put her hand on my shoulder and gave it a grateful squeeze. Whiska sighed, reached into a belt pouch, and withdrew a small vial, which she handed to Rummy. "Here," she grumbled. "Don't waste it. Make sure someone's actually dying before you give it to them."

"Thank you," said Rummy, tucking the vial into the front compartment on his own belt pouch (which, incidentally, looked like what's colloquially known in certain parts of Erithea as a "fanny pack," and I should note that fanny packs are generally considered the purview of a class of mothers who have utterly given up on trying to impress anyone and fathers who had never once impressed anyone, though it looked pretty good on Rummy). He pointed to it. "Everyone knows where it is, so if I get turned into dragon flambé, make sure you get it back so you can put it to good use. Oh, and if that does happen, and any of you make it out alive, please tell my daughter that I died a good death. You can lie if you need to. And tell her that I love her."

"I love...cockroach jelly...on toast," said Borg.

"Your *what*?" asked Nadi, eyes going wide.

Rummy shrugged sheepishly. "My daughter. Have I not mentioned her?"

"Does this look like the expression of someone who is

hearing something she has heard many times before?" asked Nadi, pointing toward the aforementioned wide eyes.

"So, no," replied Rummy. "I suppose maybe I haven't."

"Why, exactly, did you choose not to mention this little fact previously?" I asked.

"Well, this is the first time I've felt truly imminent death," answered Rummy. "It didn't seem relevant absent those circumstances."

"What did you do, pay a goblin to let you do the creaky accordion to her?" asked Whiska.

"No, no payments changed hands," replied Rummy, unruffled. "She was fully complicit."

"...but it was a goblin?" asked Nadi tentatively.

"Yes."

"Oh. That's...well, that's interesting," said Nadi.

"I'm kidding," said Rummy.

"It wasn't a goblin?"

"No, I don't have a daughter. Do you honestly think any self-respecting woman of any race would have relations with me? I don't even think the non-self-respecting ones would want to. I'm not really interested in that anyway. Besides, I'd be a terribly indulgent father. Probably annoying, though, too, what with all the prestidigitating."

"So, there's been absolutely no point to the conversation we've had for the past five minutes while we're in earshot of a sleeping, and presumably very deadly, dragon?" I asked.

"I suppose not, no," said Rummy agreeably.

Nadi bit down on the hilt of her sword in an effort not to scream in frustration. A moment later, after she had mastered her emotions, she beckoned for us to follow her. She held her sword at the ready, which suggested that she was either prepared to take on the dragon or ready to cut off the head of the next member of our group who delayed our progress any further. I decided not to delay things any further.

There's a moment before you go into a dangerous situation—a dragon's lair, a wizard's tower, the annual nuptial dress sale at Cataflan's Millinery—alongside a group of trusted companions where you almost feel giddy, like laughter is the only way to release the immense anxiety that's built up over what you're about to do. (Vomit and diarrhea are alternatives, of course, but messy ones, and they don't make for a cute footnote, so we'll just say that we all got the giggles before we went into the dragon's lair, even if we all know what Borg was doing instead, though I'm not sure that had anything to do with nerves or anxiousness and everything to do with his ridiculously overactive bowels and terrible dietary decisions.)

Once the laughter had subsided, Nadi led us into the lair, where I paused for a moment to take in the scene. The dragon lay before us, snoring contentedly, little spurts of flame snorting out with each breath. A massive treasure hoard surrounded the beast. Gold, silver, jewels, swords, armor, shields, statues, jewelry, and, inexplicably, a huge pile of carrots were scattered across the room, heaped haphazardly here and there—including beneath the dragon, where rested a pretty significant portion of the treasure.

Rummy couldn't help but let out a low whistle, which brought swift retribution from Nadi in the form of a hand slapped over his mouth with considerably more force than was necessary.

We froze as the dragon snorted, inadvertently immolating a small, purple vase near its left nostril and melting more gold coins than I'd seen in the past year. Fortunately for us, the dragon didn't wake, and Nadi very reluctantly withdrew her hand, though the glare she fixed on Rummy served as a pointed reminder for him to mind his breaking-and-entering-a-dragon's-lair P's and Q's.

I breathed out a long, slow (but silent) sigh of relief.

Whiska could barely control herself. Her eyes looked like carriage wheels, immense and round and driven to arrive at the destination before her. I tried to stop her, but half-hearted silent entreaties, it turns out, are pretty ineffective when it comes to stopping really avaricious Ratarians from getting closer to treasure.

Nadi moved to intervene, but she saw the wild look in Whiska's eyes, and, instead of trying to stop her, simply mouthed, "The plan."

I nodded and grabbed Rummy, pulling him back toward the perimeter and clearing the way for Borg to get closer to the dragon. Nadi held her sword at the ready and waited for Whiska to look at her, which took a while, given that she spent several minutes gazing lustily at the treasure. Finally, through sheer chance, she made eye contact with Nadi, who pointed toward the dragon, started to gesture for Whiska to cast her lightning bolt spell, realized that her gesture might be misinterpreted and result in a lengthy dissection of what she may or may not have meant and ultimately lead to the dragon waking up and eating all of us before we could even start to fight it, and decided instead to just nod with her chin toward the dragon and hope Whiska could figure it out.

Fortunately, Whiska figured it out. With one last, longing look at the treasure, she set her staff down on the ground so that it leaned against her, pushed the sleeves of her robe up her skinny arms (they promptly fell right back down), stretched her fingers, picked her staff back up, and began to chant very quietly, raising the staff as she neared the end of the incantation.

Just before Whiska finished, Nadi raced forward and struck the dragon across the snout with her blade. The blow didn't do a ton of damage (though it did open up a nice gash), but it did serve to make the dragon pick its head up and blink, trying to clear the sleep from its eyes. Its head swiveled toward Whiska just as she unleashed her spell.

I'll say this for Whiska: she may be rude, boorish, greedy, selfish, insufferable, and smell like a three-day-old piece of rotfish, and she may not have the most extensive magical training, and she is not good at creating decent clothing, and she does this annoying clicking thing with her teeth when she's eating, and she never picks up a bar tab, and orange is her favorite color, which is just weird, but when she wants to do damage to something, she doesn't mess around. Her lightning bolt hit the dragon square in the face, and the beast's head shot up into the air and snapped back so hard I thought its neck might break.

In case you're wondering, hearing a full-throated dragon's roar in a relatively small cavern where the sound can bounce and echo and reverberate is not good for your ears (particularly if you have sensitive part-elven ears, which tend to bleed under those circumstances in my experience).

On the plus side, we had the advantage, and we pressed it. Nadi rushed back in and redoubled her efforts, striking hard on the dragon's soft underbelly. Borg waded in and smashed his club into the dragon's left foreleg, though I think his attack produced more sound than it did damage. Even Rummy got into the act, picking up a fist-sized rock and flinging it with expert aim toward the dragon's snout, bouncing it off the upper part of its right nostril. I stood heroically off to the side, observing and recording the story of these brave heroes (mainly because I knew that my tiny knife couldn't do much harm to the dragon, and, even if it could, I had no intention of getting close enough to it to even give it a shot).

Even though we had the element of surprise and drew first blood, we were still fighting a dragon, and those things are big. Also, tough, and, in this case, incredibly angry.

The dragon's neck swiveled to the right as its head swooped back down, its gaping maw open wide to reveal row upon row of massive (albeit strangely rounded) teeth. It snapped at Borg but missed, though it did manage to bash its lower jaw into him, sending him crashing hard into the closest wall. It then turned its attention to Nadi, who danced backward and frantically tried to parry tooth with sword.

To my surprise, Whiska raced over to Borg and knelt beside him. She patted him gently on the shoulder as she leaned down and said something into his ear. He nodded, and she slipped her hand underneath his arm and helped him to his feet. It was easily the nicest, most tender thing I'd ever seen her do.

As the dragon inhaled, however, I suspected it might also be the last thing I ever saw her do, period, because I was about to become a barbecued half-elf kabob.

Borg heroically raced (well, insomuch as Borg can race... but "heroically ambled" just doesn't quite create the level of dramatic tension we're going for) right into the path of the flame, hoping to shield us as much as possible with his body, even though I'm pretty sure fire melts rocks, too. He stood tall, even as Rummy ducked and cowered like a rented mule (okay, so, he may not have been alone in doing so). I covered my face, but kept my fingers spread just wide enough to bear witness to Borg's immolation, figuring that I could literally do nothing less to help him than to play the role of silent observer—and, subsequently, incredibly beautiful chronicler of his life, assuming I didn't suffer the same fate.

It turned out, though, that Borg flambé wasn't on the menu. Instead of unleashing a rock-melting stream of flames, the dragon started coughing and sputtering, falling back on its haunches and bracing itself against the wall with its front legs as it hacked, spat, and generally made the kind of sounds a cat makes a few hours after it eats a fluffmouse. After several moments of this (and watching it cough up what looked like fiery phlegm), Borg walked over to the dragon, put a comforting hand on its haunch, and patted it gently. "Are you...all right?" he asked, sounding genuinely concerned that the creature who had just tried to turn him into char might be suffering from a case of the coughs.

The dragon hacked a few more times, sniffled mightily (sucking back in a fairly lengthy stand of orange, flaming snot, I might add), and nodded. "Yes," it said hoarsely. It cleared its throat. "Yes," it said again. It coughed softly. "I think I'm better now. Thank you for asking." Its voice was surprisingly soft, deep and resonant, and I found myself thinking that he would make a great bard...

Well, except for the fact that he'd probably eat his audience.

The dragon pawed at its nose, sniffed again, and looked at us, blinking repeatedly to clear the smoke that lingered around its face.

(Side note: would we call a dragon's feet "paws"? I don't know if you'd call dragon feet "paws." Hooves? I don't know what the actual term should be. They're definitely not hands, and not small—not in the slightest.)

"Well," said the dragon, "what do we do now?"

"I'm pretty sure this is the part where you try to eat us," replied Nadi. She raised her sword. "But don't expect us to go down easy."

"Yeah! We're not Flendarian courtesans!" yelled Whiska, raising her staff.

"Why would I eat you?" returned the dragon, disgusted. "Are your pockets lined with lettuce? Are you filled with radishes? Are your feet made of sweet potatoes?" It licked its lips hungrily. "Are they?"

"Um...no," replied Nadi, clearly confused.

"In fact," added Rummy, "not a single one of any of our body parts is made of vegetables." He paused and cocked his head. "In fact, I don't think that any of us has eaten a vegetable in a week."

"Oh," said the dragon, disappointed. "I guess I'll just kill you with fire, then, seeing as how I wouldn't particularly enjoy eating you."

"I don't...like vegetables," said Borg.

"That's ridiculous!" roared the dragon, tipping its head back and waving dismissively with its right front leg (paw?). "How can you *not* like vegetables?" It shook its head and focused on Borg. "I like you—you're polite—but you've got terrible taste."

"I've never met a dragon who likes vegetables," said Nadi thoughtfully.

"You've never met a dragon, you nitwit!" said Whiska. She pointed her staff at the dragon. "Are we going to sit here talking, or are we going to destroy this overgrown iguana and take its gold?" She cast her eyes over the piles of treasure and shivered with pleasure. "Gold!"

The dragon rolled its eyes. "The only reason you're not a tiny stain on the floor is that I had a coughing fit. That happens once every few months. It's over now. Do you really think you're going to get that lucky again?" The dragon snorted a gout of flame. "Incidentally, I understand that getting burned alive really hurts."

"Hold on," I said. "Do you *really* want to fight us? Look, I'm not delusional—I know you'll melt every single one of these jokers into candle butts. But, it's possible that you could get hurt at least a little in the process, especially by the smelly, hairy one."

"Heloise, what are you—" began Nadi, but I cut her off.

"You strike me as incredibly reasonable."

"I am," said the dragon, inclining its head forward.

"And smart," I said.

"I am," said the dragon, nodding again. "I'm also not gullible, susceptible to flattery, or easily fooled."

"Right," I said. So much for the subtle approach; oh well —I've always preferred the direct approach anyway. "Okay, you're reasonable and smart, and you have a ton of treasure here—a hoard that we won't contribute to if you kill us, incidentally, because, in case you hadn't noticed, we're so hard up that we're wearing poorly made magical muumuus that, I suspect, will just disappear at some point, and then you'll have a naked Ratarian and whatever the heck Rummy is lying around your lair. And that'll put you off your arugula for sure." I think I winced. "Trust me about that—I've seen 'em naked. It's not pretty."

"You noodle-haired lute plucker! I'll have you know I'm considered a real catch back home."

"We'll take your word for that," I said to Whiska by way of mollification. I turned back to the dragon. "All right, so in addition to all of those things I just mentioned, I'm going to suggest one more thing I think is true about you, but I need to ask you not to burn my head off for doing so."

"I make no guarantees, but you may proceed," rumbled the dragon.

"Hmmm. Well, that's a little less surety than I'd like, Mr... you know, it occurs to me that we haven't been properly introduced. I'm Heloise the Bard—it's okay if you haven't heard of me, though I'd be surprised if that's the case."

"I haven't heard of you."

"I'm surprised."

"I'm Melvin."

"Melvin?"

"Melvin."

"Hmmm. Are you sure it's not 'Dragonia'?"

"That's a ridiculous name for a dragon."

"It's just a thing I'm toying with. Never mind. Melvin—so, here's the thing I think is true about you, and I don't mean this offensively, because it's true of me, too, and I certainly don't want to offend myself. See, the thing is, I think you're lazy."

The dragon narrowed its eyes. I knew I was playing with fire—literally. "Tread lightly, elf."

"Half-elf, actually."

"Hrrrm."

"Is that a good 'hrrrm' or a bad 'hrrrm'?"

"It's an indifferent 'hrrrm.'"

I nodded. "I'll take that." I glanced to the side to see Nadi looking at me with a combination of horror and admiration. I think she knew that she'd already be dead if I hadn't been there—but, she could also sense that if I kept going, we were probably headed for the same outcome eventually. Ah, well—in for a fennig…

(A fennig, incidentally, is generally acknowledged as the smallest unit of money anywhere in Erithea—it takes a thousand fennigs to equal one Grinnarian ploufer, and it takes about ten ploufers to buy a loaf of bread. So, fennigs are pretty useless except when featured in outdated colloquialisms.)

"Maybe 'lazy' is too strong of a word—what I mean is that you like to accomplish as much as you can with as little effort as possible. It goes hand-in-hand—or maybe hand-in-claw, in your case—with being smart. Like I said, I'm the same way."

"And so modest," replied the dragon.

"She really is," added Rummy.

"Let's not forget beautiful. She's stunningly beautiful," I said. I looked at Rummy. "Are you done? I'm trying to save our lives here."

"I'm done," said Rummy agreeably. "You're doing a great job so far. Keep it up. I feel like this thing could turn on us at any minute."

"You know I can hear you, right?" said the dragon.

"Oh, yes, of course," said Rummy, nodding. "It would be rude to whisper so that you couldn't hear us."

"My point is," I cut in, trying to wrestle back control of the conversation, "you probably prefer when you can get things you want without trying too hard, right?"

"I think that's true of anyone who's reasonable," replied the dragon.

"And you're reasonable," I said.

"I like to think so," said Melvin. "The corpses of a lot of

adventurers might disagree." He gestured to the treasure pile on which he sat. I squinted to look at it more closely. It definitely contained the bleached bones of humanoid creatures. So many bones.

"Well, I'm not sure those corpses can actually disagree, technically," I replied, "unless, of course, they're undead, but that's beside the point. The actual point is that you're reasonable and we're reasonable, and there's probably some way we can reasonably help each other."

"My way of helping you, I assume, being to not burn you to a crisp?" asked the dragon.

"That would be a good start," I responded with a nod.

"And give us treasure!" shouted Whiska.

The dragon puffed out a bit of steam, which shut Whiska up, but didn't deter her from repeatedly picking up the same handful of glinting gold coins and gleefully letting them run through her fingers.

"So, you like vegetables," I said.

"Very much," replied the dragon. "In fact, they're all I eat. I'm a vegetabletarian."

"You mean vegetarian," said Rummy helpfully.

Melvin shook his head. "No, vegetarians don't eat meat, but they do eat things other than vegetables. I only eat vegetables."

"Seriously?" asked Nadi. "You must need to eat them by the wagonload if that's all you eat."

"How can you not like meat?" asked Whiska, seeming offended as she produced a piece of lizard jerky from somewhere (I don't want to know where) and tore off a bite.

The dragon looked disgusted. "I just think it's cruel to eat something that's less intelligent than you, though I suppose that's less of a problem for you."

"So you would eat another dragon?" replied Whiska, unfazed.

"I...hmmm. Well, that's a fair riposte. My statement was

intended to simultaneously insult you and suggest how far beneath me you truly are, but you've trapped me with my own words. No, I would not eat another dragon. I'm a strict vegetabletarian. I will amend my statement: I think it's cruel to eat something that's less or equally intelligent."

"What about something that's more intelligent?" countered Whiska.

"Nothing is more intelligent than a dragon—and no, there are no dragons more intelligent than I."

"So, you're trying to tell me you're the smartest being in the world?" Whiska's tone was skeptical. I wanted to strangle her.

"It would be intellectually foolish for me to answer in the affirmative, as I haven't met every creature in the world, but I am reasonably certain that's the case, yes."

"We believe you," I cut in, giving Whiska a look that she returned by daintily pretending to brush something off her shoulder, which I knew to be an obscene Ratarian gesture meant to suggest I stick my head someplace very uncomfortable.

"I am...the smartest...rock giant I...know," said Borg.

"I believe it," said Rummy, patting Borg on the arm. "You've got brainpower to spare."

I cleared my throat, glared at Rummy and Borg, and continued. "Anyway, Melvin, you're a smart guy and—"

"I'm not a '*guy*' as you so informally put it. I am a female."

"Named Melvin?" I responded without thinking.

"Yes."

"Oh. I, uh, see. That's...yeah. That's interesting." I'd lost my train of thought.

"It's a common female dragon name."

"I'm not saying it's not," I replied.

"It was also my mother's name."

"Well, that's great—family names are a great tradition."

"And her mother's name before her."

"Got it—so, sorry about that. You're a smart, ah, a smart woman."

"Melvin is a…boy's name," said Borg.

"Not in this case, big guy," said Rummy. He handed Borg a coin from the mound of treasure at his feet. "Look—shiny."

Borg took the coin and looked at it. I gave Rummy a grateful nod.

"I can't imagine," I resumed, "that it's all that easy getting vegetables into this place, especially if you're getting them all the way from Skendrick. First of all, it's not really that close, even as fast as you can fly. Second, I've seen their farms— they're not very impressive. And, they grow more grain than vegetables."

"That's true," the dragon concurred.

"Sooner or later, they're going to get competent adventurers to come after you."

"Hey!" said Nadi.

I shrugged. "Just being honest—look, you guys have got potential, but you know that Ms. Melvin here would have consumed you all before you so much as cracked one of her scales, right? And that she still could?"

"Hey!" This time, it was Whiska. "That lightning bolt I hit him—it, her, whatever—with did some major damage. You know that hurt!"

"It did," conceded the dragon. "It doesn't now. It was akin to a bee sting for a human." She smiled at Whiska. "Or perhaps a flea bite, in your case."

"You dirty, stinking, slimy mountain of useless reptile flesh!" Whiska raised her staff. "I'm going to turn you into a puddle of red goop and then drink you!"

"That's a really weird thing to say," said Rummy. "And probably unwise."

"I think," I said, grabbing Whiska's arm and pulling it down, "that we can all agree that it was unwise. And weird, yeah, come to think of it—did you just threaten to drink her?"

"It's the ultimate sign of disrespect in Ratarian society." Whiska looked at me as though I was the only one in the world who didn't know that fact.

"Well, I don't think it's necessarily a good idea to go flinging around the ultimate sign of disrespect to a creature that could eat you." I looked at the dragon, who was staring at Whiska. "And who looks very much like she wants to. Right now. So, shut up."

Whiska started to speak, but I held up my hand. "*Shut. Up.*"

Whiska actually listened.

"Get to the point, half-elf," said the dragon.

"My point is, we can make it easier on you than having to fly out of your lair, navigate tricky winds, attack a village, risk getting attacked in return, grab some vegetables—and probably not enough to actually fill you up—and then flying all the way back here, rinse, repeat."

"'Rinse, repeat'?" asked the dragon curiously.

"It's just a thing people with long, flowing, silky, honey-golden hair say," I replied, tossing long, flowing, silky, honey-golden hair over my shoulder.

"It's a stupid saying," said the dragon.

"Which is why I've decided I'm not going to say it anymore," I replied.

"How are you going to get me more vegetables?"

"Yes, that is the question, isn't it?" Confession: I had absolutely no idea how to get the dragon more vegetables. This whole conversation was a play for time in the hopes that someone (ideally someone other than me) would come up with an idea to get us out of this situation. My companions, however, didn't seem to have anything to contribute beyond insults that might get them eaten.

"Yes, it is," said the dragon pointedly.

"Well, fortunately, we have one heck of a plan," I said.

The dragon waited a moment before saying, "And your plan is?"

"Well, the plan, see...it's complicated. It would take a while to explain, and we don't want to waste your time. Why don't you just let us head out and get to work, and, before you know it, you'll be swimming in vegetables. Well, maybe not literally, because that would be hard, and you're very big. But, the point is, we'll have you loaded up in no time."

"How?" The dragon narrowed its eyes, kind of like how mine do when some schlubby patron buys me a drink after a performance and spends the next twenty minutes stammering in an effort to try to get me to go home with him. (That almost never works, incidentally.)

"I'll, uh, I'll just...Nadi, why don't you tell Melvin how we're going to make sure she has a steady supply of vegetables so that she doesn't immolate us?"

The look Nadi gave me suggested that, if we survived this encounter, I would feel considerable pain at a future date. "Well, Heloise, we've got a great plan to make sure that happens. It's so good I'm almost afraid to share it—trade secrets, you know." She laughed nervously.

"You have no plan," said the dragon.

"No, no—that's not true at all!" said Nadi. "We have a great plan. The best plan you've ever heard." She looked at Whiska, then shook her head and turned to Rummy. "Why don't you tell Melvin about it? You're so much better at explaining the plan than I am."

Rummy walked a gold coin across his knuckles for a moment before making it disappear with a flourish and then reaching into his right boot to make it reappear. I clapped. "Thank you, thank you." He bowed. "Now, the way I see it," he said, letting the coin dance across his hand again, this time putting both hands together and walking it back and forth, "your problem, Ms. Mel—may I call you Mel?"

"No."

"Fine, fine. Now, your problem, Ms. Melvin, is that—"

"'Ms.' is considered an insulting form of address among dragonkind," said Mel.

"Why's that?" asked Nadi.

"It's too human."

"Ironic, then, that it came from a half-dwarf, half-halfling, no?" Rummy chuckled.

"Not really," said Melvin.

"Tough crowd," Rummy stage whispered. No one said anything. He cleared his throat. "Right. As I was saying, your problem, ah, dragon lady, is the very same problem this coin has—your vegetables keep disappearing." He made the coin disappear again. "Only, in your case, they're going into your stomach—and a svelte stomach it is, I might add, likely on account of having such a salubrious diet—instead of, say, Borg's loin cloth." Rummy reached over and appeared to pluck the coin from the depths of Borg's garment, which prompted the rock giant to (very slowly) clap. "Now, the question we need to answer—for you, of course, since we clearly already know the answer, obviously—is how to make those vegetables reappear like this coin." He pulled another coin from Borg's loin cloth. "And this one." He pulled out another, and another, and another still. "And this one, and this one, and so on and so forth." Rummy paused. I clapped, knowing that if no one did, it would interrupt the rhythm of his patter and, right now, that patter was the only thing standing between us and a fire bath.

(On that note—if you're ever in the Bastonia region of upper Cameral, I highly recommend the fire baths, which are magical mud springs that melt years off your skin. Why do they call them "fire baths" instead of "mud baths"? First and foremost, the thought of bathing in mud is just kind of gross, so it's primarily a marketing thing. But, there are also occasional gouts of flame that spring forth from the baths. It's incredibly rare and usually happens outside the area that's roped off for bathing use, though every ten years or so, a bather gets torched. Staying beautiful isn't easy for everyone, you know.)

"Of course," continued Rummy, "vegetables, generally speaking, are much larger than coins." He looked around at the treasure surrounding him, his brow furrowed in concentration. "They're more like the size of that candlestick over there. Do you like carrots, Melvin?"

"They are, in fact, my favorite vegetable."

"You, madam—assuming 'madam' is not offensive—have excellent taste in vegetables."

"Madam is mildly offensive."

"Ah, I certainly don't mean to give offense, your dragon-ship! Is that offensive?"

"No, just ridiculous."

"I'll take ridiculous over offensive any day," replied Rummy, smiling. Dear gods; he was actually enjoying himself. He was totally going to get eaten first.

"So, that candlestick over there—let's say that's our carrot. Much, much bigger than a coin, right? And much harder to move, especially in mass quantities. It's almost...well, it's almost like you'd need magic to do it. Maybe even a magic pack that was filled with candlestick carrots and would never run out!" He unslung his pack, reached inside, and pulled out a candlestick that looked very much like the one he had pointed to a moment before, which still remained in its place.

The dragon let out a low whistle. "Now that's a pretty good trick."

"As good as this one?" said Rummy, pulling another candlestick—identical to the first—out of his pack and setting it down on the ground behind him. "Or this one?" Another candlestick emerged, which he set down in the same spot as the first. "Or this one?" Yet another appeared.

Dragons have a hard time clapping, what with those tiny arms, but this one found a way to do it. She clapped even harder when Rummy stepped to the side and, with a flourish, revealed that all of the candlesticks he had placed on the ground had disappeared.

"Oh, bra-*vo*," said the dragon, appearing genuinely delighted. "You didn't even use any real magic." She shook her head in admiration.

"How do you know that?" asked Rummy, curious.

"All dragons can detect magic—you read as completely devoid of magic, save for your pack. Conversely, that gopher creature over there is like a tiny sun."

"Gopher? *Gopher*!" yelled Whiska. "I'll show you a gopher, you jumped-up lizard-loving—"

"And that one," cut in the dragon, ignoring Whiska's tirade. She pointed toward Borg. "Do you have something behind your back?"

"I was just...going to mention...this," replied Borg. He reached up underneath his loin cloth for an awkwardly long period of time, during which time he issued a series of boisterous grunts. It was uncomfortable for everyone, the dragon included. Finally, Borg held up a small horn, about the size of a cucumber. "I think this...will help."

Nadi stepped closer and then drew back, coughing. Whiska pushed her out of the way and moved in, but was similarly overcome by a coughing fit. "Gods, man! Did you keep that thing in your rectum?"

"Yes," replied Borg. We waited for further details, but none were forthcoming.

"Not going to explain that one, big guy?" asked Rummy.

"It is...a convenient...storage place. For...rock giants."

The dragon wiggled its fingers and a jet of cleansing water shot forth, splashing the horn and dampening the smell.

"Thank you," I said gratefully.

"I didn't do that for you," replied the dragon.

"Still thankful," I said.

"What is it?" asked the dragon curiously.

"A magical...horn of...plenty," replied Borg. "Three times per...day, it can...create vegetables." He paused. "A lot...of vegetables."

"Does it do anything else?" asked Whiska.

Borg shook his head. "Not that...I know of."

"That's a pretty useless magical item," scoffed Whiska.

"...until now," I amended. Whiska shrugged. I think she still thought she could destroy the dragon if it came down to it. She is an idiot.

"I could...give it to...you," said Borg, holding it out to the dragon.

The dragon looked suspicious. "How does it work? Don't try anything funny." She got down on all of her legs and showed Borg her teeth. "I may not want to eat you, but I don't have any qualms about biting you in half and spitting you out. Though it takes a long time to get the taste of humanoid out of your mouth." She shuddered.

"Like this," said Borg. "Veggie, veggie...take a bite...make a lot...of veggies...all right?" He pointed the horn toward the ground just in front of the dragon.

A moment later, the thing erupted. Squash, carrots, kale, spinach, beets, radishes, and potatoes came flying out, along with about a dozen other varieties of vegetables I couldn't name. They piled up at the dragon's feet and, after a moment had passed, we could have completely concealed even Borg beneath them.

Melvin gasped. She cautiously sniffed the vegetables and then gasped again. "They smell...fresh! They smell...they smell...mmmmm." She let out a low moan as she gently wrapped her lips around a head of kale and chewed it slowly and softly, moaning again as she swallowed.

Dragons, it seems, eat vegetables in the most awkwardly sensual manner possible.

"Those...are...amazing," the dragon said after taking her

time to work her way through at least one of each kind of vegetable. "The best I've ever had. Without question."

"I'm glad they...are delicious," said Borg. "I don't...like vegetables. So...I just use...it as a...rectum spacer."

I later learned that rock giants have issues defecating if their sphincters get too tight, so they...you know what? It's way too gross. There's no reason you care or need to know about that. Let's just summarize what happened next by saying we all stood around staring awkwardly at each other (but pointedly not looking at Borg), bleached our eyeballs and our noses, and tried to move on by burying feelings that would resurface years later and require multiple sessions with skilled witch doctors to resolve.

"What's to stop me from killing you now that I have this?" Melvin gestured to the horn, which she held awkwardly in her hand/paw/claw, where it looked like a tiny, tiny seashell.

"That," I said, "is a very good question."

"Perhaps you'd care to answer it more quickly than other questions I've posed previously," said the dragon, with the faintest tone of menace in her voice for the first time.

Our collective gulp was, I'm sure, audible to any creatures wandering the mountain tunnels.

"If you kill us, adventurers will keep coming." Nadi looked the dragon in the eye, her shoulders back, head held high. She looked fearless—every inch the true hero. "If we don't return to Skendrick, they'll know you're still here. They will send others, and others after those—as many as it takes to slay you. Even if you kill them all, you'll never know peace. Your sleep will be constantly interrupted." She cast her eyes around the room. "Your treasure will be in constant danger."

Melvin growled. "It won't happen that way."

"Won't it?" asked Nadi. "How can you be sure? Wouldn't you prefer to avoid that possibility altogether?"

"How?" asked the dragon, her tone curious.

"We tell everyone in Skendrick that you're dead."

Rummy, sensing the import of the moment, gasped to punctuate the statement, then smiled and looked around, pleased with his performance.

Nadi rolled her eyes at him before turning back to the dragon. "Think about it—if they think you're dead, no more adventurers. No more efforts to kill you. You can sit here with your magical horn and eat vegetables to your heart's content. It sounds like that's what you really want."

"Well, that, and treasure," responded the dragon.

"Right. The treasure. Well, no one will come looking for it if they think you're dead," said Nadi.

"Or everyone will," said Rummy quietly, almost sheepishly.

The dragon's massive head swiveled toward the smallest being in the room, who shrank down another size or two under that withering glare. "What do you mean?"

"It's just...well, if I thought you were dead, and I had a rough idea of where your lair was, I'd be hunting day and night for it, knowing that there was a literal dragon's horde sitting unguarded."

Nadi frowned. "He's right. If we tell them you're dead, there won't necessarily be adventurers knocking down your door—though there may be those, too—but the treasure seekers will be endless." She turned to Rummy and nodded. "Sharp thinking, Rummy—thanks for calling that out." Nadi's equanimity in dealing with someone pointing out a flaw in her desperate plan to save us from certain death at the hands (and teeth) of a dragon impressed me. So did my ability to use the word "equanimity" as though I do it all the time.

"So, what do we do?" I asked.

"I could still kill you," said Melvin with a shrug. "Status quo for me. Only with delicious vegetables I don't have to leave my lair for."

"We'd prefer to maintain our own status quo," I replied, "which includes respiration and not being masticated."

Whiska began waving her hands around and muttering something.

"What are you doing—stop that!" roared the dragon. "I'll destroy you!" She breathed in, preparing to unleash her breath weapon, when Whiska suddenly ceased her chanting and pointed her staff at the ground beneath Rummy's feet. Rummy shot into the air as a massive pile of golden coins appeared beneath him.

The dragon glared at Whiska. "What are you about? Why did you move those coins from elsewhere in the cavern? I had them all organized! I'm tempted to burn you just because you're annoying."

"I didn't move them," snapped Whiska.

"Explain yourself, rat creature."

"I created them," said Whiska, smiling smugly (though I'm not entirely sure she had the ability to smile in any other way).

"Wait—you've had the ability to magic up treasure this whole time and we're here trying to kill a dragon *why*?" I asked, incredulous.

"So you admit it—you're still trying to kill me!" roared the dragon, her wings spreading out as she stood up to her full height, which was terrifying.

"No! Come on—no, that's not what I meant," I said with calculated intermittent pauses (okay, fine—I stammered...I'd like to see how eloquent *you* are when you're staring down a dragon who wants to bite your head off like a hangnail). "I mean, sure, we came in here to kill you, but we're not trying now. We're not idiots. Now we're trying to figure out how we can all get what we want. I'm just trying to understand why this one's been holding out on us." I jerked my thumb toward Whiska and scowled.

"Because, you pee-haired finger plucker, those coins aren't real. It's an illusion—albeit one with form and substance." She looked proud. "It'll disappear in a minute —watch."

Even as she finished talking, Rummy looked down in dismay before falling unceremoniously to the floor and shouting "Oof!"

"And how does that help us, exactly?" asked Nadi.

"I think I can tweak the spell to make it last longer," replied Whiska.

"I'm still not quite sure what you're driving at," said Nadi.

"Idiots." Whiska shook her head. "Do I have to explain everything?"

"In this case? Yes, you do," I said.

"Genius is such a burden," she sighed. "Fine. Here's what we do..."

Whiska proceeded to lay out a surprisingly ingenious plan—one that even the dragon thought had promise.

We left the dragon's lair a short time later, our packs filled with treasure (which represented an infinitesimal fraction of the dragon's total wealth, but a sizable fortune for us). Next stop: Skendrick, and an attempt to pull off one of the greatest scams of all time.

CHAPTER 26

THE CONQUERING HEROES RETURN TO SKENDRICK, VICTORIOUS!

And so it was that Nadinta Ghettinwood and her brave band of adventurers returned to Skendrick to tell the terrified populace that they could, at long last, rest easy in their beds, safe and secure in the knowledge that the great and terrifying wyrm Dragonia, the beast that had plagued their night-mares and filled their waking hours with the crippling fear of fiery death, had been slain, and that its festering corpse would serve as a warning to any other foul creatures that might set their sights on terrorizing the good people of Skendrick. Dare to follow in the foot-steps of the fearsome dragon, that inert body would warn, and you, too, shall meet the same end, killed by Skendrick's brave defenders, one of the mightiest adventuring bands ever to roam the northern reaches of Erithea.

So beleaguered were the people of the town, and so used to trembling in fear at the mere mention of the dragon's name, that at first they could hardly believe their good fortune. They gathered in the town square to hear the tale of the returning heroes and sat in open-mouthed amazement, afraid to believe too much in Nadinta's solemn declaration of the dragon's death lest it prove to be nothing more than a fleeting dream, an ephemeral hope of a better life that would be dashed upon waking by the mighty roar of the terrible beast once again wheeling about in the skies overhead, intent on dealing flaming death to any who would dare so much as draw breath in the dragon's presence.

It took the bold action of Farmer Benton, the emotional core of the town's strength, to free them from their paralysis. Casting his straw boater into the air, the town's most solid and articulate citizen let out a whoop of pure, unbridled joy, and thrust his fist skyward in a gesture of defiance. Taking their cue from a man so beloved, the other citizens of the town followed suit, and before long, the air was filled with hats, scarves, and even a few wigs—including one from comely Goodlady Maxson, whom none of the townsfolk suspected of having lost her hair, and toward whom was directed much good-natured ribbing as she blushed and grabbed for her hair, so caught up in the excitement that she hadn't realized she had cast it skyward when she tossed her kerchief.

For three days and three nights, the people of Skendrick feted their heroes. They sang, danced, and ate, and, of course, they drank—how they drank! The town council gave rousing speeches, paeans to the group's bravery and battle prowess, and not once in those three days did Nadinta, Rumscrabble, Whiska, or Borgunder sleep, not even a moment, for they felt an equal debt of gratitude to the townsfolk who had believed in them and whom they rejoiced to see set free from the burden of their fear and worry.

At last the festivities drew to a close, and the exhausted towns-folk slept for another two days. On the third day, the town council made the heroes honorary citizens of Skendrick with rights of citizenship in perpetuity before bidding them farewell, asking them to return often. Many an innkeeper and tavern owner made it a point to tell them that they need never pay for food, drink, or bed so long as they might live, even though they knew of the vast wealth the heroes had accumulated when they so boldly slayed the dragon.

Nadinta and her fellow warriors thanked the people of

Skendrick graciously and profusely, and more than one person— led by Farmer Benton, whose shoulders shook as he sobbed—shed tears as Nadinta told the assembled populace that Skendrick would forever be in their hearts and on their minds, and that if they never accomplished another deed worth recording, they would consider their lives well lived in the service of the noble folk who stood before them, honest, hard-working folk who deserved to prosper and live in peace and harmony for all of their natural days.

So it is that our tale comes to an end, though Nadinta and her band did not rest on their laurels after that grand adventure, and they performed many more legendary deeds in the years that followed. None of those mighty feats, however, gave them the same sense of satisfaction as saving Skendrick, and never did their hearts fill more with gladness and pride than they did when they visited Skendrick forever after, which they did each year on the date that they slew the dragon to mark the anniversary of their victory in a celebration still recognized today as the most important day in the great history of Skendrick.

CHAPTER 27

IT'S ACTUALLY NOT THAT HARD TO CHEAT A (DUMB) CHEATER

Our trip back to Skendrick was decidedly less exciting (and less onerous, infuriating, and dangerous) than our trip to the dragon's lair, primarily because we now knew how to circumvent the swamp and, in some small way, we weren't as stupid as we used to be.

Still, there remained the small matter of our attire, which needed an upgrade before we rode through the gates of Skendrick as conquering heroes. Thankfully, fate intervened in the humpbacked form of a wandering merchant, whose cart overflowed with bolts of cloth from a recent stop in Candaria, the region's foremost producer of cotton and silk. He cackled and slapped his knee as we approached him on the road, our first clue that he wasn't entirely sane.

"Well, looka what we ha' here—a bunch o' nippies!" he crowed as we strode up to his cart.

"'Nippies'?" said Nadi.

I shook my head. "It's a group of burnt-out, disaffected

young people, mostly from the Plafian coast, who spend their days doing mind-altering drugs and engaging in three-ways with various magical creatures. Oh, and their fashion sense is abysmal."

"And we look like them?" asked Nadi, crinkling up her nose as she looked down at her Whiska-made garment.

"Not really. We're way more clothed than they usually are. I can't even see your nipples. Why do you think they're called 'nippies'?"

Nadi blushed.

"Bet you could use summat new ta wear, couldn't ya?" said the trader, chuckling for a moment before abruptly stopping, holding his hand up as though threatening to strike someone sitting next to him (though he sat atop his wagon alone), and shouting, "Away wi' ya, or ya'll feel the back o' me hand! Bah!" He shook his head. "Ghosties," he muttered by way of explanation, with a "What can you do?" shrug.

"Big problem around these parts, I've heard," I replied, trying to sound nonchalant. The man nodded conspiratorially. "But, yes—we could use something new to wear. What have you got?"

He squinted down at me before inspecting each of us closely in turn. "Ya got gold, then, do ya?"

"More than we know what to do with," said Rummy, who then grunted when Whiska elbowed him hard in the stomach. "I mean," he continued weakly, "we have a very miniscule amount of gold that will be just enough for us to purchase some clothing and not a penny more."

"Good enough," replied the trader. "But, I ha'en't got any clothing; just fabrics."

"None at all?" Some might describe my tone as whiny, but I would characterize it as "persuasively beseeching."

"Not a single stitch."

"Do you have...thread?" asked Borg.

"Aye." The man nodded.

We stood for a moment, waiting for Borg, who looked like he had a follow-up question, to continue. At last, he did. "And needles?"

"Could probably scrounge up a few, sure," replied the trader.

"We will...take them."

"Borg, what do you have in mind?" asked Nadi curiously.

We waited for another two minutes before Borg said, "I have an...idea."

Trusting Borg, we spent the next several minutes identifying various colors and types of fabric we wanted. I did the honors when it came to haggling with the trader, who was a surprisingly shrewd negotiator for a man who paused from time to time to argue with, and occasionally laugh at, a "ghost" (or perhaps that's what made him a shrewd negotiator...he certainly kept me off balance). The old man gave Borg everything he asked for and left us shortly thereafter (though not before selling us some much-needed food as well).

Fun fact: it turns out that Borg is at least as good of a seamstress as Madame Mona La Fleur. (Seamster? I have no idea what the gender-proper way to say that is when the one doing the sewing is a man...or, at least, a rock giant; maybe seamgiant? It's telling that a word can be so gendered that you don't know what the male-equivalent might be...)

(Who's Madame Mona La Fleur? Seriously? How do you not know the premier fashion designer in Pairicee? She's so skilled she once designed a ball gown for a beholder—and it looked good! Do you know how hard it is to accommodate twenty-three eye stalks and a round, floating body? I mean, sure, the beholder lost her cool that evening and ended up vaporizing three bartenders, but, still—she looked fabulous.)

By the time he finished—which, not surprisingly, was about a week later—we looked incredible. Even Whiska looked presentable, though she had managed to capture, roast, and consume a possum just before donning her new wardrobe and still had the creature's tail sticking out of her mouth like some grotesque parody of a toothpick, which didn't exactly scream haute couture.

"Not bad," said Rummy with a grin as he surveyed his outfit, which included numerous hidden pockets and pouches to facilitate his prestidigitating. "Not bad at all—you've got a real gift, Borg."

"You really do," said Nadi as she admired her outfit, a simple, functional, supple mix of wool and leather that would stand up to rough wear. "I had no idea you could do this."

"All rock giants...can sew," replied Borg.

"Really?" asked Whiska.

"Yes. We have...contests."

"Then why do you dress like idiot barbarians wearing nothing more than flimsy loin cloths?"

"We get...warm easily. And...we look good... naked."

"Well, can't argue with that, mainly because then things would get awkward," said Rummy cheerfully.

"To Skendrick, then?" I said.

"To Skendrick," said Nadi with a nod. "Thanks, Borg." She hoisted her pack and said, "Let's go!"

To hear the bards tell it (or, at least, this bard tell it—and, let's face it, she's the only one who matters, since she wrote the tale), the people of Skendrick gathered in the town square and gave the mighty band of adventurers a rousing hero's welcome. In reality, one bored gate guard who didn't remember us and seemed only vaguely aware of the fact that the town had been beset by dragon attacks waved us into town before turning his attention to the far more important task of dealing with some dirt underneath his fingernails.

Fortunately, it just so happened to be the middle of the

afternoon on a Wednesday, the one time during the week when the town council met whether it needed to or not. We headed straight for the town hall (save for a quick stop at a bakery for some *kellgaso*) and Nadi pounded on the door.

A moment later, Alderman Wooddunny himself answered. "Yes, ah, can I help you folks?" He gave us a quizzical look. Recognition slowly dawned on his face. "Why, you've returned!" he said brightly. He blinked, and his face fell. "You didn't encounter the dragon, did you?" he asked, implicit in his tone the fact that we surely would not have survived the encounter.

I pushed past him and into the town hall where an assemblage of idiots awaited me. I rubbed my hands together and smiled—I was in my element.

"Good people of Skendrick!" I called out to the dozen councilmembers, most of whom looked bored, asleep, or murderous (or some combination thereof). "As promised, I, Heloise the Bard, renowned throughout Erithea for my peerless voice, unmatched bravery, and abundant virtue—well-earned acclaim for almost half of those qualities, I might add—have returned with joyful tidings. The brave band of heroes you engaged to slay the terrible and mighty dragon that has plagued your town lo these many years—"

I was interrupted by an unintelligible (and angry) shout of, "Haen't bin boot sivin moonths sence th' vile wyrm f'st spewed fir aboot all 'n sundry!"

"Farmer Benton?" I said, trying to recall the moron's name.

"Aye." He touched his straw hat. A tiny pig squealed in his lap. An old woman snorted and said something under her breath. In response, Farmer Benton shouted, "Crone!" The tiny pig squealed again.

"Now, now—Farmer Benton and Widow Gershon, please...our esteemed heroes have returned." Alderman

Wooddunny smiled at me. "Please, ah, continue, Miss the Bard."

"As I was saying," I said pointedly, "before being so rudely interrupted by tomorrow morning's bacon, we have returned, and we bring great tidings!"

I looked around the room, expecting jubilant shouts, or at least a high five or two. Silence. Alderman Wooddunny gave me an encouraging smile and motioned for me to keep going. "We're eager to hear your news. Pins and, ah, needles, as it were," he said, looking around at his bored fellow councilmembers.

"You seriously can't guess what I'm about to say?" I said.

One councilmember fell off his chair, snorting himself awake in the process.

"Just tell them," said Nadi, exasperated.

"Fine. We'll skip the preamble. All right, pay attention, people—here's the deal: you had a dragon problem, now you don't." (I chose my words carefully.)

"Meaning?" said a young, serious-looking woman who was one of the few paying attention; if only her intellect matched her focus.

"Meaning," I said with exaggerated patience, "that we took care of the problem. The dragon won't attack anymore. You're free from oppression. Mission accomplished. Heckuva job. Huzzahs all around. All that sort of thing."

"Do you mean to say," said the Alderman slowly, his eyes widening, "that you've, ah, actually slayed the dragon?"

"Like I said," I replied, "we took care of it. You're safe now."

It took a moment, but, finally, at long last, cheers exploded throughout the room (well, "exploded" might be a less accurate description than "wheezed"), punctuated by a shout of "Harlot!" from the Widow Gershon (I think it was directed at me, but I'm not entirely sure).

"How?" asked the Alderman. "How did you do it? I

thought that you had no chance." He grimaced. "Er, that is to say, that the, ah, dragon was a formidable foe, and that—"

"Save it, Wooddunny," I said. He looked taken aback. I didn't particularly care. "Your concern for and confidence in us was overwhelming. Truly."

A young girl stood up and gave me a suspicious look. "What proof do you have? How do we know you even saw the dragon?"

"Betty Sue makes a good point," said the Alderman, though his tone was conciliatory. "It's not that we doubt you, mind you—it's just that, ah, it's truly an extraordinary accomplishment to slay a dragon, especially one as powerful and vile as the one that has plagued our fair town."

"Village!" shouted Farmer Benton.

"Whatever!" responded the exasperated Alderman. "Gods! You people really need to get a life." He took a deep breath as he marked the scandalized looks on the faces of his constituents. "Now then," he said, his tone somewhat contrite, "we really are incredibly grateful for your, ah, assistance in our most dire hour of need, and we would love nothing more than to celebrate—and spread word of—your feat far and wide and burnish the legend of your hearty band of warriors."

"But you need to put your money where your mouths are," said Betty Sue. "We're not all as stupid as he looks," she said, gesturing to Farmer Benton. Farmer Benton didn't respond, though the piglet squealed meekly in his defense.

"Funny you should phrase it that way," said Whiska with a wolfish grin. She pulled out a large, heavy-looking sack, dropped it on the ground, and it tipped over, spilling gold coins and jewels across the floor. The good people of Skendrick had played right into our hands.

"It's no secret," I said as I stepped forward and began to pace back and forth in front of the assembled council, "that when our merry little band rolled into Skendrick, we were, well, short of funds."

"It's true," said a solemn, middle-aged man who sat next to Farmer Benton. "That one there"—he pointed to Whiska —"she asked me for a coin to purchase a small beer. Threatened to explode my bowels, she did. Waved her fingers and muttered some ancient curse, and I felt my guts turn to water. I gave her the coin, and she laughed." He shook his head. "She's an evil, powerful wizard. But a destitute one, that's for sure."

"Oh, for the love of—I didn't do anything to the loose-boweled idiot," grumbled Whiska. "I made up a few words and wiggled my fingers at him and he shat himself. And then he gave me a coin." She knelt down, picked up a coin, and flipped it to the man. "Here—I'm paying you back tenfold. Also, your village's small beer tastes like your loose bowels."

"Town!" shouted someone.

"How do you know what his stool tastes like?" asked Rummy innocently.

"The point," I said, forcing everyone to focus on me once again (we bards excel at that), "is that we did not have heaps of treasure when we arrived. Now, however, we do." I gestured to the bag Whiska had tossed down. "Whiska?"

Whiska pulled out five more sacks of treasure that she placed next to the first. For good measure, she tipped them all forward and let them spill across the floor.

"And that's only half of it," I said. I reached into my own pouch and pulled out a massive gold coin—a real one—and handed it to Alderman Wooddunny. "Take a bite of that, my good man."

He looked confused. "Is it chocolate?" He picked at the sides, trying to find the edge of a wrapper.

"No," I said in a display of infinite patience, "it's just that some people test whether or not a coin is made of gold by biting on it. Gold, as you may not know, not having an abundance of it, is a soft metal."

Alderman Wooddunny nodded and bit hard on the coin. "Ouch," he said. He grimaced. "That tastes terrible."

"It's not supposed to be a tasty treat, sir," I said, somehow keeping the exasperation from my voice. I really am a paragon of magnanimous virtue. "It's supposed to be worth a lot of money. Which it is."

The alderman nodded. "It is a rather, ah, magnificent specimen of coin. Though now it, ah, has teeth marks in it."

"I'm going to go ahead and connect the dots for you, especially that guy over there, who looks like he might struggle to count to twenty-one even when he's naked." I pointed to a gentleman in the corner whose default facial expression was perplexed befuddlement. "We came here without treasure. We went out to slay a dragon. The dragon had a lot of treasure. We now have a lot of treasure. Oodles. What do you think that means?"

"Well," said the Alderman, "it appears that you may have, ah—"

"Oh, and we have this—show them, Borg," I said, smiling (perhaps a little smugly).

Everyone stared at Borg for a moment; Borg stared back. Finally, he very deliberately removed his pack, sat it on the floor, opened it up, rummaged around inside, and withdrew a flat, red, shiny, metallic object that was vaguely circular and about a foot wide. He held it up and pointed at it. "It's a... dragon scale."

(How, you ask, had we gotten a dragon scale? Turns out that dragons shed them pretty regularly, so it wasn't all that much of an imposition for Melvin to root around on the ground of her lair and find one to give us. It was actually quite pretty to look at, which almost made up for the fact that we were carrying around someone's dead, sloughed off skin.

Okay, fine—*we* weren't carrying it, but, hey—Borg volunteered.)

Finally, Skendrick's best and brightest issued a collective gasp. "You've really, ah, done it!" shouted Alderman Wooddunny, beaming. "You've actually managed to defeat the dragon!"

"Ye kin nae argue aught wi' a right piece o' the bodkin, kin ye there, hamenpig?" roared Farmer Benton, clutching his pig tighter and eliciting a strangled squeal.

(I sincerely hope that's the only time I ever have to write the words "clutching his pig tighter.")

Various other slightly—slightly—more coherent exclamations abounded. After much back patting and an occasional shout of "Touching flesh is the devil's playground!" from the Widow Gershon, the excitement subsided and everyone returned to their seats.

"We, ah, owe you a great debt of gratitude," said the Alderman.

"Yeah, not bad," said Betty Sue, nodding approvingly. "How did you do it?"

"Well," I replied, "let's just say we can be pretty persuasive. With our weapons, I mean." I held up my knife. "We are killers, through and through." I felt some commotion behind me and turned to see Rummy, who had picked up one of the spilled coins and was making it disappear and reappear, much to the delight of Farmer Benton (Betty Sue looked bored). I cleared my throat and glared at him; he shrugged and smiled sheepishly. "Yes indeed—pure killers."

"How can we ever thank you?" said Alderman Wooddunny, his eyes on the sacks of treasure. "Perhaps we might build an everlasting memorial to your, ah, legendary achievement, though, given the economic hardship we've endured over the course of the dragon's reign of terror, we could, of course, use some, ah, seed money to build a monument worthy of your, ah, greatness." He nodded his head toward the coins scattered across the floor.

"No!" shouted Whiska. "It's mine—all mine, you hear?" She started scooping up every last loose coin...except for those that, unfortunately, had started to disappear.

"Hey," I shouted loudly, trying to draw everyone's attention away from the rather incriminating evidence that we did not, in fact, possess copious quantities of treasure and, as such, may not have actually slain a dragon. "A memorial! Wow! What a great idea. That would be flattering, and not the first time someone's suggested such a tribute to me, you know—wink, wink. Don't you hate it when people *say* 'wink, wink' instead of just winking? It's obnoxious. You need to make sure to get my good side when you build it—no, no, I'm kidding! They're all good sides. Can't go wrong—not a bad one in the bunch. Should I be holding my lute or a knife? Hmmm...that's a good question. Not sure who asked that one. I did? I suppose I did. I guess we only ask ourselves the toughest questions, don't we?" I shook my head and blew out a deep breath. "I think the bottom line is that this backside really deserves to be immortalized. 'Bottom line'—see what I did there? Backside? Bottom?"

Finally, Whiska had secured all of the coins (those that hadn't disappeared, anyway) and had stuffed them back into the sacks.

"Well then," I said in a slightly quieter, less crazy tone of voice. "Your village is safe. No more dragon attacks. We will, of course, take under advisement your exceedingly generous offer to fund our own memorial and give it proper consideration."

"Just a minor point," said Rummy, raising his index finger, "but both you and the Alderman called it a 'memorial' when I think you meant 'monument.' I'm pretty sure you only put up memorials for dead people." He looked around. "Fortunately for us, I think we're all still alive."

"Most of the people in this room won't be for long if we don't get a drink," muttered Whiska.

"Yes, let us, ah, supply our conquering heroes with, ah, libations of a celebratory nature," proclaimed the Alderman, bringing his gavel down to officially (and mercifully) bring to a close the council session.

"Harlots!" shouted the Widow Gershon one last time, just for good measure.

And so we drank and ate and drank and drank some more and ate and then drank a little more. The people of Skendrick seemed genuinely grateful for our help and suitably impressed that we had actually killed a dragon. Betty Sue kept giving me the sideways stinkeye—I think she knew that something wasn't quite right—but the nice thing about children, as a giant friend of mine once said, is that they're as easy to ignore as they are to eat.

The celebration did, in fact, last for three days, and by the time it was over, every single person in Skendrick had promised to sing the group's praises to anyone and everyone they met, ensuring, at the very least, the start of a formidable reputation. Considerably more than that would be needed, though, to spread Nadi's band's reputation far and wide (and to further convince the public that the dragon had, in fact, been killed), namely an epic tale told by a highly skilled bard, one that would be beloved and sung by other bards by virtue of its infectious melody and rhythm, compelling action and colorful characters, and the persuasive charms of its impossibly intelligent and gifted author.

⚓

IT'S hard to believe that we just marked the fifty-year anniversary of that celebration in Skendrick. It's a relief that I can now, at long last, tell the story behind the story.

I wrote the epic tale you've heard so many times at your

favorite local tavern for two reasons: to burnish the reputation of Nadi's band (which, incidentally, worked remarkably well) and to uphold our end of the bargain with the dragon by dissuading would-be treasure hunters from seeking out her lair so that she could finally get some peace and quiet.

I always wanted to tell the real story, though, which, frankly, I find more interesting, and not just because I play a central role. (Though, let's face it—that would make any story more interesting; just wait until you hear about the shenanigans I've gotten into lately with my new adventuring partner, Grimple, a hill giant who, through numerous acts of stupidity, got turned into a sickly gnome, and the insanity we had to go through to get him cured of that condition...coming soon from the same disreputable publisher as the book you now hold in your hands.) No, the real story is more interesting because it shows the human side of adventuring.

It occurs to me that "human" is actually a terrible adjective to describe an adventuring group that included an elf, a Ratarian, a rock giant, and a half-dwarf/half-halfling. Let me try that again.

The real story is more interesting because it shows the unexpected (and sometimes very personal) challenges of adventuring and how rare it is that even the bravest, most capable heroes have a smooth and exciting journey from the beginning of a quest to the treasure chest at the end. I've met hundreds of adventurers, and with some rare exceptions (notably Grimple, but that's primarily because he's epically stupid), they're just like everyone else—maybe just a little braver, and a little more foolish. They have good days and bad days, and what's inspiring about them is not so much that they slay dragons (or don't slay dragons, as the case may be); it's that they persevere through situations where they have no idea what to do, but where not taking action is not an option. My hope is that by sharing the story of Nadi and her band's efforts to save Skendrick, you'll gain an appreciation for what the adventuring life is *really* like, and maybe the next time you see an adventurer at a tavern, you'll buy him or her a drink, offer a pat on the back and a kind word, and thank the gods that it's not you who's stuck in a swamp that smells like rancid baby diarrhea.

I can sense, however, that you still have questions. "But, Heloise—how do you get your hair so silky?" Well, it's a combination of extract of krump and califor oil. That's not really what you meant to ask though, I know—what you really want to know is why I can finally tell the story behind the story, right?

I assure you that I'm not violating anyone's confidence in telling the true tale. The dragon, who discovered a new favorite vegetable in the southern region of Kolaria about two decades after our encounter with it, relocated with the bulk of its treasure and is living happily and anonymously in an entirely different part of the world (though rumor has it that she couldn't carry quite all of her treasure when she moved, so it's entirely possible that there is, in fact, gold in them thar hills for any hearty adventurers brave enough to go through the Dukbuter Swamp (or smart enough to find an orc child who can lead them around it)).

As for Nadi, Whiska, Rummy, and Borg...well, they went on to have a pretty epic adventuring career, and I'm happy to report that three-quarters of them are alive and happy.

(Wait...what, you ask? Who's *not* alive and/or happy? And what about that wizard in Velenia, the one whom humbled our heroes and who they vowed to go back and defeat when they had honed their skills? What about that little loose end, Heloise?)

Well, loose ends—let's call them "teasers"—are for sequels, dear reader, and sequels happen when a girl gets paid. So, maybe go buy everyone you know a copy of this book and check back with me in a year or so, okay?

ACKNOWLEDGMENTS

Writing is a solitary endeavor, but publishing a book is not. I'm incredibly grateful to the amazing team at Parliament House Press for taking a chance on this story even though my nose is longer than my publishing track record. Heloise would thank you too, but she's too busy working on the next book.

I'm also thankful for the Goodreads community, which has been so incredibly supportive of my tomfoolery and shenanigans thus far. If I've learned anything about the wonderful weirdos who hang out there, it's that their kindness and wit exceeds even their excellent taste in terrible books.

No one writes in a vacuum (primarily because physics won't allow for it), and no one manages to stay motivated to write books in the midst of the insanity of having a very busy job, young children, and a crazy commute without the support of a bunch of stalwart friends. I wouldn't still be banging my head against this wall if it weren't for Bret Bowman, Josh Little, Naveen Vemuri, Jeff Yates, Eric Liebetrau, Peter Martin, and Scott Weinstein. So, blame them if you hated this. (And Bret—let's inflict Cheesecalibur on the world sometime soon, shall we?)

To the good people at Grounded in Alexandria, the world's best coffee shop: thank you for keeping me caffeinated and for creating a bright, kind, and welcoming place for everyone who passes through your doors.

My parents never batted an eyelash when, more than two decades ago, I told them I wanted to be an English major. They could have told me to study something useful instead, but they didn't, and I love them for it. If I'm in any way a good parent myself, it's because I learned from the best.

And, of course, there are the people who are stuck living with me: my amazing wife Jessica and my wee rapscallions Henry and Hannah (and loyal feline Wilson, of course). To quote noted sage Bryan Adams, everything I do, I do it for you. I hope that I can make you as proud as you make me feel happy, loved, and like I'm part of the best team in the world. I love you guys.

A REQUEST...

Did you enjoy The Part About the Dragon Was (Mostly) True? *Reviews keep books alive . . .*

Leave your review on either GoodReads or the digital storefront of your choosing.

We thank you greatly!

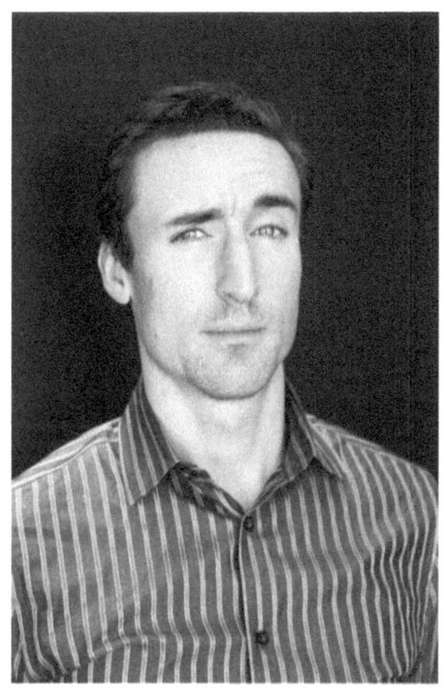

Sean Gibson is not a professional mini biography writer (if he were, this would be much more compelling). Instead, he's a highfalutin professional guy by day, hangs out with his amazing wife, son, and daughter by night, and writes somewhere in between, usually in the backseat of strangers' cars (true story). He holds a BA in English Literature from Ohio Wesleyan University and an MBA from the Kelley School of Business at Indiana University, but he really wishes he had been able to matriculate at Hogwarts (he would have been in Hufflepuff, he thinks). Sean is a fan of sports teams from

Detroit, a distressingly large number of bands that rose to prominence in the 1980s, and writing in the third person. He resides in Northern Virginia, and, given how much he hates moving, and given that his house has an awesome library that includes a globe with a hidden decanter of Scotch in it, is likely to remain there for some time. In addition to *The Part About the Dragon Was (Mostly) True*, Sean is the author of *The Chronicle of Heloise & Grimple* as well as *The Camelot Shadow* and its prequel short, "The Strange Task Before Me." He has written extensively for Kirkus Reviews, and his book reviews have also appeared in Esquire. You can befriend him on Goodreads and follow him on Twitter at @Gibknight, though goodness knows why you'd want to.